Michael Linford was born in Boscombe in 1977 and throughout his life has shown a passion for three things: music, books and people. Ten years in music retail provided a perfect opportunity to immerse himself in music all day long, before moving on to care work, where he has spent the last eight years looking after people – all with stories to tell.

With aspirations of becoming a writer since he was very young, his first attempts began with poetry. In 2011 he put over 400 poems online, before eventually releasing two small collections both in digital and paperback formats.

In 2012, Michael combined his love for books, music and people, in the writing of his debut novel *Music for the End of the World*.

Music for the End of the World

Michael Linford

Pen Press

First published in Great Britain by Pen Press

All paper used in the printing of this book has been made from
wood grown in managed, sustainable forests.

ISBN13: 978-1-78003-493-5

Printed and bound in the UK
Pen Press is an imprint of
Indepenpress Publishing Limited
25 Eastern Place
Brighton
BN2 1GJ

A catalogue record of this book is available from the British Library

Cover design by Jacqueline Abromeit
Cover photo by Jodie Chandler
Inside author photo by KittyPinkStars

This book is dedicated to my family who have always been there to support and encourage me, through thick and thin.

Also to my close friends who understand me, no matter how much energy it takes, and to my music for always being my closest companion.

Guys, I did it!

ACKNOWLEDGEMENTS

I'd like to thank the following people for donating to the fundraising page of the book on Sponsume;

Kittypinkstars, Jacob Beale, Jenny Linford, Joanna Scott, Lerryn Gray, Chloe Wood, Naomi MacKinnon, Claire Gordon, Jude Horrocks, Rhiannon Goodfield, Carly Green, Lisa Vine, Midge Maton, Ross Browne, Aki Atrill, Kerry Mountain, Laura Bough, Angie White, Helen Garland, John Macleod, Julie Evans, Sharon Garnett, Alaska Cole and Becky.

I'd also like to thank my friends for supporting me, helping to promote the idea and generally keeping me going. Special thanks go to Jodie Chandler for providing me with a perfect front cover image and all the encouragement when needed.

My heartfelt appreciation goes out to all those involved in sending me their own personal end of the world song lists, especially those in the public eye, a full list of these people can be found at the end of the book.

Finally, I would like to thank Sarah, Claire and all the team at Indepenpress for helping my dream to come true.

'Without music, life would be a mistake.'
Nietzsche

2012 – Prologue

Today is Friday 21st December 2012; the time is 9.33 in the morning and I am sat on Parliament Hill, looking out over the city of London. It is a day like no other: today will be my last day on earth. This morning the sun should have risen like on any other day, slowly melting away the early morning frost and throwing light on this busy city, but today is different; this day is still, dark and quiet. One of many cities worldwide that never sleeps, but soon that will change. At 11.11 this morning, the world will end. It has been prophesised and spoken about through generation after generation but finally my time has come, there are no more second chances.

So I sit here looking out at the last morning for this beautiful city, my city, and as I sit here and reflect on my life I have my very own soundtrack. Twenty songs that I picked to listen to: this is my very own end-of-the-world playlist. So as I start my iPod, I sit and look, and remember my little piece of the world; my 35 years. This is my story. . .

Chapter 1

January 1998 – Age 20

What does the New Year mean to you? Is it the start of something new or same problems, different day?

Thursday January 1st 1998

It was only five minutes into the New Year and already I was thinking about leaving the party and heading home. It had all been a last minute rush to come to the club for the party anyway, but after a lot of badgering from the guys at work, I had finally given in and said yes. I hated parties, social groups had never been my scene at all, and being forced to celebrate something I didn't particularly enjoy, with a large group of judgemental people, just reminded me of being back at school. I'd spent the majority of the early evening sitting at the bar chatting to a guy, whose name I couldn't remember, about music. We'd had a heated discussion about whether grunge was the new punk and if Paul McCartney was really dead or not, and eventually he had stumbled off his stool and onto the dance floor to jump around to Marilyn Manson. I couldn't help but note the irony of so many sweaty, self-obsessed, so-called alternative types jumping up and down to a song called *The Beautiful People* without the slightest trace of embarrassment. This was me, though: the guy who sat in corners, who read, thought, watched. Always on the outside looking in, but then I'd never really found a reason to want to be inside anyway. That is, until five minutes past midnight; the moment my world changed.

The year had been welcomed in by Blur, with hundreds of people screaming along to *Song 2*, and now everything had slowed down again. I called it post-New Year mass hysteria, but then people would probably just call me cynical. I guess it wasn't helped by all the happy couples – don't get me wrong; I don't want people to be miserable, but they could certainly tone down just how happy they are at times and spare a thought for the lonesome. If one more couple had asked me to take a photo of them kissing around midnight then I'd had to have started charging – not a thought was spared for what I was doing. It was like, 'here comes the single bloke, he'll take photos' – well, no he won't; he is going outside to get away from all this madness. I knew once I heard the first bars of *Don't Speak* by No Doubt that it was time to get away from the mass love-in that was happening. So at five past midnight I made my way carefully around the swell of couples, and headed for the door. I hadn't seen any of the guys from work for ages but I figured they were all wooing girls whilst the song played, providing the perfect soundtrack for their misguided attempts. Outside it was freezing, with no one and nothing around as far as the eye could see. The usually buzzing town of Camden was eerily still and quiet. I walked over to the electricity box and hopped up onto it. From here I could relax and enjoy the calm, whilst the building almost visibly throbbed from all the energy in it. I reached into my coat pocket and pulled out my cigarettes, lighting one and enjoying the rush of inhaling the smoke whilst sat in the cold air.

"They'll kill you, you know."

I turned to see a girl standing by the side of me, leaning forward on the electricity box. When I say a girl, what I mean is the most attractive girl I have ever seen. I sat staring at her, the cigarette slowly burning away between my fingers. She was beautiful. She was wearing knee high black boots, tight jeans and a Woodstock music festival t-shirt which concealed what I imagined were some lovely curves very seductively.

"Or maybe just create a vegetative state? I'm Sara, nice to meet you," she said, looking at me; confused and holding out her hand for me to shake.

Taken aback by her presence, I continued to stare at her: she looked so cool and had beautiful dark hair and the deepest blue eyes I had ever seen. In the dark of night, they were like a window to the bluest sky you could ever imagine.

"Umm, sorry, hi," I managed to stammer out. "I'm Will, nice to meet you too."

I felt I had recovered the situation well, despite the fact that this girl was looking at me with a slightly amused glint in her eye.

"So are you going to give me one of those or not?" she said, pointing to the cigarette pack. As I looked down from her to the pack, she pulled one out with her long, slender fingers and lit it before I could say a word.

"I thought you said they'd kill you?"

"Here's hoping," she said as she winked at me and briskly walked towards the door of the club.

"See you around, sorry, hi, Will," she laughed to herself as she turned and blew me a kiss, before striding through the door and into the club.

I jumped down off the box and stood there for a few minutes, trying to work out what had happened. It had all been so unexpected, yet marvellous at the same time. A completely random, gorgeous girl had come and spoken to me and then walked off, blowing me a kiss. My cigarette had burned itself out in the time I had been sitting, staring at her; and then standing, thinking about staring at her. I threw the butt into the gutter and reached for another from my pack. As I did this, I noticed a bit of paper about as long as a Rizla, but thicker, curled up between the cigarettes. I pulled it out and opened it carefully, revealing a strange message.

What Lamb would enjoy a drink, whilst heading to the slaughter?

Confused, I tucked the strange note into my pocket, and lit another cigarette before heading back into the club. I went back to my place at the small bar, all the time looking for her, and ordered another drink. The next song came on and the guy appeared next to me again.

"Seriously though man, The Offspring are the future of music, I mean what else is there?" he said with arms held open wide, as if this was the continuation of a conversation we had previously been having.

"What can I say buddy, maybe they'll play it tonight?" was the best response I could come up with, whilst I was still thinking about Woodstock t-shirts and lambs.

"Already requested it my man, it's up soon! I could quite happily die tonight," he shouted at me, wobbling on his stool as he waved his arms around. Then it clicked: lamb, slaughter, death, drink. I smiled at the genius of it and turned to the nameless lush beside me.

"You can make requests, then? Even though it's New Year's?"

"Sure can bro, just go see the man, you know what I'm saying?" And with this the guy passed out face-first on the bar. I lost my drink in the process, but at least I wouldn't have to talk to him anymore.

I made my way up to the DJ's booth and spoke to his assistant before going back to the bar. From the booth you couldn't see anything except a huge mass of people all breathing, moving and most of all, sweating, together. No sign of mysterious strangers with beautiful blue eyes anywhere to be seen. In my absence, the nameless guy had disappeared and I had my empty space back at the bar again. I ordered two shots of Jack Daniel's and sat, contemplating. I had to sit through a few more unrecognisable shouting songs, for angry teenagers to fight to, and then I heard the announcement.

"Sara, this and a glass of Jack is for you, from Will?" the DJ said, sounding a bit confused and very tired. And then it began: the opening bars of *Górecki* by Lamb filled the room and I turned on my stool to watch the crowd. As one of the most haunting introductions to a song I ever heard played, I saw a figure moving slowly through the crowd towards me. It was Sara, but she had changed her outfit: gone were the jeans and t-shirt and instead she had on a beautiful oriental dress which shone under the nightclub lights. I slipped off the stool and stood waiting for her. She moved with such grace through the crowd, until she was stood in front of me. I went to speak and she placed her index finger in front of her lips to stop me, before leaning in and kissing me fully on the mouth. I held onto the bar behind me to steady myself, not because I was drunk but because things like this never happened to me and I was feeling shaky with both nerves and excitement. Sara broke the kiss off before gesturing 'sshhh' with her finger again and taking me by the hand to lead me onto the dance floor. Something about the whole situation had a feeling of déjà vu and yet I had no idea why. It's not like this sort of thing happens to me regularly, yet there was something really familiar about the whole thing. Sara led me to a dark corner of the dance floor and we held each other tight, moving as one for the whole of the song; we didn't speak a word but it felt like complete togetherness. She was shorter than me so I had my arms around her shoulders, and she had hers around my waist as we moved slowly whilst the music played. For those six minutes, everyone and everything else disappeared; it felt like we were two souls dancing together in an empty world. Forever can go so quickly though, and soon the song was finishing, bringing me back down to earth with a bump. Sara leant up and kissed me on the cheek before whispering in my ear,

"It's nearly one o'clock, are you going to walk me home?"

I smiled at her and signalled for her to lead the way. She led me around the dance floor by the hand and headed to the cloakroom for her stuff while I visited the toilets. Whilst I was washing my hands I looked at my reflection in the mirror and everything seemed normal: no green fairies or goblins, so I figured I couldn't have had my drink spiked. I rinsed my face before drying it and my hands on the paper towels which were slowly covering every inch of the toilets as the night went on. I walked out into the corridor and she wasn't there; I glanced back into the club but there was no sign there either. I started to feel like maybe I was losing my mind, so I headed outside into the fresh air and then I saw her. She was leaning against the box I had been sat on earlier, wearing a big furry coat over her dress, smoking and grinning to herself. She looked even more beautiful than she had before and as I walked towards her, I pinched myself again, just to check that this was real.

"You want to be careful, those things will kill you," I said, as I walked towards her, smiling.

"So will my dad if I don't get home soon. Thank you for the dance, Will – it was lovely, but I don't seriously expect you to walk me home; I'm sure you have more exciting things to do. It's cool to say no. I don't live far, it's in Kentish Town."

"Kentish Town it is then," I said as I took her hand and started to walk her away from the club towards home. At this time in the morning, London's air seemed to be at its cleanest and most crisp, but luckily the alcohol kept us warm. As we walked we spoke about everything, from music to our jobs, what books we liked, what we did in our spare time and back to music again. Sara had been impressed that I had managed to work out her cryptic clue, but then a bit less surprised once she found out I had been working in music stores for the last four years. The walk seemed to take such a short time though, and it wasn't long before we were stood outside Sara's house and it was time to say goodbye.

"Thank you; I had a lovely time tonight." Sara said, looking up at me before biting her bottom lip.

"No, thank you – I hate New Year and you made tonight amazing. You really are special; I don't know why you spoke to me but I'm so glad you did. Did you want to meet up for a drink sometime or something?" There, I blurted it out. I was brave; I didn't chicken out for a change.

"I spoke to you because you looked interesting sat there on your own. Outside a nightclub five minutes after midnight, not drunk or crying or beaten up. You were just sat there because you wanted to be; I thought that was kind of cool. So I wrote the note on a bit of paper and decided to slip it into your pack when I asked for a smoke." Sara grinned, revelling in her clever scheme.

"I want to see you again," she continued. "I don't want this to just be one of those pretentious New Year things, that's all. I want to see you away from New Year's parties; when you have to want to, not when we're thrown together like tonight," she said, looking at me with those intense eyes.

"I want to see you again too, so what do you want to do? Do you want my number?" I felt like she was trying to let me down gently, and struggled to stay composed although I wanted to beg her to stay.

"January is a crazy month; so much starts and ends at the same time. I want more than that for you and me. Why don't you meet me on the last day of the month; same place, at 1 pm? If we're both there then nothing can go wrong; it's meant to be. What do you think?"

I looked at her and at that moment I would've agreed to anything. Those eyes had taken me to a place where I had never been before and I never wanted to come back from.

"I'll be there," was all I could manage.

Sara leant up and gave me a huge hug before kissing me on the lips again. She smelled so lovely and I just wanted to melt into her as I hugged her so tightly. She rummaged around in her bag and pulled out a bottle of beer, before handing it to me and skipping up the steps to her house. I stood and watched whilst she fumbled with her keys, trying to find the right one. Eventually she found it and unlocked the door, then turned to me, smiling, and blew me one more kiss.

"Until next time, William," she said with a grin, and shut the door quietly behind her.

"Until next time, Sara," I said to myself, watching the trail of lights go on and off until they reached a room on the top floor. As I opened the bottle of beer using my own house key, I stood and watched her form move around what I guessed was her bedroom. Through the lit curtains I could almost make out her shape as I saw her slip the dress over her head and throw it onto the floor. I stood, transfixed, watching as she moved behind the curtain like the most wonderful puppet show. Eventually the light went off and I realised she must have gone to bed. I took a long swig from the bottle and headed away, constantly looking over my shoulder at her darkened room.

After about half an hour it dawned on me that it was going to be almost impossible to get a taxi at this time of the morning on New Year's Day, and even if I did, it would cost a fortune. So I decided to carry on walking home. I didn't see another soul the whole time, but I figured this was just as well because I had a stupid grin on my face all the way and that might have freaked them out a little bit.

I eventually got back to my parents' house at three o'clock in the morning and had to use military precision to get into the house without waking them up. They didn't mind me coming in late as long as they knew where I was, but I always hated waking them up when I came in and I didn't need anything to put a dampener on tonight. After 20 minutes of trying to open the door quietly, I eventually made it into the hallway. Everyone was asleep, so I moved carefully up the stairs and into my room. I closed the door and threw my jacket onto the chair at the desk before lying back on my bed. I reached over and turned my lava lamp on and my main light off, before putting my headphones on and listening to my stereo. As I lay there, listening to *Everlong* by the Foo Fighters, I ran through the evening's events in my mind. I'd never had anything like that happen to me in my life, and I was starting to wonder whether I had dreamt it all up. Every time I closed my eyes I could see her face, smiling up at me and biting her lip; everything she had done tonight just made me want her even more. She was so beautiful, and her eyes were forever imprinted on my memory. Slowly the alcohol caught up with me, and my senses started swimming away with the thoughts in my mind and the music in my ears. As I drifted off to sleep, I remembered seeing Sara blow me a kiss, and I smiled.

I woke up around two o'clock the next afternoon with a banging headache and a foul taste in my mouth. As my eyes struggled to come to terms with the daylight, I realised I was lying on the bed still fully clothed from the night before, and that I must have fallen asleep before brushing my teeth or anything. This was made even more obvious by the aching in my bladder, telling me I really needed to visit the loo as soon as possible. I stumbled to my feet, almost tripping over the blanket I had wrapped myself up in during my sleep, and made it to the bathroom. As I stood there I realised how quiet the house was: my mum and dad had a tradition of going for a walk on New Year's Day, every year at midday. They didn't usually get back until late afternoon so I had plenty of time to clean myself up and look presentable again before they returned. After doing all the things I should've done last night before falling asleep, I had a long soak in the bath and tried to let the steam clear my banging head. As I lay back letting my mind drift away, it kept coming back to the same thing: that beautiful girl, Sara. I replayed the whole series of events from the night before, just to see if I could make any sense of it. I hadn't drunk that much, so surely I hadn't imagined it all in a hallucination caused by too much whisky and not enough water – or had I? The more I relaxed, the closer Sara got in my mind. I could see everything: her stunning eyes, her gorgeous body, and most of all I could feel those soft, passionate kisses. I sat up in the bath and reached over the side, drying my hands before reaching for my jacket and rattling the contents of the pockets out onto the bathroom floor. Lying in a pile were a set of house keys, a lighter, a box of matches, my ticket for the club last night and last of all, my cigarettes. I opened the pack and found one left so I decided to sneakily have it in the bath as the house was empty. I often used incense sticks in the bathroom, so lighting one of them and my cigarette would make the scent almost untraceable. As I lit the cigarette I looked at my jeans and checked the pockets of them too; there was a £5 note, 37 pence in loose change, a travel card and a tiny bit of folded paper. As soon as I unfolded the note and saw the cryptic Lamb question, it all hit me. It was real, there was a Sara, and I wasn't insane or still drunk.

After a while of relaxing in the bath I headed back to my room and got changed into some slouchy clothing – my favourite Nirvana t-shirt and some baggy combats – before lying back on the bed again. I had pinned the note to the wall next to my bed, along with the ticket from last night, a suitable reminder of the first good start to a year I could ever remember having. All I had to do was wait patiently until the end of January and then I could see her again. Sara and Will had a nice ring to it, I thought to myself, smiling. Thirty days, then I had the chance to be really happy. Surely it couldn't be that difficult?

Saturday January 31st 1998
Finally, my date with destiny had arrived. I had been waiting all month for this day and it had felt like the longest month of my life. I had done all the normal things I was supposed to – go to work, be at home, listen to music – all those things we

do to fill time; but the 30 days of waiting to see that strange and beautiful girl again seemed like a lifetime. The only thing I had done differently in the last 30 days was not go out to the club at all, and not harmlessly flirt with any of the cool alternative female customers in the shop, and the reason I hadn't done either of these things was because I didn't feel the need to. I was waiting for someone and something special.

That Saturday morning I spent so long fretting, getting changed and getting changed again, practising what I was going to say and what I wasn't going to say. I even managed to convince myself that I was becoming incontinent at one point, given the number of times I needed to wee. I had never been so nervous in my life and I had no idea why. Although Sara was a stunning girl, she was still just a girl, after all. I had spent half the month thinking that by now she must have found herself a boyfriend anyway, and probably wasn't even going to be there when she had said she would. After all the messing about, I finally made it to the club at midday. The club was converted during the day into a bar, so I was able to go in and have a drink whilst I waited; Dutch courage, I thought to myself. Before long I was sat at the window with a pint of lager and my cigarettes, smoking whilst looking out nervously towards the road and listening to Nick Cave on my CD Walkman. I was certain she wouldn't be coming; that she must have had a better offer since we met last. The words of Nick Cave assured me that love is a lot like death, and I found a lot of comfort in this concept, which was slightly worrying. I looked at the clock and it said twenty to one; I lit another cigarette and tried my best to keep calm.

I was on my second pint and what must have been my seventh cigarette when the mournful sound of my music was disturbed.

"Well, look who we have here! Same place, different time! Did you miss me?"

I felt her arms around my shoulders as she smothered my cheek and neck with kisses, before I even got the chance to speak to her or react to where the voice had come from. She slid round from behind me and lay on the settee next to me with her head in my lap. She looked up at me with those gorgeous eyes and took my heart all over again. With a wink and a grin, she twisted her lips into an over-the-top pout and demanded a kiss. I obliged of course, and everything felt wonderful again: she was here and she was real. *Will*, I thought to myself, *you are the luckiest boy in the world*.

After getting her kiss, Sara sat up next to me, still grinning. She looked amazing: her hair had been slightly layered since I saw her last, and she was wearing a flowery hippy dress over some leggings and big, bright Doc Martens. The outfit was finished off by a thick, fluffy cardigan, and once more she looked perfect; while I worried I looked like a tramp.

"What's a girl got to do to get a drink round here?" She said mischievously, before taking my pint and downing the remains in one.

"Did you want another one? Or did you want to go somewhere?" I asked, realising that these had been the first words I'd spoken since she had arrived.

"Follow me," she said playfully, before grabbing my hand and leading me out of the pub and into the cold. London isn't hot at the best of times, and especially not in January, but today the cold was made worse by a biting wind that attacked you as you tried to walk through it. I wasn't sure what Sara had in mind, but I hoped it didn't involve being outside much or I feared we would both succumb to pneumonia.

We chatted as we walked along; I told her all about the exciting month I'd had and how quickly it had gone, hoping she wouldn't be able to see through my pathetic attempts to lie and sound cooler than I actually was. Sara told me about how she had spent most of the month drawing and looking forward to today, but the month had really dragged so she was glad to finally get here. It made me smile that she didn't have to lie about it; she was cool as she was, one of those people who takes your interest without any effort at all, whose souls seem to demand to be known and loved.

"We need to do stuff today to make the last month worth it, don't you think? Let's explore the side of London that deserves its moment to shine in the sun. From the lost to the bohemian – this is the first chapter for us; let's write it with words and actions taken from the purest form of reality we know: the heart." Sara was moving her arms around theatrically as she spoke and people all around us in the street were looking, some smiling and some looking concerned before shuffling slowly away, merging back into the greyness of modern life.

"I am all yours, beautiful; wherever you want to go, I want to be there," I replied, holding her closer to me and kissing the top of her head.

The first of Sara's ideas was to do a complete square on the Tube system: surfing the Tubes and people-watching, she had called it. I actually liked spending time on the Tube anyway, so it wasn't a stress for me, and people-watching was one of my favourite pastimes.

We got on at Camden Town and made our way east towards Stratford, then south as far as North Greenwich;

west to Kensington and north to Willesden Junction before finally making our way to Oxford Circus. We had seen so many different and colourful characters, from the suited businessmen to the scruffy tramps who were spending their last few coins to find somewhere else to settle for the afternoon. We spent the whole journey observing, talking, laughing, and I was holding her close the whole time. At Oxford Circus, Sara took my hand and led me off the train.

"Here's the plan: we've got to go somewhere and buy each other something, and then we'll head back to Camden for some food, OK?" She had that look of determination in her eye, and I was never going to say no anyway.

"Sounds great; lead me wherever you want, my lady," I joked, as she stuck her tongue out at me and pulled me along the platform. In the distance I could hear a guitar playing, and I recognised it straight away. Around the corner, a busker was playing *Yellow* by Coldplay and singing the chorus at the top of his voice. I wasn't really one for buskers but this guy had a wonderful voice, and something about the way he sang just added to the authenticity and I felt like he really related to the lyrics. Sara stopped to watch the guy, and as she listened I could see her getting taken away by the emotion of the lyrics. With teary eyes she turned to me and kissed me passionately on the lips. It sounds corny but it was a perfect moment; the kind you wish you could have lots of in life. This would have been the song playing in my head to accompany this moment, had it not been playing for real. I wrapped my arms around Sara and hugged her into my chest. She felt so good against me, fitting perfectly with her head just under my chin. I was protecting and feeling protected at the same time – a perfect balance; not something that is ever easy to come by. When the guy finished playing, I threw all my loose change into his guitar case and shook his hand

25

before we headed off out of the station and onto the street. Sara still had that look of a person on a mission in her eyes as she led me along the road until she found a huge bookstore.

"I want you to wait here, OK? I won't be long; just wait here until I get back." With a kiss on the cheek she disappeared in through the doors, leaving me to sit on the bench outside and wait for her. As I sat there smoking, the strangest feeling came over me. It was a feeling of happiness: complete happiness for no reason other than that everything just felt so right. The very first time I had seen Sara I had wanted to know her, but to be apart for a month and now to be closer than before was an amazing feeling. I never wanted to let her go; being here with her felt perfect.

She came skipping out of the shop ten minutes later, clutching a bag secretively. I tried to see what it was but she hid it behind her back.

"All in good time," she laughed as she held me at arm's length from her purchase. "Your turn now – see if you can find something you want me to have that's from you." And with that she manoeuvred me round towards the shop and pushed me through the door. I stumbled into the shop, almost knocking over a display of books at the front, and turned to look at Sara stood outside, doubled over laughing at my predicament. I managed to regain my composure somehow and headed straight for the part of the shop that I loved and knew the best: the music books. I stood there for what seemed like ages looking at all the artists that they had, from ABBA to the Ramones and Sid Vicious to ZZ Top. After a bit of thought I decided to go for a book about Janis Joplin, one of my heroines – a lady with a lot of guts and the ability to outdrink most men. When I bought it, I asked the girl at the till if I could borrow a pen, and quickly scrawled an inscription inside the front cover.

Don't compromise yourself. You are all you've got. This was one of my favourite Janis quotes, and I signed it underneath with a couple of kisses. Satisfied with my choice, I left the shop and headed back to Sara. I waved my shopping bag at her playfully, and when she tried to grab it, I pulled her towards me for a long, deep kiss. It was the most passionate, yet also tender, kiss I had ever had; not at all one-sided and I felt that neither of us wanted to stop. The fact that we were stood right in the middle of the pavement on a busy London street on a Saturday meant that we had to, though, and move quickly before being attacked by the angry shoppers who were struggling to move around us as they rushed to find the next of their sale bargains.

Sara was making all the plans today, and she was soon leading me by the hand back to the Tube station. After a short journey with one change, we were soon stepping back out into the cold air that was still blowing around Camden Town.

"The plan is this: we take a look around the markets for a while, then we grab some food somewhere, have a drink and then back to mine, OK?" Sara was so vibrant and it was hard not to find her seemingly boundless energy infectious.

"Sounds perfect. On one condition, though: I'm buying you dinner and drinks." It seemed like a good deal and I was desperate to take the lead on something today; at least attempt to be a bit dominant.

Sara nodded, seemingly impressed by my stand, and led me down the road towards the lock and all the market stalls. Camden was one of those places where I had spent a lot of time over the years, always enjoying how relaxed the atmosphere was, and how all the different types of people mixed easily together. I'd spent hours sat by the lock, either reading about musicians or writing poetry in my scruffy notebook. I had also spent many evenings in the pubs and clubs with the guys from work, or on my own, just enjoying the music; but had never really spent much time shopping here. There was the occasional necessity that I required, like a new pair of Converse or a hoodie or that fur-lined jacket I had bought on sight, but that was all. Sara was obviously a far greater pro at this shopping lark than I was, bartering with sellers who I could hardly even understand; knocking down prices on everything from stripy tights to necklaces and even a novelty lighter shaped like a gun. I watched her come alive within those bustling market stores, her eyes sparkling and her smile winning over everyone within a two-mile radius. We talked and laughed as we went about our shopping trip, Sara showing me things she thought I would look good in, me making a mental note but pretending I wasn't going to come back and get them at a later date. I figured I had to play it fairly cool because otherwise this beautiful girl would know that she had me, hook, line and sinker.

Once the fun of shopping had worn off, it was time to have some food before we headed back to Sara's. Since neither of us was particularly fussy what we ate, and Sara said she fancied something simple like a pub meal, that's where I took her. Twenty minutes later, we were sat at the window tucking into the biggest burger and chips you had ever seen and quenching our thirst with a cold pint of lager each.

"Thank you," I said, watching her eat her meal, concentrating so hard on everything she did that her brow creased into a cute frown.

"Thank you for what?" she said, not even looking up from her burger.

"People don't tend to take the time to know me, let alone spend time with me and give me such a wonderful day as you have," I replied. "Thank you for everything so far this year, really; from the first until now. You've made me feel complete." Part of me immediately regretted saying that, and I worried I had come on a bit too strong and might scare her off. Sara being Sara, though, just looked up at me and smiled.

"I wouldn't be here if I didn't want to be, would I? I think there's something special about you and until that's proven wrong, then this is where I want to be, so there." She always managed to reply with such ease; such confidence, but without being arrogant. She certainly was an enigma, and one I wanted with me for a long time.

The next couple of hours involved more drinks, far too much money spent on the jukebox, and us sat together smoking, chatting, laughing and doing a fair bit of kissing too. When we were together the whole world seemed to dissolve away – we were in a bubble and it felt wonderful. I felt like I had more confidence and couldn't care less what anyone else thought or said when she was there. Eventually the Camden sky started to darken and all the street lights started flickering into life. We had just finished our last drink and selection of songs, so we decided to make the journey back to hers. Although I had only walked there with her that one time after the club, I knew the way back without any mistakes. As we walked that same path, I thought back 30 days. What a surprise it had been, her landing in my life like that; how lucky I felt to have met her and although it had been hard, just how much she was worth all the waiting. As my mind wandered, Sara was hugged up close to me, protecting herself from the cold night air. Before I knew it we were at her house again, stood at that same familiar spot outside the gate. I stood and motioned for her to come and have a hug but she looked at me strangely.

"Are you coming in or what?" she said, raising an eyebrow.

"You mean inside? Are you sure?" I stammered. My 'cool, calm and collected' mask was not slipping, but cracking into pieces as we spoke.

"Of course I meant inside, dopey. Where else did you think I was taking you?" She laughed and started to drag my arm towards her front door. "Before you say anything, don't worry – it's just me in. Dad's away in the States on business so I have the house all to myself until next week." She added a playful wink with this last sentence, and started unlocking her door.

"I, ummm, OK, cool." As replies went, I don't think that would have got me into the pages of a Charles Dickens novel. I was shocked at being allowed indoors; shocked at being on my own with Sara, and nervous, not wanting to mess anything up.

Once we were in Sara's room, my opinion of her was sealed once and for all. One wall was adorned with pictures from magazines of musicians and famous figures like Che Guevara, all in a massive collage. The second wall had a huge window that looked out onto the street below; the third wall had shelves on it from left to right and top to bottom. The shelves were filled with books and CDs; I made a mental note to check out the whole record collection later but liked what I'd already seen. The fourth wall had all the usual things against it, with the wardrobe and dressing table either side of the big double bed, but above the bed were four framed vinyl albums on the wall: The Beatles' *Sgt Pepper's Lonely Hearts Club Band*, Joy Division's *Closer*, Blondie's *Atomic* and Nirvana's *Nevermind*. Below that was her ticket from the New Year's party at the club, stuck to the wall with a big love heart drawn on it and my initial in the middle. I wasn't sure what I loved more: the amazing taste in music and love of vinyl, or the really sweet keepsake of our meeting. I think it was a combination of both.

"See, I think you're as special as my favourite vinyls." Sara caught me by surprise as she came out of her bathroom. She had changed out of her clothes and was wearing a ridiculously oversized Ramones t-shirt which looked more like a dress on her. My focus moved downwards I realised that she probably was wearing it as a dress, because she had taken her leggings off, and I wasn't sure that she was wearing anything else underneath the t-shirt. She leaned against the bathroom doorway, the light exposing her vulnerability. She was biting her top lip and her head was at a slight angle. She looked ethereal as I walked across the room and put my hands on her shoulders, hugging her into me, holding her tight as she shivered within my arms.

"It's cold tonight, so you had better hurry up and get ready. You need to keep me warm," she said, before slipping out of my grasp and jumping into her bed, pulling the covers up around her.

When I came out of the bathroom, Sara was sitting up in bed waiting for me. She had turned the lights out, lit some candles and put some music on. I smiled to myself as I recognised the familiar pop and hiss of a record player, and then the album that was playing on it: *Pet Sounds* by The Beach Boys. This girl had some amazing taste in music, and I hardly ever met anyone who liked the same stuff as me, so I was in heaven. Sara gave me an old Led Zeppelin t-shirt to wear in bed, so I changed into that and my boxers before slipping under the covers next to her.

"This is for you," she said, handing me the bag from the bookstore and giving me a huge kiss on the cheek. I opened the bag and inside was a copy of *Alice in Wonderland*. Inside the front cover, Sara had written a quote from the philosopher Nietzsche which said *Without music, life would be a mistake*, and then she had signed it *your white rabbit, Sara x.*

"It's perfect, thank you," I said, as I hugged her, kissing her gently on the forehead. "I suppose you'd better have this, then." I leant over the side of the bed and handed her my bag. When she took the book out of the bag she had a big smile on her face, and when she read the inscription she laughed and playfully poked her tongue out at me. After we both put our books on the bedside table, Sara moved over to me so that her head was resting on my chest and we hugged up tightly together. I slowly stroked down her back until my hand reached the bottom of her t-shirt; she was wearing tiny shorts and my hand found the smooth, soft skin of her thigh. She murmured sleepily as I stroked her thigh, before reaching and moving my hand around her chest, placing it near where her heart would be. I could feel the beat thumping away as she gently turned her head upwards to look at me.

"Will, I want you but I just want to take things slow, OK? I want us to enjoy taking time to get to know each other without any pressure. To trust each other enough to let ourselves go. I'm sorry if I gave you the wrong impression?" she said, nervously.

"Shh, don't be sorry beautiful, that's fine. I've had the best day of my life today and I'm just happy to be here cuddled up with you. I promise we can take things as slow as you want to. It means everything to me just to be able to wake up with you," I whispered to her, and I was happy that I meant it. I had friends who were forever jumping in and out of bed with people and it meant nothing to them, but I really liked Sara and I wanted everything to be perfect. She deserved that; we both deserved that. Laying here with my arms wrapped around a girl who was beautiful, cool and had a gorgeous body, I didn't think life could really get much better anyway. As the candles started to flicker out, *God Only Knows* began playing on the record player and as I listened to the words, I pulled Sara in even closer to me and shut my eyes.

"I think I'm falling in love with you, Sara," I said, as I started to drift off to sleep.

Chapter 2

February 1984 – Age 7

What is your favourite childhood memory? Maybe it's your first pet, a certain Christmas or maybe even a family holiday?

I don't remember a lot about my childhood and people think that's sad, but I don't ever worry about it – I know I was happy and that's all that matters. I tend to think that people create their memories from those photographs you find in faded albums of the past, and they're not really memories of the mind at all anyway. My favourite and most vivid memory from my childhood comes from when I was seven years old though, and has never faded in my mind.

Thursday 16th February
"Wake up William, it's seven o'clock. Your breakfast's ready.' My mum's shouts woke me from a very deep sleep.

I poked my head out from under the blankets and looked across at the clock. The time was seven o'clock exactly. I should have known: my mum called out at the same time every school day; she was never a minute early, or late.

"William?" my mum called again, as I carefully pulled the bed sheets off me, shivering in the cold morning freshness.

"I'm on my way, mum," I shouted back, whilst putting on my thick dressing gown and slippers before heading downstairs. I stumbled into the kitchen with sleepy eyes and found my mum hunched over the radio, listening intently.

"Mum, what are you—?"

"Shh, wait and listen, Will. It might be your school announced next," she replied, concentrating even harder on the man talking. As I watched, still confused, I wondered what she seemed so excited about. It was the same way she was on Christmas Day when she watched me open my presents from Santa. It wasn't Christmas though so I couldn't work out why she was excited.

I sat up at the table and started eating my breakfast, still confused as to what it was all about, but too hungry to be too worried at that point. I heard the man on the radio listing schools off like he was reading a script and talking about frozen pipes and dangerous roads, but was far too busy eating to pay it much attention. Then I heard the name of my school, and the man informed me that there was something to do with hazardous roads making it too dangerous to drive nearby or something. My mum hissed a 'yes' and punched the air in victory.

"That's it then, Will, no school today. So you and I are going to have some fun," she said with a childlike grin on her face. I looked up from my breakfast and questioned what was going on, but she just beckoned me over to the kitchen window with her finger. I picked my empty bowl up and put it in the kitchen sink, still confused, and saw that she was pointing at the blinds on the window.

"The reason there is no school today is a very special one, William. Today will be a day to remember: your very first snow day!" With the words 'snow day', she pulled the blinds open, letting in what felt like a huge explosion of bright light. I shielded my eyes slightly as I looked out into the garden. Everything was a blanket of white; not a hint of green grass, brown wall, or blue pond to be seen. Instead of the garden ornaments and lawn there was nothing but snow, and it was very deep snow from the looks of the few small paw prints that the neighbour's cat had left behind. I was so shocked; I had seen the odd covering of snow before, but it never amounted to more than an inch or so. This was almost a foot deep, and still falling. My mum must have noticed my shocked expression as I looked out of the window and put her arm round me. So this was what all the strange excitement was about! My first proper snow day and I couldn't wait to get it started.

Suddenly it all dawned on me: no school, so I could spend all day playing outside in the snow. I gave Mum a hug and rushed up the stairs to get changed. Within ten minutes I was back in the kitchen wearing as many layers as I could – a woolly hat, a scarf and my gloves. I was ready to hit the garden and have some fun, already worrying about when it might all be gone. My mum was busy in the front room tidying, so I called out to her and flew out the back door into the snow. Luckily there was a gap behind the kitchen door because of the back porch we had, otherwise I wouldn't have been able to open the door at all due to the snow being so deep. I tried to run through it and was knocked off my feet by the weight of it; it came to just above my knees and the strength of it when compacted together was too much for me. I picked myself up and dusted myself off, covered in snow and feeling it soak into my clothes as my body heat raised its icy temperature. I started to investigate this new, white garden, carefully leaving a trail of tiny footsteps from the house in a big circle around the lawn. It was still snowing and it wasn't long before any footsteps I had left were covered again by a clean, fresh layer. I ran my hands through the bushes and hedge, watching as the snow fell in big clumps, leaving the greenery damp and glowing in the white surroundings. I spent a good hour in the garden inspecting everything, making and throwing snowballs, writing messages in the snow with sticks, and generally losing myself in this winter wonderland. About an hour later my mum called me into the house and told me we were going out for the morning, so once again I dusted myself off and headed indoors. In the kitchen my mum was dressed up like a snowman, complete with earmuffs and a bobble hat, and I couldn't help but laugh.

"And what is so funny, hey Will?" she enquired, with a mock look of shock on her face.

"Nothing, Mum, I'm just not used to seeing you look so much like a snowman," I replied, attempting to keep a straight face but soon bursting into laughter which was made even worse by my mum's attempts to tickle me.

"Very funny William, you keep being cheeky and I'll be turning you into a snowman, thank you very much." Mum released me from her clutches and I fell to the floor, still giggling to myself.

Once I had composed myself, Mum told me that we were going to the park so that we could have some fun out in the open, where there was even more snow and I might see some of my friends from school to play with. So she locked the back door and grabbed her keys before leading me out the front door and into the garden. I was amazed to look at our street and all the trees that lined the road, everything covered in a blanket of white; even the road lay untouched and there was barely a footprint in sight. I looked at our

37

driveway and there was a huge block of snow where Dad's car usually stood. Then I realised – that was Dad's car!

"How come Dad's not at work, Mum?" I asked, excited that he might be off today, too. I didn't see my dad much apart from at the weekends when he wasn't working, and even then he often had lots of work he had to do that he brought home from the office with him. I loved my dad to bits; I thought he was the best dad in the world, and I just wished I had more time with him.

"He had to walk in, honey; the roads are far too difficult today with all this snow around. He said something about some buses running though so he might have gotten one into the office. Don't worry though, he'll be OK and home tonight as usual so you can tell him all about your day, OK?"

"I guess so," I said, sounding rather unconvincing. It wasn't that I was worried about Dad so much; it was that I wanted him to have fun with us rather than hear about it quickly over dinner before I went to bed and he hit the paperwork again. Realising, I think, that I was a bit sad about Dad not being there; Mum took my gloved hand in hers and gave it a little squeeze before leading me out of the garden and into the street.

It took ages to walk anywhere but it was lovely; everything looked like a fairy tale, all covered in white and glistening like diamonds. It took a lot of concentration not to fall over and it took a great deal of energy to walk through the depth of the snow, especially for me as it was up higher than my knees. The snow had started to fall a little heavier now, and I felt happy that it wouldn't be gone in an instant – maybe it would even last until the weekend so Dad and I could have some fun in it. Mum and I talked excitedly on the way to the park; I was pointing at all the different things I could see in the snow and how strange they looked all covered up in this thick white covering. Mum showed me how a lot of the shops hadn't opened up for the day, and we both noticed how few people were around. We figured they must all be tucked up indoors in the warm, waiting for the big melt to happen. This seemed like such a waste to me, and when Mum and I got to the park, I thought that even more! The whole of the park, as far as the eye could see, was white. It was like the world's biggest snow playground; a handful of children and adults were dotted around having fun, but there was so much room and so much snow. I looked at Mum; she looked back with the same mischievous look in her eyes, and we ran. We ran and ran until our legs gave out and we fell in a crumpled heap in the snow. I landed on Mum and she picked me up, holding me above her so it felt like I was flying over the wintery landscape, then she sat me down near her and sat up. We were both covered in flakes of white, and damp but happy. The day was so beautifully bright and everywhere you looked, you could see the snow glistening and shining beneath the sun-bleached sky.

"Haven't you two got to the top of the hill yet?" I heard his voice from behind me before I saw him and I leapt to my feet and started to run at him.

"Dad, you're here? I thought you were at work? How long are you here for?" All my questions came blurting out as I jumped at Dad and he dropped whatever he was carrying and caught me in his arms for a huge bear hug.

"Blimey nipper, what is this? *Question Time?*" he laughed, before explaining that he had taken the day off but he hadn't wanted me to know as it was a surprise for me. He slowly lowered me to the ground and showed me what it was he'd been carrying. Beside him were two homemade sleighs, one big enough for an adult and one small enough to fit a child. It turned out that Dad had been up most of the night watching the snow fall and had already decided to take today off before I even got up, so when it started to settle and get deeper, he had snuck down to the garage and made the sleighs for us to use.

I hugged him again and started to investigate the sleighs, getting my foot caught in the rope and ending up falling over and landing on my bottom in the snow again. Dad just laughed and headed over to Mum, who was still sat on the ground looking at us. Dad held out his hand to Mum like a character from one of those old movies they enjoyed watching – the ones with all the singing and dancing in – which she gracefully accepted, as he helped her gently stand. When she got to her feet, he spun her round like a ballroom dancer before pulling her in close for a big kiss. I didn't normally like seeing Mum and Dad smooching, but today it was OK. I sat and watched how happy they both were and it made me feel all warm inside. I loved my mum and dad, and they loved each other. It wasn't always easy for us; life never is, but moments like this one made everything worthwhile. I dropped the rope I had just untangled from my legs and ran over to them for a hug, just the three of us in this huge, white playground. It felt like no one else existed except for me, Mum and Dad, and this was all I needed. This was my idea of perfect.

Eventually the three of us started walking up the hill, Dad and I pulling a sleigh each while Mum walked in the middle with her hands on our shoulders. We passed a handful of people who all said hello and then carried on with what they were doing, and I didn't see anyone from my school but I was glad about that because I didn't want anyone ruining my special family day. It took us a while to navigate our way up the hill through the ever-thickening snow, but eventually we did it. When we got to the top we stopped and looked out at the view from Parliament Hill. From here you could see so much of London, and it usually looked so strong and industrial, but today it was like a giant marshmallow, all soft, white and fluffy. As I stood there looking, my mind wandered and I saw myself walking over the puffy clouds that hung above the horizon, leaping over building after building, then falling and landing in a huge soft pile of snow on the floor. So free, nothing but a soft fall from grace.

"Right then daydreamer, are we going to race or not?" Dad interrupted my thoughts with his sleigh challenge. He was sat on his sleigh with his feet on the ground either side, rocking it backwards and forwards at the top of the hill, ready to start the race. My sleigh was next to his, so snapping out of my daydreams, I jumped onto mine and did the same. Mum was the referee and we agreed to go after a count of three, so Mum stood there counting down slowly.

"Three, two, one."

We were both moving our sleighs further forward and backwards, the snow turning to ice beneath our runners and making the ground even slicker, ready for us to go flying off and down the hill. Then with an extra helpful push on my sleigh, Mum announced the last instruction.

"Go!"

And off we went, flying down the hill, both steering wildly with the bit of rope that was connected to the front of the sleigh, desperate to avoid crashing into each other and forfeiting the race. The air made a whipping noise against our faces as we flew down the hill, avoiding piles of snow. Finally the race was over and we both came to a stop in a huge snow bank at the bottom of the hill, first Dad and then me. We landed with a thump, head first into the snow, and we couldn't help but laugh at the outlines we had left in the snow. It looked like two caves that had been created by strange creatures with sleighs for bodies. After getting our breath back, we managed to pull our sleighs out of the bank and start heading back up the hill again.

"Best of three?" Dad said to me with a smile. He knew I wasn't bothered about winning the competition but I sure wanted to go down the hill on the sleigh again, and knowing Dad, he would make sure he lost the next two races just so I could win. That was the kind of dad he was: he'd do anything to see me smile and I think it hurt him that he saw so little of me through the week as much as it hurt me, if not more.

"You're on," I replied, as we started walking quicker up the steep hill.

We had two more races, and true to form, Dad let me win them both. Then he decided it was time for us to get Mum, so we headed back up the hill for the last time. When we got to the top, we found Mum lying on her back on the white ground. Her arms and legs were spread out and she was moving them up and down like a puppet, carving a shape into the snow around her.

"Look Will, I'm a snow angel," she said, smiling to herself as the flakes fell around her, littering her jet black hair and adding to the angelic effect by looking like tiny white feathers. As I watched my mum it dawned on me what was so special about today – just how much fun we were all having. I mean, we weren't a miserable family at all, but Mum was normally quite serious and Dad always worked so hard that sometimes it seemed easy to forget just how simple fun could be. Here in the snow though, everything was so easy. My dad was a champion sleigh builder and my mum an angel. In this fantasy land of snowflakes where it felt as if we were surrounded by God's pillows, everything was perfect.

My dad went to lie down next to my mum and did the same, making two angels in the snow. I stood and looked around the park: there was the occasional couple or family dotted around in different places and they were all having fun; they were all equal. In this world of children playing and adults working there is so little time just to smile, but the scene playing out before me was the magic of change, where kids and adults become the same. This was one big snowy freedom for all. I lay down next to Dad and made a smaller angel; we all lay there laughing at how silly it must look to anyone else, the three of us laying in the snow flapping our arms and legs around. We didn't care though; we were the perfect snow angel family.

After a while we could all start to feel the damp creeping into our clothes, so we got to our feet and dusted ourselves off. On the floor in front of us were the outlines where we'd lain, so angelic and smooth in the crunchy snow around them. Mum and Dad hugged before they both put their arms round me and we started to walk back down the hill, heading towards the warmth of home. It was even harder walking back home than it had been earlier and I didn't know whether that was because we were tired or whether the snow had got deeper. As we walked the last few roads home, it started to come down even thicker and faster, the late afternoon sun had started to dip in the sky and the street lights had started to flicker on, illuminating the snow beneath them so it all seemed to glow and twinkle even more. Small patches of ice on the road looked like beautiful jewels, shining in the fading light. My mum skipped into the road and started twirling with her arms held out wide; she looked like a ballerina. Dad soon joined her and they danced slowly together, moving beneath the thickening snowfall like they were trapped in a beautiful big snow globe. I held my hands up towards them and framed the scene, taking an imaginary photo for my album of memories. My mum and dad, smiling and laughing, they were my favourite people in the whole world.

When we got home, Mum changed clothes and put the kettle on, whilst Dad and I went down to the shed to put the sleighs away. Whilst we were in the garden Dad said we should build a snowman to commemorate the special day. I'd never built one before but Dad said it would be easy and set about pushing piles of snow into a big heap in the middle of the lawn. Mum watched from the kitchen window as Dad and I worked as hard as we could, pushing it all from one place to another, then packing it together and adding more, then starting the whole process again until finally we had a huge snowman body. Then we started on the head, and after lots of scraping, pushing and rolling, we had what looked like a huge golf ball which we would use for the head. Dad picked it up in his arms and pushed it down onto the body with a thump, and although I was biased, I thought it looked amazing. Dad sent me looking for something to use for the eyes and mouth whilst he sorted out some clothing for him. After another 20 minutes we had a big, smiling snowman, complete with baseball cap, scarf, two halves of a squash ball for eyes and a stone for a mouth. I wasn't sure about the baseball cap, but Dad laughed and told me it was all he had, and the snowman wasn't having any more of his clothes because he had already donated the scarf and was now stood in the garden feeling chilly. Just as I thought it was complete, mum appeared with a big carrot for the nose. She pushed it gently into his face and we were done: a great addition to the family and a great memento for our day. One quick snowball fight later and we were more than ready to get back into the warm. I went indoors and changed out of my wet clothes and into the warmest pyjamas I could find, then sat in the kitchen to drink my tea. Dad joined Mum and I a few minutes later and we all sat at the table looking out at our snowman; he stood tall in our garden smiling as the snow continued to fall around him, like a guardian of our special day.

"What are you going to call him then?" my dad asked.

"Diamond," I replied, "because he's glistening like diamond so that's his name." I sat there looking quite content with myself, and I didn't tell Dad that it was also because Neil Diamond was his favourite singer; it seemed fitting that our creation was as much a tribute to him as it was fun for me.

"Hmm, Diamond," Dad said with a smile on his face, and he patted me on the head as he finished drinking his tea.

The rest of the afternoon and evening was much more boring than the earlier part of the day. Dad sat and looked at the newspaper while Mum made dinner, and I alternated between watching cartoons and looking out the window to check on Diamond. The snow had slowed down now and was fluttering down again rather than coming down heavily like before, and in the middle of the garden stood Diamond, smiling at me from his icy white palace.

That night when I was in bed, Dad came in to say goodnight. I was usually asleep by the time he came in, so it was a lovely surprise to be able to speak to him and kiss him goodnight. To get that smell of aftershave as I lay down in bed was so comforting; we didn't get enough of those moments but today had more than made up for that. I kissed Dad goodnight and he thanked me for a lovely day. He told me to get a good night's sleep and he'd see me in the morning before slowly pulling the door behind him.

"I love you Dad," I said, as he left the room.

"I love you too champ," he replied, and switched the main bedroom light off.

I sat in bed with the bedside light on, reading my comics until mum came in. She could see straight away that I was looking tearful and gave me a huge squeeze, her arms wrapped around me, as I took shelter in her.

"What's wrong honey? Have you been crying?" she said.

"I'm OK Mum, I promise. I just had a really lovely day today and wish it didn't have to finish, and then I was thinking, what will happen to Diamond?" I started to sob again as Mum hugged me tighter.

"Oh Will, we'll have more days like today, I promise! You are only young; there is so much more time for fun, for all of us. You really don't have to worry."

"But what about Diamond?" I said. Mum sat on the edge of the bed, facing me, and took my hands in hers.

"The thing is Will, when the snow melts so will Diamond. You don't have to be sad though – he's a very happy snowman and he's glad to have had any time with you at all; he loves you very much," she said, before taking my hands and placing them on my chest.

"It's like anything in this life, you make the most of the time you have together and when you can't have any more time, you hold them here in your heart. Nothing ever really leaves you – it stays in your heart to make you smile when you feel sad; to give you company when you feel alone. That's what love is, Will. Never be afraid to love, OK?"

Then she gently laid me down in bed and gave me a kiss on the forehead before wiping the tears away with her finger. She made sure I was tucked up as usual and then slowly walked towards the door. When she opened it she turned to me and said:

"Night Will. I love you, my little miracle, and my own little piece of the world. Sweet dreams, gorgeous."

"Night Mum, I love you too," I said, before dropping my comic onto the floor and turning my bedside light off.

I lay there in the dark for ages, just thinking. Going through everything that had happened that day, from the surprise of seeing the snow, to the comfort my mum had given me before bed. I quietly snuck out of bed and climbed up onto the seat near my bedroom window for one more peek. I stuck my head up under the curtain and saw Diamond shining in the moonlight, looking as strong as he had earlier.

"Night night Diamond, I love you too," I said, before climbing back into bed and turning the light out on a perfect day.

Chapter 3

March 2003 – Age 25

If you could have time back to spend with your loved ones, how would you use it? Would you just enjoy it or spend the time telling them everything you'd meant to say but never got around to?

I remember looking at Mum sleeping soundly in her bed. She looked so peaceful, with no sign of the illness raging inside her apart from a slight loss of weight and strength. I sat on a chair in her bedroom, just watching and wishing that this would all go away. It had been six months since the day they took all our hope away. Mum hadn't been feeling well for a while, but had just ignored it and kept battling away until she collapsed in the garden one September afternoon. Dad had found her when he came home from work early and she had been rushed into hospital not long afterwards. I remember getting a tearful call at work from Dad, to say she wasn't well and could I come down to the hospital as soon as possible, so I left work and headed straight there. An hour later we were all sat together in a little private room with a doctor and a consultant talking a lot of medical jargon at us. I remember looking at Dad holding Mum's hand in his lap, both of them looking so scared and confused. I remember hearing the word 'cancer', followed by the word 'untreatable', and then finally they were talking about timespans and it was months rather than years.

I got up from my seat and walked over to the door and out into the garden area. Everyone in the room stopped and stared at me as I slowly opened the door and stepped out of the room onto the grass. I remember standing there, just breathing in the air, with my back to the room. I knew what had been said without even thinking and it hurt like hell. I swallowed hard, pushing down the lump in my throat and sucking the tears back up, then composed myself and then stepped back through the door. My mum and dad both looked at me, and it was a look that I hadn't ever seen before: they both looked lost. I went over and hugged them as the doctor and consultant made their polite apologies and left. The medical world had thrown a huge grenade into the room, then quietly left and shut the door behind them. Both my parents held on to me as if their lives depended on it, and I guess in some ways they did. I never cried though; I stayed strong for both of them. It was all I could think to do.

In the six months that followed, Mum's illness had taken hold pretty quickly and our whole life had been thrown into chaos. Although stable for the first couple of months, at the beginning of the year Mum ended up in a hospice and it looked as if her time was nearly at an end. Mum hated it there, and I remember how she and Dad used to argue about what was best for her and how they could look after her better than he possibly could at home. Mum was having none of it though, and within a month was back at home where she wanted to be. She was given less than three months to live when she left the hospice, but Mum wasn't bothered by that; she was coming home to die and that was her wish.

Before she came home, Dad and I had sorted all the plans so everything would run smoothly. Dad had taken compassionate leave from work and would look after Mum from Monday to Friday; I would take over on the weekends if he needed me to and he could have a break himself. It never happened though; he rarely left the house anymore, let alone left Mum for a day. The whole event had been a lot more difficult than we ever expected, even with the specialist nurses and carers coming in. It was strange to open our lives to the complete strangers who would come in to offer assistance, but we were always so grateful for their help and empathy in such hard times. It was clear to see that what they did was more than a job, it was almost a calling. Together we were proud to say that as a team we had made sure she was always comfortable.

In the last week Mum became a lot sleepier and the nurses said that with the drugs she was on and how weak she was, it was only a matter of time now before she passed. I found it so hard to make sense of any of it; during the day mum would sit up slightly and talk. Admittedly she wasn't strong in voice or body and sometimes did fade back into sleep again, but I couldn't believe that we were going to lose her so easily.

Sunday 2nd March
That morning, I let Dad have a lie-in. I got up at seven o'clock and had been sat with Mum ever since. As I sat there staring, she shifted slightly in the bed and opened her eyes.

"Will, are you there? Will?" She was so breathless, and the urgency in her voice snapped me out of my daydream. I walked over to the bed and perched on the edge of the mattress next to her, took her hand in mine and with the other I gently stroked her hair.

"I'm here Mum, don't worry everything's fine. You should be resting, it's still early." I spoke in hushed tones so I didn't wake Dad up; I really wanted him to get some rest before this all got even harder.

"I had to tell you, Will – I saw Sara today," she said with the hint of a smile on her face.

"Mum, don't, please," I said, the emotion causing my voice to break.

"Shh," she said. "She looked so beautiful, Will. We didn't get to speak for long; she said she had to come and find you. She was rushing around, so busy." The smile on Mum's face broadened and then she slipped back to sleep again, her breathing so soft and subtle. I tucked her hands under the covers and kissed her on the cheek.

"I love you Mum, with all my heart," I whispered into her ear, and sat watching her drift back off to sleep before gently getting off the bed and returning to my chair. After a while of sitting there, I put my head in my hands and sobbed, quietly at first but then louder and louder until I felt an arm around me.

"It's OK Will, it's OK, let it out son, please. You can't always be the strong one. It's OK to cry." My dad was hugging me now and I collapsed into his chest, months of hurt flowing out of me in one go. I had tried so hard to be the one that kept everyone going, but I just couldn't do it anymore; I was breaking and it just hurt so badly.

"I'm OK Dad, sorry. I just need to get some fresh air, please, I'm OK," I said as I hugged him back and headed downstairs and out through the kitchen door into the back garden. I sat on the bench that Dad had put there for Mum and lit a cigarette. As I blew the match out I saw a hazy vision of the garden through the smoke, and it made everything look white, like it was covered in snow.

"It's like anything in this life: you make the most of the time you have together and when you can't have any more time, you hold them here in your heart." These were the first words that came into my head as the memory of all those years ago came flooding back. At the time I thought that my mum was so brave for being able to deal with a loss so easily, and all these years later I needed some of that strength for myself. I sat reminiscing about the times I had had as a child and how lucky I was, until a howl pierced through the peaceful silence. It was Dad's voice. I bolted back indoors and up the stairs to Mum's room.

Dad was laid on the bed cradling her in his arms, and I knew straight away that his world had ended in that very minute. It was an all-too-familiar sight: a man with all the pain of the world in his red eyes, holding onto something or someone for dear life. He was hugging her to his chest and tears were streaming down his face.

"She's gone, your mum's gone," he cried out through the tears.

I stood at the top of the stairs feeling completely numb; everything was spinning and the walls were closing in fast. Nothing ever prepares you for something like this, whether it's a complete shock or you knew it was coming – there is never any sense in loss. I walked slowly into the bedroom; my legs felt like lead and I was hardly moving no matter how hard I tried. I walked over to the bed and put my arm around Dad's shoulder, gently easing Mum's body back on to the bed. Dad looked at me with such sadness in his eyes and he collapsed into my arms.

"Oh Will, what am I going to do without her? She was my life; I don't know how to exist without her." He was sobbing so hard that I could feel his pain rattle through my entire body.

"I know Dad, I know. I'll help you, OK? Together we'll get through this; it's what Mum would have wanted." I tried to reassure him but I didn't know if he could even hear me through his sobs.

We sat there for what felt like hours, Dad crying his heart out until he was exhausted. He looked so pale and tired, so I helped him back to his bedroom and gave him a couple of Mum's sleeping pills that she'd had stashed away from the end of the last year. I sat with him until he fell asleep and then started working through all the harsh realities of any death: the phone calls, the paperwork, the official details.

By late afternoon it had all been sorted; every form and certificate that needed to be signed had been signed and Mum had been taken to the chapel of rest until the funeral. Dad had slept through the whole of the day since Mum had passed away; I tried waking him when they took her away but he hardly stirred – all the sleepless nights over the past few months had finally taken their toll, and with the sleeping tablet he would be out cold until the morning. When I looked at the clock it was almost 6 pm, and the house was silent. I stood in Mum's room staring at the bed where less than 12 hours earlier we had spoken. I couldn't believe she was gone. I climbed onto the bed where I had been before; I could still smell her perfume and feel the warmth where her body had been, and I laid down as if next to her and cried. I cried for all the loss; all the broken dreams; all the missed opportunities, but most of all I cried for her, my mum.

Friday 7th March

The next few days passed in a blur, and everything seemed so clinical to me. The funeral directors had come and spoken to Dad; all the arrangements had been made and all the paperwork sorted out. We only had a small family anyway, but any relatives and other family friends had been contacted about the funeral, and although there was a big hole in our home where Mum should have been, it felt like we were just getting on with things that needed to be done. Dad had been like a ghost the whole time, forever on the verge of tears, and together we struggled to talk for fear of upsetting each other. One of the things I had wanted to do was sort Mum's room out, but Dad had just shut the door and wanted nothing else done with it, like he was locking it away somewhere it wasn't allowed to be reached again.

On the day of the funeral, Dad and I spent the morning together in complete silence. We had both gotten dressed far too early and were sat waiting for what felt like hours. It seemed so strange to be waiting for something that you had never wanted to come, but now you were wishing it would be over already. The service was beautiful and I'm sure Mum would have been proud of it. I chose the music as it was a topic that Mum and I had often spoken about, and I was the perfect person to choose songs that would suit the occasion and Mum's taste: the Carpenters, Kate Bush and Phil Collins. The song *This Woman's Work* by Kate Bush took on an even more ethereal quality when played in the little chapel, and although there were only a handful of guests, there wasn't a dry eye in the house when that was played as we said goodbye. During the service, Dad said a few words about meeting Mum and how she was the best thing that ever happened to him; about the ups and downs of married life and how you come through it all in the end if you respect each other. He thanked Mum for making him feel like the luckiest man on earth, and finished his speech by saying "God bless you, my sweet Elizabeth; please wait for me and I will come find you. I love you and will miss you every day." He kissed his hand and laid it gently on her coffin. I was so proud of him – I never thought he'd be able to speak without breaking down but he did; he reminded me of when I was a kid and how I never needed superheroes, not when I had my dad.

I had written a little piece but had asked the vicar to read it out for me as I knew I would never be able to say it aloud. I had thanked Mum for being the greatest mum in the world and for putting up with me no matter how much of a pain I was; for always supporting me, but most of all for being herself. She was the most amazing woman I had ever known.

After Dad and I had shaken hands with the handful of visitors, he put his arm around my shoulder and led me back to the car; it was time to go home. I remember staring at the sky the whole time we were driving home; it looked so beautiful yet so empty, mirroring how everything felt to me at that point. It was now time to return to normal, to go to work and pay the bills, to smile and laugh, to live. As I looked at Dad and then my own reflection in the mirror, it struck me how neither of us looked like we had anything left in us that wanted to live. That night as I lay in bed listening to Mum's old Simon and Garfunkel album, I realised that I hadn't just lost my mum that day – a piece of my dad had died with her, too. I could hear him quietly sobbing to himself in the next room until the early hours of the morning, and my heart ached even more.

Friday 14th March

Dad cried himself to sleep for the next six days after the funeral, whilst I lay in bed listening to music. I wanted to say something or do something, but I knew my dad's pride wouldn't let me see him like that so I was forced to just carry on as if I hadn't heard it.

A week after the funeral, I returned home from work to find Dad sitting in Mum's old bedroom. He had moved the bed right into the corner, then brought the settee in and placed it in the middle of the room, where he sat on it with his back to me. As I entered the room I heard Neil Diamond playing on the stereo, and I could see that he was drinking. I knocked on the door and Dad turned, looking at me with tired, red eyes.

"Hey there champ, how was work? I dug out a load of your mum's records today so I thought we could listen to them and have a drink to celebrate her life, what do you reckon?" He seemed almost upbeat, but that ghostly look in his eyes gave him away as being full of whisky-tinged bravado.

"Sure Dad; let me grab a shower and change out of my clothes, then I'll join you OK? I'll ring for a takeaway too if you like, save either of us cooking?" I was trying to seem calm and unconcerned, but at the same time I wanted to make sure that he was still eating.

"Sounds good champ, go on. Don't be long, there might not be much left," he said, waving the half-empty whisky bottle in the air as the record reached its end.

Half an hour later I was sat with Dad on the settee, drinking whisky and listening to The Beatles. Dad had another two bottles unopened next to him on the floor, and it didn't take me long to realise that this might be a very long night. The drinks kept coming; the records kept being played, and we talked about Mum and how great she was, how lucky we were, all the wonderful memories we had, and most of all how much we both missed her. Dad had even taken a cigarette off me and lit it, sat there indoors smoking and smiling to himself when he told me how he had stopped smoking because Mum had hated the habit.

"I did it all for you, I did everything for you," he said, almost to himself as he slung back another whisky. Then he turned to me again.

"The thing is Will, I feel guilty. Your mum was always there for me, she carried me through so many bad times; got me back on my feet and fighting again, and she made me who I was."

"I don't understand though Dad, why do you feel guilty? None of this was your fault," I replied, feeling confused as to where this conversation was going.

"After everything your mum and I had been through, both good and bad, there was one thing I didn't do and I cannot forgive myself for it," he said, his eyes welling up with tears as he spoke.

"What is it, Dad? What's wrong?"

"I never said goodbye Will, I never got to talk to her and tell her I loved her one last time. I never got to say goodbye and now it's too late, she's gone and I don't know how to live without her." It all came flooding out and he howled like he had on the other nights I heard him, except this time it was to me, his son, and he was crying in my arms.

I hugged him so tight and tried to console him, but I had a pain inside me; it started in my stomach and travelled through my heart until it stuck in my throat. As I hugged him, I whispered, "It's not your fault Dad, it's mine, I just realised. I should have woken you up that morning; it shouldn't have been me that Mum spoke to before she died, it should have been you. I am so sorry, so sorry." The pain was immense as I realised I had been the one to hear her last words. Dad had no need to feel guilty; it was me who had let him sleep in. I should have woken him at the normal time and he would have had his chance to say goodbye; I had taken that from him and I could never fix that.

After a while Dad stopped crying and slumped back on the settee again. The whisky bottle was almost empty now, and a combination of the drink and the emotion seemed to have worn him out. I watched as he slowly sank further and further down until he was asleep. I sat there for a while making sure he was definitely asleep, and once he was, I lifted his legs onto the settee so he was laid down and put a blanket over him. I finished the last of the whisky as the last few bars of the music played, and then I got up and groggily headed to bed myself. I remember looking at the clock as I stumbled into bed and noticing it was well past two in the morning, and then I closed my eyes and fell asleep.

Saturday 15th March
When I woke up the next morning it was ten o'clock and the house was silent. I showered and got ready very quietly so I wouldn't wake Dad – I figured that the amount he had drunk the previous night meant that he would be asleep until at least midday, if not mid-afternoon. I didn't have to work as it was Saturday, so I had decided that later on I would see if Dad wanted to do something; maybe even go out and get some fresh air. After being up for nearly two hours I decided to go and check Dad was OK, otherwise he would be asleep all day and then awake all night again. I quietly walked down the corridor past his bedroom to Mum's old room. As I

walked in I noticed that the settee was empty, and it didn't look like anyone had been there for a fair amount of time. The empty bottle of whisky was still sat on the floor, but there was only one full bottle left near the chair where he was sat the previous evening. I looked out the window but couldn't see him in the garden; I checked the front room and the kitchen but there was no one there either. I called out, but the words almost echoed around the silence of the building. As I searched I suddenly realised that his bedroom door had been shut when I walked past, so he must have gone to bed and taken the other bottle with him for a nightcap. I went upstairs and knocked on the door of his bedroom, quietly at first and then a bit louder, but no reply, so I carefully opened the door and peered in. The curtains were half-drawn and there was Dad, lying on his side cuddling Mum's dressing gown. Quietly, I walked over to him, and as I did I felt something crunch underneath my foot. I looked down and saw a small pile of white powder on the floor. Next to that was a lid, and then I realised what it was.

"Dad, don't you dare – I can't lose anyone else," I screamed as I jumped on to the bed, turning him over onto his back. I was too late; my dad was already gone. His eyes were staring at me with that same ghostly expression they had held for the last two weeks, but there was no life at all behind them. I checked for a pulse; I checked his breathing, but he was gone. I rushed over to the bedside cabinet to phone for an ambulance, and as I did I noticed the empty bottle of Mum's sleeping tablets on the floor beside the bed. Next to them was a half-empty bottle of whisky and a piece of paper torn out of a notepad. As I was dialling 999 I looked at the paper and the erratic-looking note written on it.

I'm so sorry, Will. I love you but I have to be with your mum.
Love, Dad x

As the person on the other end of the phone started speaking to me, everything went blank: my head started spinning and I plunged headfirst off the bed and onto the floor with a cracking sound. Then the white went black and I was out cold.

I woke up in a bright white room later that day; my head was throbbing but for a split second I thought everything had been a bad dream and I would see my parents sat next to the bed, waiting for me to wake up. My heart felt so heavy when I looked at the bedside and there was no one there; this was my life now, with nothing and no one but me. Tears began to roll down my cheeks and from somewhere deep within me a huge painful scream came from my mouth as I realised that nothing was ever going to be right again; I was lost and alone. Minutes later two nurses came rushing into the room. They reassured me as best they could, and explained that I was in hospital because I had taken a large bang to the head and lost consciousness. It was only the call I made to the emergency services which had alerted anyone to a problem before I had passed out. The nurses were so sympathetic and spent ages at my bedside looking after me, but I just wanted to get home; I needed to get home. After a few hours and checks by the nurses and doctor I was allowed home. I was advised to rest and they gave me some painkillers for the headache, but other than that I had a clean bill of health, so I made my journey home in the fading London evening light. London by day was so busy with people, traffic and noise, but London at night could be the loneliest place on earth, and it could appear like a huge concrete jungle that would swallow you whole, given half the chance.

When I got home I found the front window boarded up where the emergency services must have broken it to get into the house, and there was a note on the side explaining that someone would be round to replace the glass in the morning. Other than that, everything was normal. I got myself a carton of apple juice and walked upstairs. I stopped outside my parents' bedroom and looked in – everything was calm and tidy; the shape where my dad had been was still imprinted on the bed but other than that everything was still. It was almost like nothing had ever happened there at all, with no sign of the pills or the half-empty whisky bottle, and I closed my eyes and wished that it hadn't. I pulled the door closed and headed to my bedroom, the bedroom that I had known for 25 years, but now felt like a stranger to me. I walked over to the CD player and put *The Ghost of Tom Joad* by Bruce Springsteen on, lit a cigarette and sat on the edge of my bed. My whole world was spinning around in my head: people, places, voices and conversations all mixing together in one huge jumble. I was feeling dizzy and I wasn't sure if it was the headache or the cigarette, so I stubbed it out and decided to lie down, and before I knew it I had fallen asleep.

Friday 21st March
The next week was the same as it had been after Mum died, with all the paperwork and phone calls that had to be made. As I was now the last member of my immediate family I also had the added problems of sorting out all their financial things. In the first few days I made some phone calls to people that Dad had worked with who understood finances, and his colleague Kevin came round to see me and talk me through all the options so I knew what to expect. The hardest thing was dealing with how people looked at me: that sympathetic look in their eyes that showed how much they

pitied me. I know they were all just being kind but I didn't want pity from anyone, I just wanted my life back.

After all the paperwork was done, the day of the funeral came around. There was exactly the same crowd there that had been at Mum's funeral, except there was one person missing and that person left a huge hole at my side and a massive empty chasm in my heart. I had chosen Neil Diamond, John Lennon and *Freebird* by Lynyrd Skynyrd for the service. Dad had always loved *Freebird*, and I couldn't think of a more fitting song for him to leave us with. As much as I had wanted to avoid it, and as much as I hated the thought of doing it, the vicar had spoken to me about saying a few words, being that I was the only surviving relative, and I couldn't really say no. I had spent ages writing a huge, long speech but once the time came to read it out, the emotion of the event got too much for me and I could only say what was in my heart. I remember how I felt standing there, with everybody's eyes on me as I spoke.

"Firstly I'd like to thank you all for coming today. I know my dad would be honoured to have you all here, and with it being so close to the last time we were here, I appreciate it all the more. Most of you here knew Dad from working with him, and I think that is how most people remember Dad: as a worker. I spent a lot of my childhood wishing that he didn't have to work so much, but I look back now and realise that if anything, it just made the time I did have with him even more special. He gave everything he could to provide for his family, and I'm sure you will all agree how sadly missed he will be at work, though there is nowhere in the world he will be missed more than by my side. He was my best friend, my hero and above all else, my dad. He wasn't the world's greatest dad, but he was the greatest dad in the world to me. I want to apologise to him for anything I ever did wrong; I want to curse him for leaving me to fill shoes that I will never be good enough to fill, but most of all I wish I could hug him and tell him how much I love him. He and Mum were destined to be together and it killed him to lose her; I hope he has found her and himself again, and in a far more peaceful place than here. I spent a long time trying to think of something to say as a big enough send-off for him but all I came up with is two small words: *thank you*."

As I finished I couldn't hold the tears back any longer, and they came flooding out. I walked over to the coffin and laid my hand on it.

"I love you Dad, I'm so sorry I couldn't save you."

After the service I stood in the doorway shaking the hands of everyone that had come to pay their respects, and they all thanked me and told me I had done Dad proud with my speech. The last person to leave was Kevin, and he shook my hand, thanked me and told me he would phone me in a couple of days regarding all of Dad's financial matters.

"I've decided what I want to do. I'd like to put any money left into my bank account, and I want to sell the house and all the furniture as soon as possible," I said; I had been thinking about it all week.

"Your dad worked hard for that house though, Will. I know this is a really hard time for you, but don't you think it'd be better to take some time and think about it before you do anything rash?" he said, appearing quite shocked at my plan.

"Kevin, I really appreciate everything you've done for me and I know Dad thought very highly of you, but you know what I've been through and now I need to get away from all of this. I just want the chance to start again, without all the memories and all the sadness following me around. I'm haunted by enough ghosts already."

Kevin listened carefully to what I had said, then looked me straight in the eye, nodded and shook my hand.

"That's what I'll do, then; I'll have the paperwork drawn up for you and bring it round in the week. Take care Will, we know you've been through an awful lot, but we're all here if you need us." He smiled and headed off to the car park, leaving me on my own outside the chapel.

In the days that followed I moved quickly, desperate to keep busy and wanting to sort everything out so I could leave the house. It turned out that there was a lot of money in Dad's different accounts and bonds from work, as well as the money in my parents' joint account and in Mum's, so selling the house wasn't an immediate issue financially. With Kevin's help I had everything transferred to my account and had the house cleared and on the market before the end of the month. I had managed to find a flat in Camden for rent and was ready to move in at the first of April, so all I had to do was move my stuff over and then I could say goodbye to all the sadness for good. It had all seemed so quick, but that was what I needed – I felt like the only way I could survive would be to have a fresh start and the sooner the better, but there was one thing left for me to do.

Monday 31st March
On the last day of March, I sat on Parliament Hill, looking out at the beautiful view over London. In my bag I had two containers: Mum and Dad's ashes. I had thought about where I should sprinkle them and the most obvious place for all of us was here at Parliament Hill. As a family we had spent a lot

of time here, and it seemed the most fitting place for me to finally say goodbye to them both. At ten o'clock that morning I emptied both jars into the wind, watching the ashes blow around like tiny angel wings in flight. Mum and Dad, together again, both floating away into the beautiful clear sky.

"Safe journey. I love you," was all I said as the wind blew the remains high into the sky and out over London. I sat back down on the bench, lit a cigarette and looked at the view. Tomorrow would be the start of my new life and I had never felt as alone as I did at that point.

Chapter 4

April 2005 – Age 27

What is the bravest thing you've ever done in your life? Was it to help someone else, or something personal?

Thursday 21st April

"My name is Will, and I'm an alcoholic. I first came here a year ago when my life had hit rock bottom and the only way I knew to cope was the drink and then drugs. I used drink to escape from the pain I was holding inside, and to take me somewhere that I thought I wanted to be. When I first came here I had no life, no self-respect and no dignity. I was living like a tramp and was heading towards an early grave, but now, a year later, I can stand here and say that I am sober. I haven't touched a drink for 12 months and I feel so much better for it. I want to thank all of you here for your support and encouragement, and to a special someone who isn't here: I couldn't have done it without you. So thank you."

I sat amidst a standing ovation, feeling both proud but embarrassed at the same time. The lady leading the group offered her congratulations, and then discussion moved on to other things related to our meetings. I quietly got up from my chair, headed towards the coffee machine, walked straight past it, and out onto the road outside. I didn't want a lot of huge emotional goodbyes and congratulations; I had completed my year and now I had to stand on my own two feet. I turned the corner, got into my car and drove back to my flat. When I was inside I slumped down onto the settee and let out a huge breath. I had been more nervous going to the AA meeting today than I had when I first turned up there, over a year ago. I never thought I would come this far, and it was such a strange feeling looking back and seeing myself as a stranger compared to who I was now. I always thought of alcoholics as being washed up sixty-somethings with a string of broken marriages and children to their name, but I had been proven wrong and it was probably the most valuable lesson I had ever learnt. Here I was, not yet 28 and a recovering alcoholic. I hadn't even seen it coming; I mean, I always liked a drink but I never realised it had become a problem. In the early days it was a drink for confidence when I was going out to gigs or a pub, then it was the years of drinking for fun and having a bit too much every now and then, but the last four years had taken me on a very dark path, downhill and fast. Looking back I know now that the seeds were planted in late 2001, but after losing both my parents in March 2003, that's when it took control of me. I was no longer gaining escapism through the bottle; the bottle was using and destroying me.

I remember the first big drinking session I had in April 2003. It was a Monday morning and I had just signed the paperwork that finalised the sale of my parent's house, and the six-figure sum was due to be in my account by the following week. Since that was the last loose end to tie up, I decided to go out and have a drink, partly because everything was still so raw and painful. I left the solicitors and headed back to Camden at around eleven o'clock, arriving at the pub in decent time to grab a seat by the window and have lunch. I'd resigned from my job the previous week and was taking some time out to think about what I wanted to do with the rest of my life. When all my parents' finances had been sorted out and transferred to me, it was fair to say I had a huge amount of money and that was before I'd sold the house, so I could afford not to work for quite some time and I figured it was my right. My workmates had understood and they wished me luck; I was told that if I ever wanted to come back I could, but they hoped everything worked out for me. Kevin and a couple of other people from Dad's work had rung me a few times and told me how well I was coping and that Dad would've been so proud of me, and some people even thought that it was as if nothing had happened. People deal with grief in different ways though, and I always bottled things up – I'd had to hide things from my parents for the last two years of their lives and now it just seemed to come naturally. I don't think anyone ever truly realised how much I was hurting; only Sara ever saw the real me and I would've given anything to have felt her arms around me right then. I sat gazing out the window, twisting the ring I had on a cord round my neck between my fingers, lost in my thoughts when the music came on the jukebox. As soon as the song started I knew what it was: I had listened to Coldplay's *Yellow* so many times in the last seven years and every time I heard it the memories came flooding back. I looked over at the jukebox and there was a couple choosing songs; they were laughing and playfully wrestling with each other, and I couldn't help but feel jealous. I don't know where it came from, but I felt a rush of panic as I watched these two young lovers being so close. I quickly finished my pint of cider and headed to the bar and ordered another pint and a whisky chaser before getting back to the safety of my window seat away from all the happiness around me. Before I knew it the pub had started to fill up, and my anxiety levels got higher and higher. I alternated my time between drinking and heading back to the bar to order more drinks, until eventually I was fairly tipsy and feeling more comfortable. I'd given up travelling between the bar and the window, taking a seat at the bar instead and attracting the attention of Jodie, the alternative girl who worked behind it. In between serving, she had been chatting to me about the music that was being put on the jukebox, and we had ended up talking at great length about our musical likes and dislikes. It turned out we had lots in common, especially with music, and that was a favourite subject of both of ours. She had even been a regular in the shop where I worked, but it had been a while since she'd been in. The time ticked by as we chatted and before long it was six o'clock and her shift was over.

"I fancy listening to some music and having a drink tonight; I'm not working tomorrow so what do you reckon? Let's go get wild?" She had a wicked smile and was obviously hoping to get out of her workplace so we could carry on getting to know each other elsewhere.

"Sure, why not, did you want to meet me somewhere after you've freshened up?" I was doing my best to sound convincing but was finding it hard to think about spending time with a girl that wasn't Sara – it just didn't come naturally to me anymore.

"I've got it all here," she said, as she pulled a rucksack from behind the bar. "Meet me out front in five minutes; I'll get changed and we can hit the bar down the road. It's rock night tonight with live music, but they open at seven and have an hour of DJ requests." With that she disappeared through a staff door and was off to change.

I finished my drink and headed to the toilets. As I washed my hands and face I looked up at my reflection, and it looked right through me. I felt the panic start again and drew a deep breath to try and keep calm.

"What are you doing here? Just go now, quickly, you don't need this," I said to my staring reflection, before drying my hands and face and heading outside. I stood outside the pub smoking until Jodie appeared; she was wearing torn jeans and baseball boots with a Sonic Youth t-shirt and a battered-looking leather jacket. She looked great as she bounded over to join me by the streetlight.

"Do I look respectable enough for you?" she joked as she led the way to the club down the road. She started telling me about working at the pub and her dreams of becoming a photographer one day; she was so full of energy and it had been so long since I had met anyone like that, it made me smile. I didn't tell her much about me except that I was taking a break from work to decide what I wanted to do with my life, and I skipped the usual parts of the conversation about family and general life, choosing to steer the conversation back to music and books where I could. From the minute I had left the pub I had noticed how tipsy I was feeling, and before I knew it we were sat in the club listening to rock songs from the '90s and doing tequila slammers together. The club was pretty empty when we arrived but before long it was over half full, with most people waiting for the live music. I had seen the flyer though and the two local bands playing were heavy metal and I didn't fancy seeing either of them, so I figured we could have a couple of drinks before heading off. My mind was wandering as I looked around the club, my vision becoming heavier with every drink.

"Will, are you still with me? I don't think you heard a single word I said." It was Jodie talking to me; she leant across the table and took hold of my hands. "I was saying we could do a couple more slammers and then head back to mine? I'm sure I can sober you up." She winked at me and moved my hand up to her face.

"Sara." I said it; I don't know why but it came out. I wanted to tell Jodie to stop but there was only one name that always came straight into my head and it was Sara's. I pulled my hands from hers straight away and clung on to the table as the room started to move from beneath my feet.

"Sara? That's really nice, Will. You can't even remember my bloody name. Thanks a lot. Who the hell is Sara anyway?" Jodie was understandably hurt and fuming, her arms crossed and her eyes narrowed angrily, staring at me.

"I'm sorry, I really am," I said as I pushed myself away from the table and stumbled back through the club. It felt like the floor was tilted as I knocked into people stood by the bar; I struggled to keep my balance but eventually fell through the door and out into the street. The air outside hit me immediately and I convulsed, vomiting into the gutter at the side of the building. I had a million thoughts flying through my head but none of them made any more sense than any of the others. When I'd finished being sick I stumbled away from the club towards home; it wasn't far and I managed to make it without any more problems. When I got in I was feeling better, so I freshened up in the bathroom and made my way to the lounge. It was nearly nine o'clock now and I was thirsty so I poured a big glass of orange juice from the fridge and sat in front of the television. As I sat there I started to feel awful about the nights events: I felt really sorry for Jodie but most of all I felt guilty. I started to think about Sara and the tears started rolling down my cheeks; I missed her so much and I didn't want anyone else. I had known she was the one for me when I first met her and now everything seemed so pointless. As I sat back on the settee my heel caught something under the coffee table that clinked, and I looked down and saw half a bottle of vodka lying there. I wanted to sleep; I hadn't slept well for months, let alone years. So picked up the bottle and took a big swig, washing it down with orange juice, then another and another before finally emptying the rest into the glass of juice. That night ended with me passing out on the couch, but the last thing I remember before that were the tears rolling down my cheeks once more.

Looking back at that night, it's amazing that I didn't kill myself through alcohol poisoning alone. The nights had gotten much worse though, and the cracks really started to show in October that year with an incident at the church, and carried on until March 2004, the last time I drank.

I remembered that night in March well because now I can look at it as being the start of my new life. I'd spent all day in the flat watching films, drinking cider and getting high. I'd started to use drugs recreationally in the past few months and the habit had gotten a bit out of control, more so when I drank than when I was sober, though. I had wasted three quarters of the day and it was only when I ran out of drink that I even thought about leaving the house. I was wearing a scruffy pair of combat trousers, my Converse trainers and an old Pixies t-shirt, so I pulled on my hoodie and headed to the shop. Twenty minutes later I had bought another three litres of cider, a small bottle of whisky and 40 cigarettes, and was sat on the bench outside the shop opening the cigarettes and starting the cider. It had gotten to the stage where my behaviour became very erratic almost as soon as I started to get drunk, and this night was no different. A quick trip to the shop turned into me thinking that I should go to Parliament Hill and visit my parents' special place, so off I walked, swigging the cider as I went. I made it to Parliament Hill in good time, considering, and as I sat down on the bench in the dark night air, the city of London was lit up all around me like a huge fairground. The night was quite warm, and a mixture of the alcohol and the temperature made me feel fuzzy and my eyes heavy.

"Look Dad, is that a tramp?" The boy was whispering, in the loudest voice I'd ever heard, to his dad.

"Don't stare son, come on let's keep walking. Quickly now, come on," the dad replied, pulling his son by the arm and leading him down the hill.

I had opened my eyes when I heard the voices, shocked at the thought of two strangers stood in my flat. When I saw the two sideways figures stood against a backdrop of trees though, I knew I wasn't in my flat; in fact I wasn't even indoors. My head was pounding as I lifted it up slowly, and my body ached; I moved into a sitting position and felt the hard wood underneath me. I slowly opened my eyes again and that familiar London view was staring back at me: I was still on the bench at Parliament Hill from the night before. On the floor was an empty cider bottle and in my pocket was the last bit of the whisky I had bought the previous night. I slowly screwed the bottle cap off and held it to my mouth, closing my eyes to the sun that was making my head throb more. As I went to tip it into my mouth, I felt a hand grab mine and I opened my eyes immediately.

"You need to stop this, Will — it is Will, isn't it?" The stranger took the bottle from my hand and emptied it onto the dirt.

"Wait, you don't understand," I protested, trying to grab the bottle back. I just need one more drink, and—"

"And you'll be fine, I know Will, I've heard it all before. I'm going to give you something and I want you to go home, sober up and look at it, OK? You need to sort this mess out before it's too late. I know what you're going through and you can get through this, I promise. If not for me or yourself then do it for your parents — they never would have wanted to see you like this." The strange man put a small card in my hand, patted me on the back and walked off.

I don't know whether it was the hangover blues or something else, but the kindness of that strange man brought me to tears, and as London woke up that morning, so did I. Sitting there with tears pouring down my cheeks, I knew something had to change. I thought about Sara, Mum and Dad, the old job I loved so much, and how everything was gone but I had to change my life around; I needed to get myself back on my feet again. Slowly the crisp morning air helped shake the cobwebs from my head and I was ready to walk back to the flat. It was time to start living again — I owed it to the people I had lost if nothing else.

"I'm sorry," I said, more to myself than anyone else, and I turned from London's skyline to walk home and start repairing my life.

Once I got back to the flat I had a shower and got dressed; I wouldn't let myself return to bed no matter how tired I was, not until I did something positive about this mess of a life. I sat down on the settee with a cup of tea, staring at the small piece of card on the table in front of me. On it were two capital letters — *AA* — and a phone number. I rang the number and the man who answered politely introduced himself and asked how he could help me. It was now or never, fight or flight, and only I could choose.

"Hi, my name's Will and I need help with my drinking. I just want to know how to stop and I was told you could help me." The words fell out without me even thinking about them and that was it; I had made my start of a new life. The man asked me if I wanted to give him a brief idea of the problems and listened intently as I told him how bad things had gotten, including the blackouts and the general deterioration in my mental state, and how I needed help to turn my life around. He took my number and said he would ring me back as soon as he could sort out the best venue for me to attend a meeting and explain where we went from there. He rang back just ten minutes later and told me some of his own story regarding alcoholism and how AA had been so beneficial to him in his recovery; he told me where the closest meeting was to me and when they were held, and I agreed that I would attend one which was in two days' time at the local church hall. When I had finally finished on the phone I went to my bedroom and put some music on before rewarding myself with some much-needed sleep.

Two days later I was stood outside the church hall, lurking in the shadows, shaking like a leaf and chain-smoking. The last two days had been really challenging: I hadn't had a drink and my body had reacted to the change. When I slept I had been having the most vivid nightmares and waking up drenched in sweat, whilst during the day there were times when my hands were so shaky that I struggled to complete the most simple of tasks. It would have been so easy to have just taken a drink, but I had made my decision and was going to stick to it. I realised now though that I needed this support more than ever.

As I stood in the dark watching people being greeted at the hall door and welcomed in, I stubbed my cigarette out and followed suit. The hall was larger than I thought and the chairs were nicely arranged in a circle so that everyone was involved in any discussion and no one was isolated. I chose a chair near the door and as far back as I could and watched quietly. The man on the phone had explained that as I was a newcomer it would be best for me to come to a first meeting as a spectator; this way I could get a feel for it, find common ground with others' stories and gain myself a sponsor to help me with the process. He had explained that a sponsor would be someone whose long-term sobriety and lifestyle appealed to me; someone who would help me with the 12 steps to sobriety and also act as a one-to-one support when I needed it. I was also encouraged to go to as many regular meetings as I possibly could in the first few months, so the support network and platform for my recovery was as strong as it possibly could be.

So there I was, the newcomer at the AA meeting, eyeing up possible sponsors and facing my demons at last. There were such a variety of people at the meeting and I couldn't get my head round the different sorts of people that suffered from alcoholism: all the stereotypes were blown away by these normal people with this nasty problem. As I sat looking at the people around me, I noticed a guy coming in the door. He looked like an old rock star: long hair, beard, leather jacket, leather trousers and a scruffy heavy metal t-shirt. Everyone welcomed him when he entered the room and it seemed that he was hosting the meeting tonight. He said how good it was to see some new members, and when he turned my way I suddenly recognised his face. He was the stranger who had handed me the card two days ago; the one who had poured my whisky away and helped me face up to reality. He smiled as he saw my face and carried on greeting everyone with a friendly nod. It dawned on me that he knew what he was talking about when he spoke that morning, and when he said he understood, he really did understand because he must have been in the same position as me at some point. Suddenly that stranger gained a huge respect from me and I had a feeling I had already found my sponsor.

The meeting was profoundly inspirational and yet heartbreaking at the same time. So many tales of sadness, of lives lost to the bottle, of broken marriages and broken families. It turned out that the stranger who had led me here was called Joey, and he had been sober for over six years now and had been adopted by the group as a sort of chairperson, he structured the meeting so well and was so sympathetic to the tales of woe without being condescending at all. That first meeting lasted nearly two hours, and everyone relaxed afterwards and socialised with cups of tea if they wanted to. I was still feeling nervous so I decided to slip away quietly and head home, but just as I got to the door I heard a voice.

"I'm really glad you came tonight Will, I hope you've seen enough to want to stick with us?" Joey was stood behind me smiling, holding out his hand for me to shake it. "I don't believe I properly introduced myself. I'm Joey; I used to work with your dad until I lost my job."

"You knew my dad? I don't remember ever meeting you." I was startled by this new revelation.

"I worked with your dad for about 18 months, but I lost my job and didn't see him again until about a year before he died. The whole time I was working with your dad I was going through some emotional problems at home and I turned to drink to shut all the problems out, but in the end I lost control and couldn't function properly. I was turning up at the office still drunk, losing paperwork – everything started to fall apart and I just became a mess. I didn't stand a chance with the management; they fired me on the spot and no one from work bothered to check on me and keep in touch, except your dad. I heard about his passing from someone else that used to work with him and since then I've tried to keep an eye out for you and what I heard and saw worried me. Then I found you on the hill that morning and wanted to try and help you. I'm so glad you followed the advice and came here; I feel like finally I've repaid a small bit of the debt I owe your family." He spoke so honestly about his problems that I had a huge respect for him and I owed him more than he knew.

"I didn't know. I'm really sorry you had such a hard time but I'm glad you're coping now. It makes me smile to think of Dad doing something like that; that's exactly the sort of man he was, always putting others first. I know he would want to thank you for getting me here; I hope I can get as far as you have. Tonight was the first step though, and I've done that, so I'll have to see where it leads me. I do have one question for you, although it's probably a huge thing to ask." I knew it was now or never; I had a feeling I needed Joey more than he knew.

"I'd love to be your sponsor; it'd be an honour," he said, smiling. "My advice to you, Will, is to come to another meeting tomorrow and gain more understanding and confidence. Don't underestimate what you've done here, it's a huge step and you need to give yourself credit for that. Then by the start of next week, maybe you'll want to tell your story? I'll see you tomorrow night; here's my number in case you have any problems." He handed me a card with his number on and shook my hand, before heading back off into the crowd of people. I noticed how they were all drawn to him like he had some kind of power, and smiled to myself as it dawned on me that he was my sponsor. I left the building ready to take on the world – a fresh start; I had started the fight of my life.

Over the next few days I went to a meeting every evening, some of which Joey was at, and some he wasn't. We talked every day on the phone or met up for coffee, and it turned out that we had more in common than Dad, too. Joey had been in an old rock and roll band back in the seventies who had achieved moderate success throughout London, and he was really passionate about music. He even took me to his flat one afternoon and we spent time listening to old vinyl records together and drinking coffee. He opened my eyes to some old bands that I had never gotten around to listening to properly, like the Stooges, the New York Dolls and The Clash, whilst I gave him an education in their early nineties equivalents, like Sonic Youth, Dinosaur Junior and the Pixies. As well as having the perfect sponsor, I was glad to say that I had made a new and very good friend.

It was the second meeting in the second week when I finally spoke. I remember putting my hand up, and when it was my turn I stood up and spoke the words I never thought would apply to me:

"Hello, my name's Will and I am an alcoholic."

I ended up speaking at length about the issues that had led me to drink, and was extremely aware of the emotion in the room as I told them of my losses. When I finally sat down after speaking it was a huge relief, like sharing had eased a burden from my shoulders and now I might be able to gain some momentum in my recovery. At the end of the meeting most of the people there made a point of coming up to me, offering their condolences and extra support if I needed it. I had been worried at first that AA was going to be a huge cult full of brainwashed zombies with no spark left, all talking about how good water is for you. The truth was that it was just a group of normal people who weren't afraid to say that they had a weakness, and who were brave enough to try and seek help to rid themselves of it. I learnt more about others and why they had turned to drink too, and it opened my eyes to how something can be so destructive, especially something that is so clearly linked to British culture. I stayed away from all my old haunts in the first few months, too scared of what might happen if I went into one of the pubs or clubs, and instead I went for walks, had coffee with Joey, listened to music, read – all those things that I had lost from my life during my drunken stupor, and now I was getting them all back.

After six months I had decided that I needed to work again, so I spoke to the guys at Love Music and they all said they'd love to have me back, as long as I was OK and ready for it. I explained that I didn't want paying; I had money, but I just wanted to be doing something again and I could think of no better way to spend time than being surrounded by the music I loved. So a week later I was in the shop again, doing odd jobs and just enjoying the camaraderie of being with the guys and using my time positively. As I wasn't on the payroll but just helping out, it also allowed me the freedom I needed for my recovery: I could go to meetings at any time and I could also spend time with Joey and talk through the lows.

By the end of my first sober year, I had lost touch with Joey. Somewhere around the tenth month he had started to come to fewer meetings, and when I had phoned him to meet up he had either been busy or not answered the phone at all. Then at the end of the month I received a parcel which contained a copy of a Velvet Underground CD, the AA twelve-step book and a postcard. On the postcard was a picture of clouds, and as I ran my finger over the texture I realised that it had been hand-painted with great patience and precision. On the back was a small note that read: *Will, you have done me proud, you have done your family proud, but most of all you have done yourself proud. I have some things I need to do, so it's time for you to open your wings and fly solo. Onwards and upwards my friend! Forever in music, Joey.*

In a way it was a good test of my strength to keep on my sober journey without Joey. It had been easier to think of him as doing all the work for me rather than actually giving myself any credit, but now there was no hiding place and I continued to win the battle.

Thursday 21st April
Sat on the settee after the meeting where I had celebrated being sober for a year, I turned on the television for some background noise and sat drinking a cup of tea. My mind wandered through all the various stages of staying sober and just how easy I had made it look, even though it wasn't all plain sailing at all. My mind wandered to Joey, and I wished I'd had the chance to thank him in person for everything he'd done for me, but I knew that he would be proud of my achievement, wherever he was now. I had set my mind on two celebrations to mark the event, so first I started rooting through my CD collection in search of the Velvet Underground. As I looked through the pile of CDs that I had collected over the last few months, a report came on the

local news about a man who had been found dead in the lock. The reporter talked about the unnamed person appearing to have taken his own life after a night out in town, and how more tests had to take place before they could identify the man or be completely sure of his cause of death. As I found the CD and put it into the player, I was thankful that I had survived my fight with alcohol so far; I realised how easily it could have been me, and I felt pain for the lost soul whose life had ended like that. I turned the telly off and let Lou Reed's voice ring out around my front room. I sat there listening to the raw emotion of the music whilst smoking a cigarette, my one remaining vice, and drinking another cup of tea. I listened to the whole album from start to finish and thought about Joey; I wondered what he was doing now, where he was and if he was OK. I never did understand why he just disappeared – I always put it down to being busy with AA stuff, but then he appeared to have stopped going to that too. In the end I figured he must have gotten himself a girlfriend and made a happy new life for himself. I glanced up at the postcard on the shelf and a shiver travelled down my neck. I felt a bit uneasy, but had no idea why.

Once the album had finished I grabbed my jacket and headed out to Parliament Hill. I sat for an hour or so, on the bench overlooking London as always, gathering my thoughts and taking in the fresh air. It was the place I felt closest to my parents, and I often went there when I wanted to talk to them.

"I did it guys – a whole year and still no drink. I promised I would and I've done it. I wish you were here to see me; I'm working again, getting on with life again and I'm sober. I'm just glad you weren't here to see all the bad times before; I wouldn't ever have wanted you to see me like that. I have one of your old friends to thank though, Dad – Joey found me when I needed someone and he helped me all the way. I just wish I could thank him; maybe one day I'll get the chance. I miss you guys, and I love you, more every day." Wiping tears from my eyes, I stood and took one last look at the view before heading back home, stronger and sober. Wherever Joey was, I hoped he had found the peace I had.

Chapter 5

May 1993 – Age 16

Were your school days the best days of your life? Did you form lifelong friendships, or were you glad to leave them all behind?

Wednesday 5th May

The last exam I sat at senior school was French, and all I remember about it is when the bell rang for the final time and I was a free man. My years at school had been pretty enjoyable until I reached the age of 12; this was the time that I really discovered a passion for music and literature and a dislike for sport. Those final years at school I had spent as an outcast, really, with most of the other kids playing football every break time and more interested in fighting than art. I remember lunchtimes in the summer when I would find a shady spot beneath the tree in the playground, put my headphones on and listen to cassettes whilst reading a book. I loved the escapism of music and books, and although it separated me from my peers, it led me into fantastic worlds I never would have visited otherwise. My mum had always said that I was a deep child, and so the beautiful works of

Sartre, Camus and Bukowski fascinated me from the age of 13 upwards. I got called so many names in those last few years, and although I wasn't bothered about not fitting in, it did hurt me to be thought of as such a freak, especially when I wasn't hurting anyone.

I had a couple of friends in those final years but they wouldn't ever stick up for me when I was getting bullied – it was easier to stay quiet or leave the scene of the crime than stand up for me and risk making themselves targets. I had my music though, and that was all that mattered. I worked hard and although I wasn't the cleverest boy in the world, that got me through most of my studies. I was also terrible with exams, what with my nerves often getting the better of me, but I coped overall. The moment that last bell rang though, I felt a freedom like never before. I got up from my desk, headed past everyone else as they were signing each other's books, emptied the contents of my locker into my rucksack and left. It was such a strange and quiet end to what had been a really difficult few years, but I was just glad to be leaving. I left all the name-calling and social groups behind me and walked home, ready to start a new chapter in my life; one where I could finally make my mark on the world and become something I wanted to be.

Monday 10th May
The following week I started job hunting. I think Mum and Dad had hoped that I might go on to college and then university, but that wasn't what I wanted. I didn't want to be in a school-type environment anymore, and I was looking forward to getting myself a job so I could earn some money and start thinking about my long-term plans. So first thing that Monday, I started looking. The local paper was full of

adverts looking for staff for various jobs, but they either wanted some form of higher educational qualification or experience, and I had neither. Both Mum and Dad were supportive of my decision to go straight into work rather than further education and were prepared to help me as much as possible, but I wanted to do this on my own for a change. I felt like this was my chance to really grow up and stand on my own two feet. I had started working on a CV that I could take to any potential employers, and all I had left to do was fill in my exam grades, which I was due to get at the end of the week. As always, music was my companion that morning. For my sixteenth birthday my parents had bought me a five-CD changer music system and I hadn't stopped using it since. Early that morning I had loaded it up with the five albums I was listening to most at that point, and put it on shuffle to keep me occupied whilst I worked. When it got to lunchtime I decided to go out and get some fresh air and get a break from job-hunting, so I headed out into Camden to clear my head.

Camden high street and the markets were my favourite places in all of London; I loved that there was such a melting pot of different people mixing together without problems. Nobody seemed to judge anyone and most people walked around with smiles on their faces. It was one of those places where you could be yourself without fear of ridicule – that was what everyone did there; it was an alternative haven in a world full of standard expectations. As I wondered down the high street I noticed one of the old shoe shops was boarded up and had a sold sign on it, and it made me realise how long it had been since I had come to town and walked around. The thing that really caught my eye though was the sign in the middle of the boarded-up window.

Coming soon — Love Music, opening May 31st. Application forms available now.

My brain clicked into gear and my eyes lit up — this would be perfect for me, working with music in a place that I loved. Attached to the wood covering the window was a plastic holder with application forms in it, so I took one and decided to cut short my trip and head home. As soon as I got home I made myself a cup of tea and headed upstairs to fill out the form. The form was folded over like a pamphlet, and on the front it had the shop's logo — which was a big heart with a CD in the middle — the contact details and date of opening. On the back was a section where you filled in your personal details and exam grades, but it was the middle two pages that interested me the most. At the top in big letters it said *Ten questions to test your love of music.* It didn't state that you would need to pass the test in order to get a job, but I had a feeling that this was exactly what the test was for. I decided to go for it; music was my life so I looked at the ten questions that followed.

1) Where did The Beatles record most of their songs?

2) Which hotel was made famous by Leonard Cohen and Sid Vicious?

3) What Bob Dylan song did Jimi Hendrix have a hit with in 1970?

4) Who was the founding member of Pink Floyd who also inspired Shine On You Crazy Diamond?

5) Which rock star fronted the E Street Band?

6) Which band recorded the album The Joshua Tree?

7) Which group flew into the Hotel California?

8) R.E.M. cut the number one album 'Out Of...' what?

9) Which US boy band featured three members of the Wilson family?

10) Which band knocked Michael Jackson off the Billboard number one spot in 1992?

Ten minutes later I was happy that my answers to the questions were right, and I just had to fill in my exam scores when I got them and then send the form in. The more I thought about working in a record shop, the more perfect it seemed. I imagined myself listening to music all day, surrounded by the love of my life and getting paid for it. I just had to hope that I got an interview, and then a job. All I could do now was to wait for my results to come through and then the rest was up to fate. I finished my tea and lay back on my bed with the sound of Nirvana's *Nevermind* filling my ears.

Friday 14th May
At the end of that week, my results came through in the post. I had achieved the marks I wanted, passing six out of eight exams and all at grade B, so I filled the form out and sent it off in the post with a quiet prayer that I'd at least get an interview. My parents were really pleased with how well I'd done and even supported my idea to get out and work in the end. Ultimately, they just wanted me to be happy, and they knew that wasn't going to happen if I spent any more time in a classroom environment.

Monday 24th May
Ten days passed, and I was starting to give up any hope of getting an interview at the record store. I had sent the form off but heard nothing back at all, and I figured they must have already found what they were looking for. It wasn't until

later that afternoon when I was making myself a snack, that the phone rang and the guy on the other end told me he'd like to see me for an interview. I arranged to meet him the next day at ten o'clock, and he said that the back area of the shop was all completed now, so I could be interviewed there by him and another member of the management. The thing that interested me the most, though, was his praise when he told me that I got full marks on the music test.

Tuesday 25th May
I barely slept all night; I was far too excited about the possibility of a job, and nervous at the thought of being interviewed. My mum and dad were really pleased for me, and gave me pep talks in the morning to prepare me for whatever the outcome was and to let me know I was supported by them both; all that mattered to me though was getting the job. I dressed as smartly as I could, in black trousers and a white shirt with a black tie, and the only giveaway of my scruffiness was the Converse boots I was wearing, but I hoped that made me even more of an obvious music lover.

The walk to the shop was nerve-racking; I was trying to guess what questions would be asked and what the people would be like, but it just made me feel even more nervous. Before I knew it, I was stood at the door to the shop, ringing the bell and awaiting my fate. The next couple of hours seemed to fly by. I remember meeting the manager John and his assistant Shaun, and I remember getting on really well with them, chatting about my love of music and what it would mean to me to work in a store like that. I learnt a bit about the independent status of the store and how they were more geared for selling music that was interesting rather than just popular – they didn't sell any obvious chart albums, concentrating more on alternative bands and music that was critically acclaimed, rather than massive sales. After a brief chat about my music tastes and knowledge, they thanked me and said they would be in touch. The next thing I remember is being at home and getting the phone call to tell me I had the job, and that they wanted me to start on Monday the 31st. My mum and dad were so happy for me, and I was celebrating the fact that I could stand on my own two feet rather than asking for handouts all the time. My clearest memory of that day and those that followed is spending a lot of time reading as much of the music press as I could, researching all sorts of bands that I had heard mentioned before, but never gotten around to hearing or learning about.

Monday 31st May

"Don't go asking him to smile at the customers, man – he's one of those teen grunge kids; all he'll do is sit around gazing at his shoes and writing on his arms in biro," Steve was shouting across the storeroom to Mattie, who had come out back looking for someone to help him.

"Oh man – *I hate myself and I want to die*, you mean? Jeez, don't we all when the weather's as nice as this and we're stuck in here? Grab me a copy of *Copper Blue* by Sugar whilst you're there Steve; I need something to make me smile." With that, Mattie disappeared back through the door and into the shop again. Minutes later the music could be heard thumping loudly throughout the shop, and I could picture Mattie rocking out behind the counter in front of a handful of bemused customers.

"Hey kid, don't take it personally. We're like this with everyone until we get to know them. You seem cool so we'll all get on fine I reckon." This was directed at me, and probably the closest I was going to get to a compliment from Steve on my first day.

The start of the day had flown by and whilst all the banter was being thrown around, I was sat in the corner of the storeroom eating my lunch and reading *Melody Maker*. I hadn't really stopped working from the minute I'd arrived that morning, so was glad to be able to sit, eat and recharge my batteries for an hour. I had been shown the entire shop layout and the storeroom and how it was organised, and then helped to file the overstocks of the more popular albums in alphabetical order in the stock room before heading to lunch.

The shop itself was amazing; it looked like the alternative record stores in America which I had read about. Old, faded gig posters and band photos decorated the walls, whilst some of the coolest music got played in the store regardless of any bad language in the lyrics. This was a music store for real music lovers; people who were as passionate about music as the bands who had made it in the first place. The store was quite obsessed at this point with American alternative and indie bands: ever since Nirvana had shaken music from its foundations upwards, more and more bands were gaining recognition and Love Music was devoting a large amount of space to helping people find what they wanted. I was in my element; it was a dream come true for me to be able to work in a shop that really cared about music and let you wear your own casual clothes, and where you could listen to Pearl Jam whilst you worked. The guys there were all really cool too, and although I was clearly the baby of the bunch, I was made to feel welcome and knew it wouldn't be long before I blended in seamlessly.

It turned out that the manager, John, had opened six of these stores at the same time. There were stores in Manchester, Newcastle, Liverpool, Brighton and Sheffield as well as this one in London. He wasn't a hands-on manager at all, and the staff had been told from very early on that they would only ever see him in the store if there was a major problem, and other than that he was available on the phone or by fax. Shaun, the assistant manager, was in his late thirties and obsessed with music in general. There wasn't a pub quiz he could go to in which he wouldn't get full marks for the music questions, and it turned out that he was the person behind the ten questions on the application forms. It was never used to stop someone getting a job, but he let me know that whenever someone got full marks he was almost certain to employ them. I had met him early in the morning when he had introduced me to the other team members, but then he had gone off on errands. Again, he wasn't that hands on really either, but he was always around in case of any problems, and able to come to the shop if needed.

I had met the three members of staff who worked there and instantly liked them all. Mattie was the most experienced in music retail who worked in the shop on a daily basis; he was the unofficial person in charge really, and was a really lovely guy with a sharp sense of humour and very good taste in music. I knew from the instant I met him that we would get on, and I would learn so much from him. He was in his mid-twenties but had the enthusiasm of a teenager for all things music-related. Steve was in his early twenties, with a very deadpan and sarcastic sense of humour, but a really caring guy too. He loved all things English when it came to music and didn't care what was cool; if he liked it then it was cool as far as he was concerned. He was the joker of the shop who often tried his best to embarrass the other members of staff, but somehow it nearly always ended up backfiring and he only embarrassed himself. Steve was also the resident musician in the store and was constantly trying to form bands in the hope of one day playing live gigs and getting his music released. The last member of staff I had only met briefly – her name was Kelly, and she had popped into the shop during the morning to find out her hours for the week. She was the stereotypical riot grrl: torn Babes in Toyland t-shirt, scruffy jeans and purple Doc Martens. She had her nose pierced, and so many different colours in her hair that it looked like a rainbow. She was 18 years old and breathtakingly attractive; I imagined that she would never really have to do much work when he was in because all the men would be falling over themselves to help her. We had exchanged a smile and a nod, but then she headed back out into the high street again, a joint in one hand and a Patti Smith album in the other, off to meet some friends and party all afternoon.

The people that came in to the shop were the epitome of cool for me too, from some original punks to the more modern day lo-fi listeners, but we somehow catered for all. The motto of the shop was basically *if it's alternative, it's for us*, and I think we managed to produce a really good atmosphere and mix of musical tastes amongst ourselves, which added to the feeling of togetherness. All the staff were able to joke with regular customers the same way they joked with each other, and at the heart of it all was a collective passion for music.

After I finished my lunch I was met by a serious-looking Steve, standing at the stockroom door.

"I've got some bad news for you Will – this just isn't working out." He shuffled his feet and looked at the floor.

My heart sank; I was trying to work out what I could possibly have done wrong. I had a horrible feeling that I was going to be told that they didn't want me after all. Tears started to well in my eyes, and for the first time since leaving school, I felt like a child again.

"Have I done something wrong? I don't understand, what do you mean?" I could feel myself getting redder and redder as I spoke, desperately trying to hold back the tears.

"I mean it's time for you to hit the shop floor, my little grunge boy. You have been hiding out here for too long – to the deep end you go!" A massive smile as he pushed open the door to the store, and motioned with his arm for me to enter. I felt so stupid, and as I walked past him he patted me on the back and whispered in my ear, "Chill out man, it's just my sense of humour. I like you and Mattie is well impressed so you've got no worries there. Just be yourself; I think you'll fit in well."

"Mattie's impressed with me? Really – but why?" I wasn't sure if Steve was playing another joke on me.

"Something to do with you mentioning Dinosaur Jr this morning. He's another one of you mopey grunge folk and that totally impressed him – oh, along with your Converse." Steve winked at me and made his way behind the till as I smiled to myself. It hadn't dawned on me that I might impress any of these guys; I thought they were all so cool but I guess when it comes to music most people are equal!

For the next hour Steve showed me how to work the till; I was pretty good with electronic stuff so I picked it up pretty quickly. It was just a case of remembering all the different codes for special offers and things, but they were all listed on a note stuck to the till so it wasn't too hard. After a while Steve got bored and decided it was my turn, so he turned down the music and made an impromptu announcement to the half-a-dozen people who were stood in the shop.

"Ladies and gentlemen, here at Love Music we pride ourselves not only on our outstanding ability to provide you with music you want, but also to provide you with the friendliest and coolest retail staff on the planet. Today as we enter virginal territory behind the counter, I would like to introduce you to our newbie. He is a Converse-wearing, grunge-loving music enthusiast and his name is Will. Give him hell!" He turned to me and grinned before turning the music up again and heading out of the front door of the shop. I stood nervously behind the till with the sound of Suede's debut album filling my ears. I watched the few people in the shop shuffle around from rack to rack, looking at the CDs and searching for specific things they had in mind. Steve was stood out on the pavement leaning against a lamppost, staring at me whilst smoking a cigarette. He motioned with his hands as if to tell me the floor was mine, and then I realised what he was doing: he was giving me my chance to make my mark on the shop and on the customers, and most of all in my own mind. I had a look at the CDs behind the counter and found what I needed, so I turned the track down and addressed the shoppers.

"Hi guys, as Steve has already announced, I'm Will and hopefully you'll see more of me over the coming months, but just in case you don't I really don't want to waste time here listening to music I don't like, so apologies for anyone I upset now but this one's for me." I was a bit shaky, but managed to sound convincing enough as I turned back to the player, swapped discs and pressed play before returning to the till. After a few seconds the opening bars of *Them Bones* by Alice in Chains filled the store – one of my new favourite albums, *Dirt*, and my message to the store and to Steve. This would show that I had arrived and that I planned to stay. The few people in the shop smiled at me and carried on looking at the CDs, although I'm sure a couple of them started nodding to themselves whilst they looked, quietly appreciating the music.

"Bravo, young prince." Steve applauded as he walked past me towards the stock room, and that was all he needed to say. It felt like he was telling me I'd done well, and now we could start a relationship as a proper group of music-loving comrades. For the next half an hour I stood there serving people as they came and went, with confidence and a big smile on my face.

"I knew there was a reason to keep you," laughed Mattie as he came out onto the shop floor later on. "You wouldn't believe how much I've longed for someone who understands this stuff like I do; there's nothing I love more than to talk to someone who enjoys the same music as me. Although you're young, Will, you may well turn out to be my saviour."

"Thanks. I know it's only my first day but I'm really enjoying it here. I hope I can get to know all of you guys better, I think you're all really cool." I felt stupid for saying it but couldn't think of any other way to put it.

"Cool? You should see Steve dancing around to some poppy English crap; you'd soon change your mind. Except for me, though – you're right there." He laughed to himself and chucked me a cassette before heading to the front of the shop and starting to move things around. The cassette was a mix tape with *Mattie's musical education* written on it; the mock cover was a mixture of stars and swirls, and the track listing inside was all handwritten – I only had a quick look at it but it included acts that I'd heard of but not got anything by, including Sonic Youth, Sebadoh, the Lemonheads, Hüsker Dü, and many more.

"Thanks Mattie. When do you want it back?"

"I don't want it back – I made that for you this afternoon. I need to teach you a thing or two about the other things I listen to, especially if you're to be my wingman." He had such a serious tone to his voice but his smile always gave him away, and from that first day I was sure that I would get on with Mattie most of all.

The rest of the afternoon went quickly, with Steve taking another turn behind the desk serving people and Mattie explaining various plans for different promotions that would happen over the next few weeks. He showed me the staff rota and all the little details I needed to know, like how to book time off and what days or times I was working. That week he had me in for five days in a row; he wanted me to jump in at the deep end and take as much in as I could, and I was glad because this place really felt like home to me. The hatred and name-calling of school was quickly becoming a distant memory – I had found a place where I felt like I belonged. Eventually it got to five o'clock and Mattie told me I could get off home early whilst he and Steve did all the cashing-up and shut the shop.

"I'll see you tomorrow, OK. If you get here for ten then it gives us time to set some stuff up and you can dive straight in again. You did well today though, and it's been a pleasure." Mattie shook my hand and smiled at me as he said goodbye.

"Thanks Mattie, and thanks for the tape too. I'll see you at ten." Off I set, walking home; tired but glad the day had gone so well.

"Oi grunge boy – don't forget, none of that pitiful self-hating crap tomorrow, OK? It's going to be the Kinks all the way," Steve shouted after me, laughing out loud as he helped Mattie put the signs to the shop away. I turned and saluted before heading back towards home – I wouldn't tell Steve I actually liked the Kinks when I saw him tomorrow or I might get something I really didn't like instead.

When I got home I told Mum everything about my day, and explained how great it was to be working somewhere that I thought was so cool. She smiled and nodded, blown away by my high-speed assault on her ears, and her own lack of understanding as to who Alice in Chains were in the first place. Mum was eating when Dad got in from work. I ate mine as quickly as I could and retired to my bedroom to do some more research through the various music magazines I had littered around my room: copies of everything from the *NME* to *Spin* magazine occupied most of the shelves that didn't have CDs or tapes on them. I put the tape that Mattie had given me into my player, and let my musical education begin.

Chapter 6

June 2000 – Age 23

Does absence make the heart grow fonder, or make it easier to part? Can true love really cover any distance?

Monday 12th June

"You need to calm down beautiful; I can't understand what you're trying to say. Where are you – can I come over, or meet you somewhere?" I had been struggling to understand a word Sara had been saying since I'd picked the phone up and figured it would be a lot easier face-to-face.

"It's all ruined, I just don't know what to do," she said, sobbing her heart out over the phone. I hated it when she cried; it always felt like someone was tearing me apart.

"Meet me in half an hour at the hill and we can sit and talk, OK? It'll all be fine beautiful, I promise. I love you."

"I love you too," she croaked, and then the call ended. I started to panic as I grabbed my jacket and keys – Sara was always so level-headed that I couldn't understand what would cause her to be so upset, and I just hoped it wasn't anything to do with us because she meant everything to me. Ever since that first strange meeting on New Year's Day in

1998, we had gone from strength to strength. We had slowly built a relationship as lovers and best friends, and neither of us had ever been happier. My parents had loved her from the minute they met her and although I had been scrutinised more closely by her father, we had managed to find common ground, which had eventually led to a good relationship. Sara's mother had died in childbirth so that had made the bond between Sara and her father even stronger: he had been there for her constantly from the start and had to do a lot of things which most men would've found awkward. In return for all his help and support, Sara had taken the time to learn skills like cooking, and kept him well-fed after his long days at work. Her dad travelled a lot with work and worked long hours; I didn't really understand what he did, but I knew it involved large sums of money and a lot of hours working. He was similar to my dad in that respect, but luckily for me I had always had Mum there when Dad was at work.

After our first six months together, both our parents had let us stay together in their houses, which meant that we spent a lot of time together, enabling our bond to grow strongly and quickly. We had worked through all those strange early moments of a relationship where you are both excited and nervous in equal measure, and now it wasn't Will and Sara anymore, it was *us*.

One of the things I loved most about seeing Sara was that fluttery feeling I got in my stomach every time we met; I never wanted to lose that sort of excitement and have things become mundane. As I trekked up Parliament Hill I saw her sitting on the bench staring out at the view; she had her hair loose and was wearing a big pair of sunglasses. When I reached the top of the hill she saw me and came running over to give me a huge hug. Wrapping her arms tightly around my shoulders and sobbing into my neck she let everything spill.

"I'm so sorry, I really am – I love you with all my heart but now Dad's going and I have to go with him, so it'll all be over and it's all my fault. I don't want to lose you but I can't stay here; I don't know what to do, I'm so sorry, I really am."

"Ssshhh, it'll be OK beautiful, don't cry, please. Come sit down and we can work this all out; there's nothing we can't beat together. Just calm down and tell me everything from the start." I slowly walked her to the bench; she was clinging to me like her life depended on it and I tried to keep calm despite my stomach knotting itself over and over again. We sat on the bench and Sara explained how her dad had managed to get a promotion at work that was worth a lot more money and less working hours, but the problem was that it meant relocating.

"You know I won't let a bit of distance stop us from being together – I'm driving now anyway so I can visit all the time. Where is he going: Manchester; Liverpool?" I was trying to find the positive in what was becoming an increasingly negative situation.

"It's New York, Will – they've asked him to head the office there. I'll be halfway across the world." As she looked at me with those beautiful blue eyes, my mouth dropped open in shock and I felt the tears welling up. As I tried to stand up, everything started spinning: London's skyline turned sideways and upright again, while the noise suddenly became deafening: I could hear every footstep, train and car in the city, all at once like an operatic finale. I struggled to stay on my feet and slumped back onto the bench, head in hands, crying my eyes out.

"Oh God no, this can't be happening. I can't lose you Sara; you're my world and I'm nothing without you." My strength had gone; I couldn't pretend everything was going to be all right. I was losing the one person who made me feel human; the one person who had given me a reason to keep battling away through any problems. I called her my northern lights – she was more beautiful every time I saw her and it didn't matter how many times I saw her, she would never be anything other than a miracle to me.

We ended up crumpled together on the bench for about 20 minutes, just holding each other tight and crying until we couldn't cry anymore. I wanted to ask her to stay; I wanted to tell her that her dad should go alone and she'd be fine here with me, but I knew it was pointless and I didn't want to put any pressure on her. If her mother had been alive then she wouldn't have needed to go, but I understood the relationship she had with her dad and I think she had always felt guilty about his loss and would do anything to look after him and be there for him.

"When?"

"We leave on Thursday 29th at two in the afternoon. Dad's getting an apartment in Greenwich Village; it's all included in the job. He's going to keep the house here until he decides what to do with it. We've only got two weeks – he told me early this morning and it's all confirmed and booked. I don't want to lose you; I just don't know what to do."

I could see that her heart was breaking and I knew I had to make this better for her. She was my world and I wouldn't let anything hurt her if I could stop it. I took a deep breath and spoke the words that would change my life forever.

"I'll tell you what's going to happen: we're going to have the best two weeks of our lives together, and then on that

Thursday I'm going to see you off at the airport. Whilst you're in New York starting your new life, I'm going to pick up extra shifts at work and then in six months or so, I'm going to fly over and visit you. This isn't over unless you want it to be; I would wait for you forever." I managed to speak without my emotions betraying me; I sounded so calm and confident and even managed a smile before I kissed the top of her head. Sara was searching my face with her gorgeous blue eyes, looking for any bit of fear or disbelief, but found none.

"I love you so much Will, I want you to know that. Just because I'll be in New York, it won't change a thing between us. It's you I want and one day I'll be back in your arms again, and then it will be forever." Tears started rolling down her cheeks again and I wiped them away with my fingers before taking her face in my hands and kissing her deeply on the mouth. I wasn't going to let her go without as many reasons to want to come back again as possible.

Eventually the two of us, both exhausted by the emotion of the conversation, wearily made our way back to my house. Dad was at work and Mum was out for the day with a friend, so before long we could collapse into bed together and cuddle up tightly. Sara had phoned her art college and explained the situation so she didn't have to go there again, and I had phoned Mattie at work and asked for the time off. He wasn't overly pleased at having to get cover with such short notice, but when I told him what was happening he said not to worry about it and he would sort it out. It meant we had the two weeks to ourselves with no work or any other distractions, so phone calls made, we climbed wearily into bed and made a pact to sleep before starting the most wonderful couple of weeks we could possibly have together.

Friday 16th June

Although we hadn't done much in the few days since Sara had told me she was leaving, we had managed to spend the time together so that was all that mattered. A lot of time had been spent watching films in bed or listening to music; hours had slipped by whilst we kissed and cuddled, both of us trying to make as many memories as we could before we parted. We would stay up late talking, and then end up making love before falling asleep in the early hours of the next morning. It was wonderful to have so much time together just to be close, but the shadow of her leaving was never far away and occasionally it got too much for both of us and we'd end up hugging and getting upset together.

That Friday morning I was woken up by Sara sitting on top of me and leaning in close to my face.

"Wakey wakey, sleepy head — I have a plan for the weekend." She was kissing me all over the face in an attempt to wake me up.

"Hey," I said dozily, "what's up beautiful? What's your plan?"

"I want to go to Brighton for a couple of days. We can get the coach there if you don't want to drive, and spend a couple of nights in a bed and breakfast. We can go to the Lanes and do some shopping; go for a few drinks, maybe hit a nightclub, walk on the beach, whatever you want. Can we go, please?" She was bouncing up and down with excitement now, and I could never refuse her anything when I knew how happy it made her.

"Anything you want gorgeous — can I at least shower first though, please?" I replied with a cheeky grin on my face, as Sara rolled off me and started bustling about, packing her stuff.

Two hours later we were travelling down the M25 in my Mini with Hole blaring out of the speakers and Sara singing along to *Malibu* at the top of her voice. Every now and then I glanced over at her, and as always the sight of her filled my heart. These few weeks were a struggle for me because I wanted to have a lovely time with her, but I couldn't shake the horrible fear of what I was going to do without her. Her leaving day was coming ever closer and there was nothing I could do to stop it; all I could hope for was to save these small snapshots in my mind so I'd still have a reason to smile when she was in New York.

"Hey you, is everything OK? You're so quiet," she said, snapping out of her best Courtney Love vocal and leaning over to stroke my face.

"Sorry beautiful, I got a bit lost in my thoughts then. I'm OK, I promise; just enjoying your singing." I smiled at her, taking her hand and kissing it.

"Oh William, you are such a flatterer," she said, laughing before turning back to the window and carrying on her rock karaoke.

Between the thoughts of Sara, the cigarettes and the music, the journey went quicker than I thought it would and before long we had arrived at the hotel near the seafront. The day was beautiful so we decided to check in and then head straight out into the sunshine, saving our unpacking for later. This was easier said than done though, because the minute we made it to our room Sara lay down on the bed, looked at me with those beautiful blue eyes of hers and started grinning.

"This bed is so comfy; you really should come and lay down for a while, you know? All that driving must have been stressful, maybe you need to relax before we go out?" Sara patted the gap next to her on the bed and pouted at me.

I climbed on to the bed next to her and rolled in close, breathing in her scent and feeling her body wrapped closely around mine. We started kissing, and before we knew it we were under the sheets, naked and exploring each other. The sound of the waves drifted through our window as we made love passionately – there was something so natural about the whole event, and it was so different to the sterile atmosphere of the city, where there was hardly any nature around. Afterwards we stayed wrapped around each other, both content and quiet.

"I love you so much," Sara whispered into my ear, before pulling me closer towards her. I could tell she was crying; I could feel the silent sobs against my chest. "I never want to lose you; I don't know how I'm going to cope without you."

It's OK beautiful, it'll all work out, I promise. You are going to go to New York and make a wonderful life for yourself, and the minute I can, I will come over and be with you again. You won't lose me, I promise – you mean everything to me." I had to stop myself from getting too upset, so instead I clung to her with every bit of energy I had left, wondering if it was possible to hold onto her so tightly that I'd never have to let go. This all seemed so wrong: I'd spent my whole life wanting this feeling and now I was going to lose it.

"Anyway trouble, you haven't fulfilled your passenger obligation yet," I said, lifting her head and wiping away the tears. I had a million and one pet names for her; she thought I was mad but I liked the intimacy of it.

"What's that, then?" She looked at me quizzically.

"You need to help me get presentable so we can go out." I was sweaty after the drive, and even more so now. "Come on." I pulled her up from the bed and towards the bathroom, and her sadness lifted slightly and she started giggling as we fell into the shower together, kissing and fumbling to get the water started. When I looked at her as the water poured over us, I saw such love in her eyes that I knew it didn't matter if I lived to be two hundred – there was no way I would ever forget her.

Eventually we managed to tear ourselves away from our room and make it out into the mid-afternoon sun. We went for a walk along the pier, spent an obscene amount of loose change in the arcade, ate ice creams and walked along the beach. Any amount of time spent with Sara was wonderful, but it was made all the more special by getting away from London for a while and being so close to the sea. The air felt fresher here and it was so relaxing to be anonymous – despite the size of London it always amazed me how often we would bump into people we knew, and in the strangest of places. Here we were just two lovers strolling along the beach without a care in the world. The only strange thing was that in all the time we talked, neither of us mentioned New York. It was always going to be hanging around above us, but it was as if we had made a silent pact that if we didn't mention it, it didn't exist. We managed to spend the whole afternoon strolling in the sun, carefree and relaxed; just us in our own little world.

That evening we watched a bad movie on the hotel television and filled ourselves with snacks and drink. It was like being a kid again, enjoying simple things without any pressure. Eventually a combination of the sun and all the walking caught up with us, and we started to drift off to sleep curled up together.

"Thank you," Sara said sleepily, kissing me on the cheek.

"I didn't do anything," I replied, holding her so close I could feel her breathing roll through me.

"You're you, and that is all I could ever need," she replied, before snuggling into my chest and falling asleep.

I lay there looking at the ceiling of the hotel room as she slept; the streetlights outside cast a shadow through the gap in the curtains, projecting a strange shape above us. As I studied it I noticed more and more how it looked like an angel, its wings spread wide and at such an angle that it appeared to be hugging us from above. As I looked at the shadowy angel a single tear rolled down my cheek and onto the pillow. Before I could make sense of anything I was thinking, I fell asleep.

The rest of the weekend went so quickly. On the Saturday we got up early and went out into town - it reminded me of our first proper day together in Camden, with Sara buying the strangest items and attempting to get a better price for most of them. We walked for hours, looking in the most curious of shops with the quaintest of items in them; Sara was always looking for that magic box in a junk shop, as I called it. We chatted, we laughed, we kissed and held hands during our marathon walk around Brighton. When it got dark we had dinner at a restaurant near the seafront, before heading out onto the sand to enjoy our last night of the sea air. Although the sky was clear and we could see all the stars above us, the air was warm and it was perfect for just sitting and appreciating the beauty of the sea. Above us we could hear the clatter of people on the pier and see the lights flashing away with all of the electronic machines that the modern world provided, but down on the sand it was like a faraway world; a world with nothing but the sand, the sea and the stars. As we sat together looking at the stars, a plane flew overhead and caught our attention.

"Twelve days and that could be you, beautiful – flying off to a brave new world. Are you excited? There must be so much stuff to see in the States; all those places with the coolest music." I had to speak about her trip – it wasn't going to go away and I was tired of pretending it might.

Sara shifted slightly and moved so she faced my side, gently putting her hand on the back of my neck.

"I have so many emotions I don't know where to start. It's always been the land of opportunity and you know how much I want to get somewhere with my art – New York is just a small part of a huge country full of amazing things and amazing possibilities, so yes, the thought of that is exciting. The place we'll be living is beautiful and I can't imagine ever living somewhere that special, but – and there is a huge but," she said, her fingers tracing my jawline, "opportunity, excitement, a future – none of these things would be worth anything without you. I want us to have all this together, and I'm so damn scared that someone will come along when I've left and sweep you off your feet. You are so special and you don't even know it; it's lovely but bloody infuriating at times, Will. You deserve to be so happy and it makes me so sad to think that will be with someone else." Sara stood and walked towards the sea, talking over her shoulder, "You don't need me, Will; you are so wonderful and you could be with anyone, doing anything. I won't blame you for getting on with your life. I wouldn't expect you to give everything up for me."

I was so surprised to hear her talking without her usual confidence and wracked with insecurity that it took me ages to react. I'd sat up listening, and then as she walked towards the sea, I got up and ran after her.

"Sara, wait. I didn't mean to upset you; I just didn't want you to think you couldn't talk about it with me, that's all. The whole New York thing is fantastic; I just wish I was able to go with you." I caught up with her and turned her towards me, my hands cupping her face. "You're right to feel excited and you're right to be thinking of opportunities and where else the move might lead you, but you're wrong about us. There was a girl once who swept me off my feet – she made me as lovely as you think I am; she made me happy, and she made me who I am. That girl is you, and whether you are in America, New Zealand or the North Pole, it will always be you. Without you there isn't really a life to be getting on with; everything I do will be to get me through until I can see you again. I'm yours Sara, and although you can be a pain in the ass, you're my pain in the ass." I pulled her tearful face towards me and we kissed as passionately as before, our hands entwined and our bodies pressed close; a romantic scene played out under a beautiful night sky. I couldn't stop time but I could stop wasting it by worrying.

That night in Brighton was a huge step for Sara and I, and we spent the rest of the time making crazy plans to cover all the possibilities of us being together in America. Most of them were pure madness, but it allowed us to talk about the forthcoming trip without any sadness or Sara feeling she shouldn't be at least a bit excited. As always with time away though, before we knew it we were heading back to the normality of London and the clock continued to tick.

Sunday 25th June
I couldn't believe we only had four days left. I looked at the calendar on my wall over and over again, just willing it to be earlier in the month, but it wouldn't change. A week

previously we had travelled back from Brighton, and now that seemed so far away; this last week had been quite hectic as Sara had needed to spend time packing for the trip and sorting out her passport and all the required papers. As usual she had also needed to sort lots of similar things for her dad, who had returned on the Monday and was here now until they both left together. It had meant a few nights coming home alone to my house, but in my mind I knew it would be better to get used to that sooner rather than later.

As I sat staring at the calendar, my mum knocked on my door and handed me the phone.

"Will, it's Mattie; you need to go down to the shop as soon as possible."

"What's up, Mattie? You said it was OK for me to stay off until next week? I'm meant to be seeing Sara today; I can't work." This was all I needed with just four days left to spend with Sara.

"Hey man, I didn't say anything about working, did I? Now how about you stop whingeing and get your dopey ass down here ASAP. That's all." And with that he put the phone down.

I was up anyway so I figured it wouldn't take much to stop by the shop before heading to see Sara, so I grabbed my jacket and headed to find out what was going on. When I reached the shop I noticed everyone stood outside looking at the door: Mattie waved at me and Steve stuck his middle finger up, grinning; Kelly was there too and acknowledged me with a cool flick of the head.

"Hey guys what's going on then?" I said as I met them outside the shop. I watched as all three of them turned and pointed at the door. Pasted above where the open sign usually sat, there was a handwritten sign that said *Due to*

sickness and diarrhoea, this store will remain closed until Monday!
Sorry for any inconvenience.

"What's this all about? You guys aren't ill, are you? I don't get it."

"Well, apparently Steve here came in with a bug and gave it to me and then in turn to Kelly, so I had to ring Shaun and he said to stay closed for 24 hours and then try again Monday. He wasn't able to spare anyone from anywhere else to help out, so here we are." Mattie was grinning from ear to ear, whilst Steve alternated between giggling and coughing 'bullshit' loudly to himself. Kelly was just stood there looking cool, and it dawned on me that I hadn't ever seen her do anything else.

"You see, young William, the plan is to take you and your lovely lady out for the day, to get right royally drunk and show you both why Camden life is the best life in the world. So what do you say, are you up for it?" Mattie patted me on the back, still smiling.

As usual with the guys from work, once something was planned, it happened with no messing around. So before I knew it we were all sat in the pub and the drinks were flowing. Sara had arrived about 20 minutes after us, and it turned out that Mattie had already phoned her to let her know and she had jumped at the chance to have one last group meet-up. As usual the time spent was dominated by conversations about music, arguments about who should be allowed to put what on the jukebox, and Steve generally poking fun at me. I loved how Sara could mix with so many different types of people without feeling awkward; this was another one of her many talents and made life a lot easier when socialising. As the conversation turned to Mattie telling us all about the Muse gig he had gone to earlier in the month,

I found myself sitting and staring across the table at Sara. As I studied her face I reminisced about the first time we met; that strange twist of fate that led us to be outside the club so early on that New Year's Day, and how everything in my life had seemed to get better and better from that point onwards. I still remembered the first time we hugged and how good she felt against me, the smell of her hair filling me with a feeling of such happiness. In four days' time that would all be gone, and I would be here trying to fill the huge void that her absence would leave in my world. As Mattie talked excitedly about the gig and how great Coldplay had been as a support act, Sara turned and our eyes met. She looked at me quizzically and forced a smile, but her eyes gave it all away. I knew she was thinking the same things I was; I could see the sadness lingering behind the surface. Luckily our sad little moment was soon broken by the larger-than-life Steve knocking the remainder of his pint on the floor by accident and slapping me on the back.

"Come on then you miserable sod, it's your round so stop making moony eyes at your missus. Mine's a pint!" And then up and off to the toilets he went. In another life I'm sure Steve and I wouldn't have been friends, but there was something about him I found endearing, even though he spent most of his time making jokes at my expense. The thing I always noticed about Steve was that he really cared deep down; he just had this façade of nothing being important and life being a joke. I remembered walking in on him sat in the staff room once when it was my day off: he hadn't known I was there, so I stood and watched him for a while as he was listening to Arab Strap and doing the most beautiful drawing I had ever seen. He hadn't ever told me about his talent, but as I stood there watching him I realised that he was drawing a picture of an old lady who obviously had meant a great deal to him, judging by the effort he put in, and I saw just how talented he was. I only watched him for about five minutes, but the beautifully sad song lyrics and his drawing with such emotion and passion told me a lot about what Steve was really like underneath that slightly rough exterior. I never told him what I saw that day, but I always kept the memory as a reminder that people aren't always what they seem and I knew that if I ever needed his help, he would be there.

I found out what everyone wanted, including Kelly's latest odd concoction which I always thought she did just to be different – this week it was Guinness and a shot of blackcurrant, but for the rest of us it was our usual pints of cider – and then stood at the bar waiting to be served.

"Hi handsome, haven't I seen you somewhere before? You're not on telly by any chance are you?" Sara whispered in my ear as she playfully squeezed my bum.

"Actually, yes I am. I was on last week's *Crimewatch* in fact. The Camden ladykiller, breaking hearts wherever I go." I tried desperately hard to stay calm and straight-faced, but it wouldn't work and I ended up bursting into laughter.

"You dope; you sure you're OK though honey?" Sara suddenly looked more serious as she put her arm around me.

"Yes and no – I'm really trying not to think about Thursday, but sometimes I find it really hard. It's getting closer and closer and it scares me, that's all. I'll snap out of it though, I want to concentrate on the last few days and make sure we don't waste them being miserable. There's plenty of time for that after we part." I brushed the hair from her eyes and gave her a big kiss, hopefully reinforcing how positive I was trying to be.

"Well there's a lot more to do today; these guys think it's going to be one big pub crawl but I have other plans for you mister," she said playfully, before helping me back to the table with the drinks.

We spent a couple more hours in the pub; enough time for Steve to spill another pint and then get a fake pound coin jammed in the jukebox. Mattie being the leader of the group as always decided it was time to leave before we were kicked out, so at some point in early afternoon we all spilled back out onto the streets of Camden again.

"Well I don't know about you lot but I'm in the mood for another public house, and another and another until I don't remember my own name," announced Steve, more than happy with his stereotypically English drinking habits. Mattie agreed and Kelly gave a nod of the head, which was generally about as emotive as she got without giving her coolness away.

"Looks like you two lovebirds are free to go then, unless you want to come along," Mattie already knew the answer but was offering anyway out of politeness.

"Thanks guys, we're going to head off and go do some things though. Sara's only got a few days left so we said we'd have a tourist afternoon and see the London we sometimes take for granted." I looked at Mattie and smiled to thank him for what he'd done today.

"Well, I guess it's time you gave me a hug then, Sara? You owe me that much in advance, for looking after this miserable git whilst you're away." Mattie was joking but as he grabbed Sara for a hug, you could see he was sad to see her go. "Seriously though, we'll take good care of him I promise. You go show those crazy New Yorkers what us Brits are all about. Stay safe and don't forget us. Maybe we'll open a shop over there and come see you?" He always had the knack of knowing what to say at the right time, and sometimes it made me jealous that I wasn't that good with words.

"Thank you Mattie, thank you for everything. I'll hold you to your promise of looking after him, OK? I want you to make sure he's working every hour under the sun so he can visit sooner rather than later." Sara smiled and kissed him on the cheek before stepping back next to me. This was followed by Steve giving her a high five and saying "Go get 'em" and as expected, a nod from Kelly and one word: "Laters." These were my people; we had been together for seven years now and still had as much fun as we did back then, if not more. As they stumbled off in search of their next pub they looked back and waved to Sara, who stood waving back with tears welling in her eyes.

"Hey beautiful," I said, gently wiping the tears from her cheeks, "quit those tears, there's fun to be had."

I hugged her and then, hand in hand, we headed off towards the Tube station. The rest of that day was spent doing the craziest things I had ever done in London, from the open-top bus journey to the boat down the Thames; we even went on the London Eye and up St Paul's Cathedral before finally ending up at Parliament Hill. We sat on our bench watching London closing down for the day; the night was rolling in and the city was starting to become illuminated in front of our eyes. It wasn't natural, but it had a strange sort of beauty to it anyway. All the lights twinkling on like a beautiful starlit sky; Sara and I sat cuddled up together, watching the world get ready to relax before sleeping.

"It sounds really silly, Will, but it doesn't matter where I am in the world – there won't ever be a view I love as much as this one," Sara said, sleepily, as she nestled close into my shoulder.

"I know what you mean beautiful; this place holds so many memories for me too. We've spent a lot of time sat here watching the world drift by. Every time I look out at the city I'll be thinking of you, I promise." The words caught in my throat as I said them; the realisation that I would be here without Sara caught me off guard.

"You and me, always," she said.

"Always," I replied.

Thursday 29th June

After one last beautiful night together, the day I'd been dreading finally arrived. Early that morning I had kissed Sara goodbye and headed home so she could finish getting her last things packed and I could shower and then meet up with her again at Gatwick Airport. As I walked home I reminisced once more about the first time I met her, and the walk home that morning and how happy I was. This time couldn't have been more different; my heart ached and I felt sick at the thought of being without her. Over two years ago in January I had made this same walk knowing that within a few weeks I would be seeing her again, but this time all I had was an airport goodbye and then nothing.

The early morning air was crisp and sharp, and my tearful eyes were stinging as I tried to swallow down all the sadness that was bubbling up inside me. When I got home I spoke quickly to Mum and then headed to shower; usually Mum would've made more of an effort to make sure I was OK, but I think she realised how hard I was trying to hold everything together, and didn't want to upset me by talking about things. That was the thing with my parents: they never forced me to talk about things, but I knew I could always rely on them to comfort me and look after me if I was sad. It was that kind of support which made me feel so lucky to have them both and I knew I would need it more and more once I was left alone without Sara to keep me smiling.

After showering and getting dressed I pulled a bag out from my wardrobe and started to get everything ready. As a going-away present I had made Sara a mix CD with meaningful songs by all the different sorts of artists we'd shared in our time together, bought a journal for her to doodle in or write her thoughts, and got my favourite Pearl Jam t-shirt which I sprayed with my aftershave so she could remember my smell. I packed all the gifts together and wrapped them up for her with a good luck card, in which I wrote a long emotional message, thanking her for everything she had done for me and basically saying 'until we meet again'.

I looked at the clock on my bedside table and it said 10am; I figured that Sara and her dad would have to be at the airport in a couple of hours so there was no point waiting, so I grabbed my coat and got in my car. I put *August and Everything After* by Counting Crows on the player, and headed to Gatwick Airport. The journey was eerily quiet, and the music was a perfect melancholy backdrop to both the event and my mood. I made it in plenty of time, and after parking I sat in my car for a while, smoking and listening to the music, trying to both gather my thoughts and keep a lid on them. I didn't want to upset Sara any more than she already was, and I knew I had to be brave, for both of us.

Eventually I wandered over to the airport entrance and sat outside waiting for their arrival. About ten minutes before midday, I saw a woman walking towards me, pulling a suitcase behind her. My heart fluttered like never before: my beautiful girl walking towards me for the last time in a long while. Sara was wearing the same outfit as when I had met her, and it was like two-and-a-half years had vanished in a second. She dropped her suitcase handle when she got near me and threw her arms out wide, hugging me more strongly than I could ever remember. She repeatedly kissed my face, searching out my mouth and we embraced passionately with the shadow of the airport entrance looming large behind us. Her dad appeared not long after, so we quickly calmed down to avoid any embarrassment for anyone. After a brief handshake and a quick goodbye, he made his way into the airport with us following. I took Sara's bag for her and she linked arms with me; I felt like a movie star heading off on some expensive holiday with the love of his life, but sadly this wasn't the case. After baggage checking and all the usual things, Sara's dad headed off and told her to meet him at the departure gate in half an hour.

We found a quiet corner in one of the bars, ordered a drink and sat talking, hugged up closely together, desperate to get as much closeness as we possibly could before parting.

"Here's to the most beautiful girl in the world, her new life and all the possibilities that the world has to offer," I said, clinking my pint glass against hers.

"And here's to the most amazing boy; one who is my life and better damn well be joining me again soon," she replied, clinking my glass and forcing a smile.

"You know I will, beautiful. I've already spoken to Mattie and he said I can do as many as six days a week if I want, and I can always get extra work in out of hours, stocktaking and stuff. Once I've saved enough I'll fly out and see you, but until then we can speak on the phone loads and email each other."

"I don't want you burning yourself out honey, but I must say I like the thought of you not having any spare time to be mixing with any other women." Sara laughed as she spoke

119

but I knew her; I knew her deep, hidden insecurities, and I knew that this was really a fear of hers.

"Why would I want to mix with other women? I've got the best there is to offer and all I care about is seeing her again. Remember, there's no me without you, beautiful." I pulled her close and gave her a huge hug and kiss before reaching behind me and handing her the package.

"What's this?" She seemed shocked as she took it in her hands, feeling the shape and tracing the lines of tape.

"Just a little going-away present, but you're not allowed to open it until you get on the plane." I suddenly felt like I was blushing, and Sara just sat staring at me and smiling.

"Oh Will, thank you so much. You are so special. I've got something for you too; it's only small and the same applies – not until I've gone, OK?" With this, Sara handed me a small envelope with something flat and curvy in it.

"Thank you; I love you," we said in unison as we hugged one more time.

We finished our drinks and then it was time for Sara to meet her dad at the departure gate, so I walked with her hand-in-hand, ready to meet our fate. The queue at the gate was fairly long but moving quickly, and her dad was stood near the end of it, waving at her. She waved back and held up a finger, signalling that she wouldn't be long, before turning to me. She took my hands in hers and we stood facing each other, both on the verge of tears and feeling more awkward than we ever had before.

"Well mister, I guess this is it, then. I don't know what to say," she said, struggling not to cry.

"You don't have to say anything beautiful, I already know," I replied.

"I'm going to miss you so very much Will, but I want you to know that there won't be a minute when I'm not thinking about you and us; you'll be with me every step of the way as I am with you. I love you and will count every day until I see you again." With her last words she threw her arms around me and cried into my shoulder.

"I love you too beautiful, and I feel the same. You will be with me everywhere I go and I won't be happy until I'm in your arms again. You're my life, my lover and best friend and I owe you everything. Never stop believing, and before you know it we'll be together again." I was in pain from fighting back the tears, but I'd promised myself that I wouldn't make it more difficult for her.

Sara kissed me hard on the lips, before trying to wipe the tears away from her eyes. "You and me," was all she could manage to say before turning and running to meet her dad.

"Always," I called out after her, and she turned and blew me a kiss before carrying on and getting a comforting hug from her dad.

I stood there in the middle of the huge airport space and as I watched the queue move further and further, the room got smaller and smaller. The last thing I remember is seeing Sara turn quickly and wave, her cheeks stained with tears but managing a smile for me. I waved back and then she was gone, through the door and on to the next stage of her life.

I stood there for about ten more minutes just waiting for something to happen that never would, before turning and making the lonely walk back to my car. I sat there with the music on again, and waited until I saw the plane that I thought she was on, taking off and leaving for her new home. I changed the album in the car over to *The Joshua Tree* by U2, and as the song *With or Without You* came on, my eyes welled up and I pulled the envelope out of my pocket. Inside was a note which said *You know where home is; unlock the door and let your heart stop being so brave.* The note was wrapped around a key which I knew straight away was to her house in Kentish Town, so with the sadness building in my head and heart, I drove straight there.

When I arrived at her house I went in and made my way up to her bedroom. There wasn't any reason to think there could be anything for me in the rest of the house, and her bedroom was where my heart could be as sad as it wanted to, so I entered her room and froze. Her room was exactly as it had been the whole time I had been dating Sara: nothing had been changed or taken down whilst she'd prepared for the move. On her bed was a note which I sat down and read.

To my darling boy,

By now I am probably flying over the ocean and already missing you whilst you are sat reading this and hopefully missing me too. Knowing you, you have a very sore head from being brave for me and not crying, and a sore throat from swallowing all your sadness down for the last few hours. I have left two gifts for you and I want you to read this carefully so there is no confusion.

Firstly, the house is staying as it is for the time being, so your first gift is my room, and all our memories that are stored in it. You can come here whenever you want and stay as long as you want: whatever you need, and whatever makes you happy. Dad has got a cleaner coming in once a week to keep everything tidy but they have strict instructions not to do anything with my room, so it's all yours. Look after our memories and I hope they keep you happy whilst I'm gone.

Secondly, I want you to press play on the video recorder that you always found so amusing, and lay back and watch. You need to cry Will, and then you need to smile.

Forever yours,

Your little trouble girl, Sara.

I turned the television and the video recorder on, lay back on the bed and pressed play. After a few seconds, Sara appeared on the screen, dressed in the same oversized Ramones t-shirt from our first night together. She sat cross-legged on the bed with scruffy hair, smiling at the camera. As I watched, I felt the lump in my throat grow, and then she spoke.

"Hey mister, if everything has worked out as I hoped then you should be lying on my bed watching this. Do me a favour and press play on the CD player when this finishes, OK? You might think I'm mad but I worked out that the hardest part of us being separated will probably be at night, so I decided to make this video for you to watch as you go to sleep when you are feeling low. I want you to know that I'll miss you with all my heart and every time you close your eyes and sleep, I will come find you and keep you safe. I love you Will; this is my present for you. Now press play." Sara smiled cheekily at the camera before blowing a kiss and getting into bed and turning her light off. As the screen went black, I leant over and pressed play on her CD player, turning the lights down and laying on her pillow, breathing in her scent. After a few seconds, the familiar sound of *Górecki* by Lamb filled the air. I smiled to myself and imagined her in bed beside me, then I grabbed a pillow tight and the tears started to flow. I didn't know what I was going to do without her being around; she was my world and I felt so lonely without her. As the music played on I spoke out loud, to no one.

"Sweet dreams beautiful, I love you."

As the exhaustion took hold and the tears flowed, I grabbed her pillow tight and cried myself to sleep.

Chapter 7

July 2001 – Age 24

What would be your ideal holiday? Would you rather experience things alone or would you prefer someone special to share them with?

Sunday 1st July

I woke up with my head pressed against the cold glass, and the movie on the screen having ended long ago. I looked at my watch and it said 1 am, but I had no idea what the real time was, or where I was at that point. All I knew was that the plane had taken off from London at about four o'clock in the afternoon, so there were only a couple of hours left before I landed at John F. Kennedy International Airport in New York. It would be late in the evening when I arrived but I had already arranged it with Sara and she would be there waiting for me.

My neck ached from where it had obviously been lolling during my snooze but I was happy in the knowledge that the next two seats were empty, so no one had to witness me dribbling down the window whilst I slept. As I tried to get my head together I noticed the stewardess had brought me another tomato juice at some point, so I quickly drained the glass, enjoying how it soothed my dry throat. This was my first time flying and I had loved it, except for the dry air on the airplane; my throat felt like it was lined with sand.

It had felt so strange entering Gatwick Airport earlier in the day – it had been a year since I had last been there to say goodbye to Sara. It was strange to think that the same place which tore us apart was now helping us get back together again, and it was amazing to see how much more of a spring I had in my step walking that same path through the airport this time around. I couldn't believe it had only been a year since I'd seen Sara; it had seemed like forever, even though we had spoken on the phone at least every other day. She had been doing so well in New York, enrolling in college and taking all sorts of classes like photography, painting and all sorts of other arty things. Her dad had helped her out financially so she didn't have to get a job because he preferred her to be safe at home rather than roaming around the city, especially at night. He was very wary of letting Sara do anything, which I always thought was a result of him losing her mum like he did, and because he spent most of his time in the office he really had no idea how safe or unsafe the city was anyway. Sara enjoyed this freedom though, and made the most of her spare time drawing, creating photography projects and speaking or writing to me. She always told me how much she missed me even though things were going well for her, and this meant the world to me because it was hard being so far away and imagining all sorts of things. I had done nothing but work whilst she'd been gone. Mattie had been good enough to give me as many shifts as possible so I could start saving some money, and he had even let me help out at a few local music gigs he was doing the sound for, as an extra earner. Everyone at work had been really supportive, pestering me constantly to get out of my house for the night, but I had refused most offers so I wouldn't miss Sara's calls and spend any of my important savings. It took time but eventually I had got here, booking the flight and the hotel and finally getting closer to seeing the love of my life again. As I sat reminiscing over the strange journey that had brought me here, I got the little box out of my rucksack and held it in my hands, closing my eyes and quietly thinking things over. With my eyes shut I soon felt myself starting to drift off again, so I returned the box to the rucksack and made myself comfortable for the last bit of the flight.

The next time I woke up was during the announcement that we would be landing soon, and to make sure we were all seated and wearing our seatbelts. I looked at the world below me; it was lit up so brightly with neon lights and traffic as far as the eye could see. Somewhere down there was my beautiful girl and I couldn't wait to see her. I watched the landscape below disappear quickly behind us, and then the lights of the airport were in sight. I'll never forget the feel of the plane landing, the way it circled in the air to get into the right path and then headed down to earth at such an angle that the world seemed to be racing up to meet you; the bumps as the wheels touched down and then the high-speed rush to the end of the runway before we slowed right down and eventually stopped. Before long we were all gathering our belongings and making our way off the plane and into the airport itself. This was the first time I had ever been on a plane; my first time abroad and possibly the most important holiday I was ever going to have. My nervousness was a huge contrast to the calmness of the other passengers. After all the usual security checks I was in the swarm of people entering the arrivals lounge, and everywhere I looked people were waiting to greet others. Some were families getting excited every time they saw someone come round the corner, hoping it was their relative returning home. Others were drivers for businessmen holding signs with names on, desperate to attract the attention of their fare so they could do their job and then get home themselves. As interesting as all these new sights were though, there was only one person in the world that I wanted to see and I couldn't see her anywhere. As I passed the biggest group of people waiting – some kind of local sports team all decked out in their team colours – I saw some kind of commotion near the entrance. As people were walking out, pulling their luggage behind them, they seemed like they were being bowled over by something heading straight for them. Then I saw what it was, and my heart fluttered. Sara was rushing towards the arrivals gate, inadvertently knocking people out the way in an effort to get to me. I passed the last bit of fencing and she saw me immediately, she shouted my name and came hurtling towards me, jumping up into my arms and wrapping her legs around me.

"I'm really sorry; I got held up in traffic and didn't think I was going to make it in time. I ran all the way from the car; I didn't want to miss you. I can't believe you're here, you look great; I've missed you so, so much." Sara had a tendency to speak quickly when she was excited, so that you could barely catch a word she said. She was smothering me with kisses, and I had forgotten just how good it felt to have her so close.

"Hey beautiful, you couldn't get rid of me that easily," I replied coolly, but then the emotion got the better of me and tears welled up in my eyes. "I can't tell you how much I missed you Sara, just seeing you again feels like coming home. I love you and hate being apart from you."

We both managed to compose ourselves and headed to the baggage carousel so I could pick up my luggage, and then it was out of the airport to a car that Sara's dad had arranged for us. As the driver headed off to the hotel I was staying at, Sara rang her dad to tell him I had arrived and everything was OK. Whilst she spoke on her phone, I looked at her properly for the first time in a year. She looked more beautiful than ever: her hair had grown down to the middle of her back and she was wearing a tight black top and skinny black jeans which clung to her curves beautifully, and she'd topped it all off with a pair of leather Converse and a short leather jacket. She looked amazing and would've fitted in anywhere in the world, and as I looked at her I got that familiar feeling of butterflies in my stomach, and the overwhelming pride that I was with her. Here we were again, Will and Sara, different country and different year but the same beautiful feelings. When Sara finished her call, she turned and leant against me, holding me tight. The driver fiddled with his radio as he headed towards our destination, only stopping when he came across *L.A. Woman* by The Doors on one of the stations. I sat there with the sights of New York flying past me, listening to music I loved and with the most beautiful girl in the world in my arms and I figured life couldn't get much better.

I hadn't told Sara which hotel I was staying in and I wanted it to be a surprise for her, so when we arrived at our destination I asked her to cover her eyes, stand in front of the building and wait. I walked behind her and held her shoulders, before whispering in her ear.

"You can open them now."

Sara looked up at the sign and gasped in excitement, before squealing and giving me a huge hug. "Will, really – the Chelsea Hotel? How very rock-and-roll. How on earth did you afford this?"

"Ask Mattie and Steve — I've practically been living at work for the past year. I wanted this trip to be as special as possible, and we've only got five days so I thought why not do it in style? I want nothing but the best for my beautiful girl."

It didn't take long for us to check in and find our way upstairs to the room, which was almost like a huge bohemian apartment. When I locked the door behind us, Sara noticed two of her suitcases already sat next to the bed.

"How come my suitcases are here? What's going on?" She turned to me, confused, so I walked over to her and put my arms round her, smiling broadly.

"OK, so I didn't do it all on my own. I spoke to your dad and he said as I'm only here for five days that he was happy for you to stay here with me. He sent your bags over earlier and will have them picked up for you when I check out on Friday. So you're all mine for five whole nights — do you think you can cope with that?"

"Hmm, I'm sure I can find ways to struggle through," Sara replied, smiling before slowly unbuttoning my shirt and leading me towards the bed.

Monday 2nd June
At six o'clock that morning, the sunlight streaming through the open curtains woke me. I rolled over to look at my watch on the bedside table and realised how early it was, so I rolled back and cuddled up to Sara again. We had gone to bed within minutes of entering the room last night, and then fallen asleep after making love for the first time in over a year. We had been so preoccupied that we hadn't drawn the curtains, unpacked anything or even looked at the room properly, but none of this mattered. As I laid next to Sara,

my chest pressed against her back and her thighs resting on mine, my mind drifted back to last night. It had felt so perfect being with her again and being intimate; two souls joining back together as one, and in the most passionate way. I loved watching Sara sleep; she was so peaceful and always curled herself up under the covers like a little mouse. These few days would be some of the most important of my life, and I hoped everything went as planned and that the days would go by slowly enough for me to remember them properly. Although I hated the idea of having to leave her again at the end of the week, I needed to concentrate on the days I had with her and make the most of them. I fell back to sleep wrapped around Sara, with my heart feeling lighter than it had for months.

A couple of hours later I was awake again and Sara was stirring next to me.

"Good morning gorgeous, did you sleep well?" I stroked her hair out of her eyes as I kissed her on the cheek.

"Mmmmmm, I had the best night's sleep in ages, thank you, baby. You should be there at bedtime more often," she said as she yawned and rubbed her eyes sleepily. As I looked at her I realised that I could happily spend the rest of my life watching her sleep, and I hoped she felt the same about me.

"What are the plans today then? Where is my hostess taking me?"

"Well, first things first Will – we both need to shower, then I'm going to take you for breakfast New York style before we head to Central Park. It's supposed to be a lovely day today and I've got so much to show you." She rolled on top of me and nuzzled her head into my chest playfully.

"You know, as a visitor to this fine country I wouldn't want to be a drain on resources, so what do you say we share a shower? I'm only trying to save on water wastage of course," I said, winking at her.

"Oh William, that's so very thoughtful of you," she replied, grinning. "I think that's a fab idea." And she rolled off the bed, pulling me into the bathroom with her.

Eventually we managed to leave the cosy bubble that was our bedroom and head out into New York for breakfast. We were both starving and I had yet to experience eating in a foreign land; I was desperate to see if all those old stereotypes about America were true. Even though I'd grown up with so much exposure to American culture, it was amazing how fairly similar things could be so confusing. I used the Tube in London every day of my life, but when faced with the maze which is the Metro in New York, I was completely baffled. Sara did brilliantly as a tour guide, trying to explain where all these underground trains ended up, but I was lost and so grateful for her assistance. Sat on the train heading towards Central Park, I caught a glimpse of us cuddled up together in the window opposite and realised just how perfect we looked together. I was so proud to be able to call her my partner, and my mind wandered to the next step of our relationship: I wanted her to be next to me forever.

"Hey daydreamer, I hope you're thinking about me and not some hot city girl?" Sara snapped me out of my thoughts by gently punching me on the leg.

"Actually I was thinking about breakfast," I said, poking my tongue out at her. Then she mimed biting in my direction, so I shrunk back in my chair quietly.

"I love you Will, I just want you to know that."

"I love you too beautiful." Hearing her tell me how she felt always warmed my heart; she could be a woman of few words sometimes but I never needed doubt her – she was a straight talker.

Eventually the train got to our station and we departed at the corner of Lexington Avenue and 63rd Street, out of the stifling underground air and back up into the sunshine. I followed Sara across the street to a waffle house and smiled to myself; I figured all we needed now was doughnut-eating cops and all the stereotypes would be correct. Half an hour later we were well fed, possibly overdosed on sugar and heading into Central Park.

The strangest thing about Central Park was how different it was to the city. When you stood in the park, surrounded by the many acres of green, you would be forgiven for forgetting that the bustling concrete city even existed. Not only did the city exist though, but it circled this beautiful garden of Eden and dwarfed it in height and density. We walked through the park hand-in-hand; Sara talking at length about her projects and how much she had enjoyed spending time doing them without the pressure of deadlines and the fear of failure around every corner. New York had proven to provide her with an amazing basis for a very human art project that could reveal the city from the viewpoint of an outsider looking in. She told me of the many hours she had spent in the park, drawing or sketching, listening to music and just wishing I could see it all with her. Even though I hadn't seen any of it before though, it felt strangely familiar to me, almost like I had experienced it through her.

Sara guided me around the park like a professional, showing me some of the most wonderful sights I could ever hope to see. I wasn't usually one for taking pictures but I made sure I had my camera for this trip so I could show everyone back home the things I saw, and so I could also get lots of pictures of Sara to keep me smiling when we had to part again. Sara spoke of her love for this park and how much time she had spent sitting here, whatever the weather, just enjoying the sights and sounds of the place. We looked at the statue of Hans Christian Andersen and posed for obvious cheesy tourist photos. Even better than that for me though was the *Alice in Wonderland* bronze, which I had seen in the guidebooks but was far more breathtaking in real life. Sara and I shared a love for the book and its strange story, so to be stood by huge bronzes of all the main characters was very surreal. I took a lovely photo of Sara sat on the small toadstool at the front, looking so content as she smiled at me; it was small memories like that which I could keep forever and although Sara didn't like having her photo taken it meant a lot to me that she would let me do it anyway.

From the statues we made our way to the Ramble, a huge wooded area crisscrossed by paths and streams, and after walking for what seemed like hours, we sat on a bench and watched the world pass us by. Even in a serene place like this there was still the bustle of people, either jogging or racing from one place to another on their lunch break, and I felt lucky that we could just sit and time wasn't an issue for us. We had the ability to sit comfortably in silence and just be relaxed together – not something that everyone gets to experience in the modern age. Looking out across the water it felt like our own private paradise, and there was no better way to experience it than cuddled up with the one person who meant the world to me.

"Do you think if we just stay here, that time will stop for us?" I asked Sara as I looked at the birds swooping to the surface of the lake for fish.

"It feels like that every time I'm with you, Will. I've loved spending time here alone, watching the movement and the stillness blending together, but having been here with

you I'm not sure I ever want to come back without you."
Sara held my arm tightly and nuzzled into my neck, kissing
me softly before getting to her feet.

"But mister, I have something that you have to see and I
know it will blow your mind. So come on, we've got some
walking to do." And off we went again, trekking through the
park to our next destination.

When asked what the best song ever written was, I always
said *Imagine* by John Lennon, and I knew about the New
York connection and his death here, but what Sara showed
me next touched me in a way I hadn't felt before, and gave
me a great idea.

"This is Strawberry Fields; it's strange because it's one of
the most visited parts of Central Park, but also one of the
most peaceful. The whole section is shaped like a tear drop
and Yoko Ono arranged it as a memorial to John." Sara was
still in full tourist guide mode and I found it really cute how
serious she looked when describing everything to me in
detail. The place itself was beautiful, and we were quite
lucky because there were only a couple of other people there
at the time. I stood and looked at the beautiful mosaic with
the word *Imagine* inscribed in the middle, surrounded by
candles and notes that people had left, as well as a small
guitar with a handwritten tribute on it. It was so touching
and it made me think about how much of an impact one man
can have on the world through his music. Sara was busy
telling me that the mosaic had come as a present from the
city of Naples in Italy, before moving on to other bits of
information. I took hold of her hand and pulled her into my
arms.

"You are too damn cute, you know that? And as I'm the tourist and you're my official guide, there's one thing I really, really, want you to do for me, please."

"What's that?"

"Shut up and kiss me," I said, smiling at her. Sara looked me in the eye and blushed before giving me the longest, most beautiful kiss I had had in a long time. "I've missed every part of you, and being here with you again is the best thing of all," I said, feeling the lump rise in my throat.

"I feel the same Will; nothing feels right without you. I want to be in your arms every night, not thousands of miles away, just left with my dreams and an empty bed. I don't care how we do it; I want you back with me as soon as we can." Sara's hands were on my shoulders, and as she held my hair back our eyes met so intensely that we didn't need to say anymore. We both wanted to be with each other, and we just had to find a way to do it without upsetting her dad or my family. The thought entered my mind that we should just run away together, but we knew ultimately that it wouldn't work as we were both so close to our families.

As I looked one last time at the mosaic, everything in my head came together perfectly: I'd made my plan and just had to work out when to do it. I smiled to myself as we walked out of the park together, hand-in-hand. Overlooking Strawberry Fields was the Dakota apartment where John Lennon was shot outside, and Sara asked if I wanted to take a closer look but I didn't feel the need to. Outside were hoards of people taking photos and posing where he was shot, and it felt ghoulish to me and eerie enough just being that close to it, so we walked on in search of a place to eat.

The rest of our first proper day together in over a year passed by so quickly it was almost like a blur. After eating, all the walking we had done had finally taken its toll on us, so we decided to crash at the hotel for the evening and just enjoy some time alone. We got the boring unpacking job out of the way first, with much hesitancy on my part, and then we curled up together listening to music and enjoying being close to each other again. I wasn't sure whether it was because I had been starved of her for a year, but to me Sara looked even more beautiful than ever and I couldn't stay away from her. Again that night, we fell asleep curled up tightly together.

Tuesday 3rd June

That morning we were far more organised than the day before, and we got up, showered and dressed before a quick breakfast at the hotel and then out into New York again for the day. I'd managed to save a little money apart from what I needed for the trip, so I decided to take Sara shopping and spend some money spoiling her. I wasn't quite prepared for some of the prices I saw in the shops, but Sara informed me, in true holiday rep style and with that knowing grin of hers, that "On Fifth Avenue you get what you pay for". She was an expert at winding me up at times but I even loved her for that. On the second full day I was starting to settle in to the way New York worked, and even had thoughts about whether I could move to be with Sara and survive the place. I came to the conclusion that wherever Sara was I could happily live, and with my own plans in my head, I was hoping that this would be something we'd have to start talking about.

Sara didn't find anything she wanted on Fifth Avenue, so we visited Soho, which reminded me so much of Camden it was just like being back home again, before everything changed. Within minutes, Sara had started her old trick of haggling with the different traders in order to get the cheapest prices, and the feeling of déjà vu for me was overwhelming and brought a huge smile to my face. We finished our shopping morning with Sara carrying two bags full of all sorts of clothing. She had managed to get an awful lot for the money though, and I was happy because I'd been able to spoil her.

"Right mister, you have two choices for the afternoon: we can either go hang out, have a few drinks and then head back, or do the last few touristy things so you've had the complete Englishman-in-New-York experience. What do you think?" Sara knew I wasn't really bothered what I did as long as we were together, but her asking gave me the chance to sort some plans out in my head.

"Tomorrow's the fourth of July so I reckon everyone is going to be partying most of the day, so why don't we do the last few tourist things today? On Thursday I have plans for you beautiful, so that's already taken." I winked at Sara and she shook her head, laughing at my attempt to take control of anything.

"OK boss, whatever you say. Staten Island ferry, here we come." She held her arm out and looped it round mine, walking us towards the Metro.

I've never been overly keen on boats or being on the water in general, but the experience of the ferry was something I wouldn't have missed for the world. Having seen pictures of the Statue of Liberty in books and magazines was impressive enough, but seeing it in real life was exceptional. Sara clung tightly to me as the ferry moved across the harbour, protecting herself from the strong, cold winds that blew out there on the water. I listened intently as she told me about her experiences of New York so far, revealing the things she hated about the place like the smog and the prices of things, before telling me the things she loved like Central Park and the New York skyline. It was obvious that she loved living here and although I missed her so much, I was glad that she had found somewhere where she could be happy.

"I won't tell you the thing I hate most about New York though; you'll have to wait for that," she said, snuggling deeply into my body, and there we stood for the return journey to the city: two young lovers holding each other close as Lady Liberty loomed large behind us, the noise of the city drowned out by the gentle splashing of the waves as the ferry cut the harbour water in two.

The rest of that Tuesday was spent with Sara once more enjoying her role as tour guide. She showed me the Empire State Building, the Rockefeller Center and the Metropolitan Museum of Art before finally finding somewhere to eat and then heading back to the hotel for the night. Like London, there was so much to see in New York, and even with the Metro there was still a lot of walking involved, so I was more than grateful to make it to bed each night and have some intimate time with Sara. In the year apart it had been one of the most difficult things; not being able to touch her skin, kiss her deeply and feel us move together. To have that back for these few days had meant so much to me, and just being with her again made everything feel complete.

Wednesday 4th July
"Happy Independence Day beautiful!" I shouted to Sara above the noise.

"And to you, my adorable boy," she shouted back as we clinked glasses together in a toast.

We'd started drinking around three in the afternoon, and by the time it had got to seven we were in a hugely busy Irish bar in the centre of the city, with a great atmosphere, but having to shout at each other over the noise in order to have a conversation. That morning we had slept in late and hadn't finally gotten out of bed until lunchtime, but we'd packed so much into the time we'd spent together so far that it didn't feel like a waste. Today was American Independence Day though, and was always going to be a huge party day, especially in New York, so after a large lunch we had started partying and we didn't plan on stopping until late. We had drunk in fancy wine bars, dingy little backstreet dives and now the biggest Irish pub we could find. I don't think I'd have felt brave enough to go in alone but Sara had that sort of effect on me, making me feel like I could go anywhere, do anything and feel confident doing it. There was something strange about being in the middle of New York and surrounded by English and Irish people too, like a secret little tribe hiding out in the big city, although with all the noise in the bar it was difficult to tell where anyone came from; all the voices merged into one big mass of volume that drowned everything else out.

"Hey gorgeous, what do you say we go have a private party somewhere?" I gave Sara that look she knew all too well.

"I'm sure you could persuade me to go with you – you're not thinking about breaking any state laws though are you?" She smiled back.

"Only one way to find out, I guess?" I took her hand and led her out into the busy night.

We headed downtown, stopping only for me to pop into one of the more posh bars we'd been to earlier to grab a bottle of champagne, then found ourselves at the foot of a tall office building. At the back of the building was a tall, winding set of stairs to be used as a fire escape, so we climbed up to the very top and found ourselves a space to sit on the roof. We both giggled nervously as we slumped against the wall of what looked like some sort of caretaker's hut at the very top; neither of us were very good at crazy stunts, but the alcohol we had consumed that day and a desperation to be alone had definitely fuelled our bravery. The view from up there was fantastic, looking out over the Hudson River, and below us we could see thousands of revellers enjoying the celebrations.

We passed the champagne back and forth as the conversation got sillier and sillier with each drink. Even though our time together was nearly over it was lovely to be able to forget everything for a night and just laugh. Sara had such a beautiful laugh and I always told her I didn't get to hear it enough, but tonight we fell about at every opportunity, huddled up on the roof like a couple of naughty teenagers escaping their parents for a night. At around nine o'clock the fireworks started and the whole of the New York sky was filled with explosions, colours and light. It was the most amazing spectacle I had ever seen, the whole city lit up and celebrating together; the crowds seemed to grow with every second and I felt privileged to be a part of it all. I watched as Sara traced the rockets into the sky, blinking when they exploded into colour above us. She was mesmerised by the display, and as I looked at her my thoughts went back to tomorrow and how it would be the most important day of my life so far. I patted my jacket pocket, just checking that everything was still safely tucked away, and once satisfied, I smiled to myself and wrapped my arms around Sara to watch the rest of the display.

Thursday 5th July

The morning of my last full day in New York started with us both suffering from raging hangovers. Somehow we had made it back to the hotel but neither of us remembered how. It appeared that I was missing a shoe and Sara had somehow acquired a large Hawaiian-looking flower garland around her neck. All we remembered was waking up just a few hours after falling asleep and finding ourselves still fully clothed, so between us we drunkenly undressed each other and fell back into bed, naked and worn out. We eventually surfaced around lunchtime, had a big greasy cooked lunch, and then made our way back to Central Park at my request.

"I just want to experience the Lennon tribute again gorgeous, and take some photos. You know how much the guys back home love music history and this will blow their minds. You don't mind do you?" I was always checking that everything was OK with Sara, and I knew it drove her mad at times but I couldn't help it.

"Baby, it's fine, honestly. Today is your choice, I already said that. Whatever you want to do is good with me, and after last night I'm in no fit state to make any decisions." Sara pulled a sorry, sickly face and clutched my arm tighter as we walked through the park towards Strawberry Fields.

When we got there I chatted briefly to a guy who was playing his guitar to entertain the visitors, and then walked over to Sara who had found an empty bench on the edges of the circle.

"What are you up to, young man? Who was that guy you were talking to?" Sara was an awful person to keep anything from; she was so perceptive and it made hiding anything almost impossible.

"I saw him here the other day and I just asked him to take a photo of us, that's all beautiful; I wanted someone trustworthy so they wouldn't run off with my camera. You can't be too careful these days," I said, desperately trying to sound convincing.

"I'm sure you can't," Sara said, and her eyebrow rose slightly as she stared straight at me.

Luckily for me the guy came over and took the camera from me, getting Sara and I to sit together cross-legged on the ground so he could fit us, and the circle, in at the same time. We both lay back slightly and the big circle framed us beautifully in the picture, with roses and candles scattered around the edges. I thanked the guy and then motioned Sara over to the bench again to sit down. Whilst Sara was looking at the picture on the camera with me, she didn't notice the guy talking to the few people visiting the site and getting them to quietly stand together in a far corner. I turned to Sara: it was now or never.

"Sara, I need to speak to you." Somehow my nerves had gotten the better of me, and I was sounding like someone at a business meeting.

"What's wrong honey? You look really serious, are you OK?" Sara turned her body to face mine and looked concerned.

"Since I met you, everything has made so much more sense and I've enjoyed life like never before. Being away from you for the past year has been the hardest thing I've ever had to do, and the thought of leaving you again tomorrow is killing me. These last few days together have shown me how much better my world is with you in it, and that's all I want from life."

"I feel the same Will, you know that. You shouldn't think about tomorrow though – why waste today?" As Sara spoke, I signalled to the guy subtly and he started to play his guitar.

Sara looked up confused, as *Something* by The Beatles filled the air.

"I guess what I'm trying to say is that if all we have is now, are you happy?"

"You're here with me Will, how could I not be?" As Sara spoke, I reached into my coat pocket and held the tiny box tightly in my fist.

"Then why not join me in a lifetime of todays?"

"What are you talking about, Will? I don't understand." Sara seemed genuinely confused as I finally made my move.

"What I'm saying is, Sara, will you please do me the honour of being my wife?" In one swift motion I had slipped down to one knee, and held the open-lidded blue box out towards her, so the ring sparkled in the early afternoon sunlight. Sara's hand flew to her mouth as she gasped and tears started spilling down her face.

"I will – I mean, yes!" The tears were flowing down her cheeks now, and Sara let me put the ring on her finger before throwing herself on me and smothering me with kisses.

"Oh goodness Will, you don't know what you've just done. Thank you so much; since I met you I've been the happiest I have ever been and I'd give anything to spend the rest of my life with you. I love you so much more every day." And as Sara squeezed the breath out of me on the floor next to the memorial, the handful of tourists all cheered and took pictures of us: the happy couple.

On the way back to the hotel I told Sara how long I had been planning my big surprise, including how I had phoned her dad and asked his permission, and how he had agreed and been happy for us both. I then told her about speaking to the guitar-playing guy earlier in the week at the memorial and had made sure he would be there today, and finally, how I had been carrying the little box around with me the whole time, so desperate not to lose it, or for her to find it randomly. Sara was impressed that I had managed to arrange so much without her having any idea of it, and couldn't stop staring at the ring and smiling to herself.

When we got back to the hotel we had a few drinks at the bar before phoning the record shop and leaving a tipsy message on their answerphone about us getting engaged. I could just see the look on Steve's face as he heard the loved-up couple being all slushy and mocked putting his fingers down his throat in response. Then the evening was ours to spend cuddled up together and start making plans for the future. Although we had said we wouldn't have any more drink, we decided to spoil ourselves as a celebration of our future together. The plans we made got crazier the more we drank, and in the end I'm pretty sure we had run out of time left compared to all the things we had decided we must do.

"There's one more thing we need to do tonight though, baby," Sara said, flicking her hair back from her face as she lay on the pillow. "We need to consummate the marriage."

"I think that's after we're married, beautiful."

"We've never done things properly though, Will." And with a grin, she leant over and turned the lamp off, pulling me close towards her as the lights of New York cast shadows through the hotel curtains.

Friday 6th July
The dreaded morning had come around far too quickly. I woke up early and snuck out of bed to do as much packing as I could before Sara woke, and then climbed back in and snuggled up to her again. I knew how bad it would be having to pack everything and didn't want it to take up too much of

our time, which we could be spending on nicer things, like cuddling up together. The next couple of hours saw Sara and I waking up and nodding off again at various points, before making love one last time and laying there in each other's arms.

"I've got a surprise for you too, Will," Sara announced out of nowhere, climbing on top of me and smiling. "I'm going to come visit in September; I already arranged it with Dad and he's paying for me to come home for a couple of weeks, so you only have to survive a couple of months or so without me this time."

I could barely contain how happy I was. I pulled her towards me and kissed her passionately and for as long as I could before she broke away for air.

"Thank you beautiful, that's the best news I could have possibly had. I hated the thought of being away from you again but if I know you'll be back that soon then I can keep smiling. That means I'll get to show my beautiful fiancée off to the city of London!" I grabbed her face and kissed her once more, rolling her over on to the bed again.

By the time we were getting into the car, it was nearly nine o'clock in the morning, and I had two hours before I had to check in at the airport. The car had been arranged by Sara's dad again, and the driver had strict instructions to take me on a quick sightseeing tour of New York before I flew back to the UK. The car took us south from Chelsea, around the city and then back north towards the airport. Sara was pointing out all the sights so I didn't miss anything; she was so used to where everything was and it was all still a mystery to me. She showed me the Twin Towers where her dad's office was, and I was speechless at the height of them, dwarfing the whole of the city and seemingly stretching high up into the clouds. We hit a bit of traffic in the city itself but before too long we were heading on the expressway direct to the airport. I was staring out of the window, taking it all in, when Sara slipped her hand into mine and gripped it tightly.

"What are you thinking about honey? You're very quiet."

I turned to her and kissed her on the cheek. "I'm OK beautiful; just thinking about how good it's been having you back in my life again this week and I don't want to go back to nothing. Every time I have to say goodbye it just gets harder. I'm nothing without you." I felt so emotional but fought back the lump growing in my throat – the last thing I wanted to do was upset her.

"Don't say that Will, you are everything; my everything and I love you. It's only 11 weeks before I come back to England, that's all. I know it seems like ages but with work and life in general it'll be here before you know it, and who knows, maybe I'll be coming back for good. Things are different now, after all." Sara looked down at her engagement ring and smiled up at me, hugging me tighter. I smiled back at her and we kissed as the car continued its long drive to the airport.

At the airport, Sara came in with me and we sat talking for a while before I had to make my way to board the plane. We managed to keep it together this time because we knew that in less than three months, we'd be together again. I looked at her and couldn't believe how lucky I was: she was my princess and this was a fairytale that I could believe in. The announcement about flights boomed out over the speakers as we stood there making the most of our last few moments together.

"I love you beautiful; September cannot come quick enough for me, and I will spend the whole time waiting to have you back in my arms again. I'm always with you though, more than I am ever away from you. I'd wait forever for you; I want you to know that."

"You won't have to wait forever Will, I'm already yours and when I get back we have a lot of planning to do. I don't want to waste time; I want to be your wife as soon as possible. You are my future and I want to commit to you and then we can start building a life for ourselves. You gotta go and earn some serious money; your fiancée expects spoiling when she returns." Sara punched me playfully on the arm, and although she was smiling I could see the tears in her eyes. They never looked as blue as they did at that moment; the wetness making them look like a deep ocean I could just get swept away by. She really was the most beautiful girl I had ever seen and she was mine.

The announcer shouted one last warning regarding the flight I was on, so it was time to make that walk away once more. I hugged Sara tightly as I could and we kissed so deeply that I felt like I was floating on air.

"I love you, have a safe flight. When you get home, watch the tape!" Sara winked at me; she knew that was the first thing I'd do when I got home anyway.

"I love you too beautiful, see you soon. Seventy-seven days and I'm counting already." One more kiss and then I headed towards the desk, the ticket in my hand.

"Will, wait – I almost forgot to give you this!" Sara came running up to me, handing me a wrapped parcel before kissing me on the cheek and whispering in my ear. "By the time you get home it'll already be 76 days until you see your fiancée again."

She blew me a kiss and stood as I made my way through the gate and headed out of sight. The last view I had of her was her waving to me as she let herself start to cry. As I made my way down the corridor it hit me that all my dreams had come true: not only had I met the love of my life, but she'd actually agreed to marry me. I held the parcel tightly to my chest and inhaled the smell of her perfume that emanated from it. All I had to do was get through the next 11 weeks and life would be perfect.

Chapter 8

August 1996 – Age 19

What role does music play in your life? Is it just an enjoyable pastime, or essential as a soundtrack to your existence?

Thursday 22nd August

After weeks of planning the big day was finally here; I was waiting for the car to arrive that would take me to Reading Festival. I'd been to a few gigs before, but ever since last year's Glastonbury, Steve and Mattie had both been telling me how I needed to lose my festival virginity by experiencing my own very first, bona fide festival. They came home with some mad stories about all the different sorts of things they'd got up to and all the bands they'd seen, and had decided that we would go to Glastonbury as a trio this year. I remember the look on their faces when they broke the news to me that Glastonbury was taking a year off due to the fields needing time to recover, and how they thought all our plans were ruined. It wasn't until Kelly had said how lame any festivals apart from Reading were anyway that we found our answer. We all knew that any of the festivals were worth experiencing and there wasn't anything lame about any of them, but we didn't care about the opinion, just about the fact that it had given us the idea of the perfect alternative.

At ten o'clock I heard the sound of loud rock music being played through car speakers, and the honking of a horn. I looked out the window and saw Mattie waving from behind the wheel of his VW Beetle, and Steve in the passenger seat, a can of lager already in his hand, fiddling with the stereo. I could hear Led Zeppelin as I grabbed my rucksack and tent and opened my front door. I had one of those huge army-style rucksacks which could fit more in it than you could ever believe, or need. The only thing I didn't have was alcohol because I wasn't much of a drinker anyway and knew that Steve and Mattie would have more than enough for the three of us. I waved as I struggled down the path with the weight of the rucksack, and Mattie got out of the car to meet me.

"Hey bro, you ready for the time of your life? I hope you said goodbye to your mum because when her boy comes back, he's going to be a man. You'll have to take your rucksack in the back with you, but I'll chuck the tent in the boot with ours." Mattie high-fived me and put his seat forward so I could get in the back; it was cramped with all the bags and my rucksack but I managed to make a bit of space so I could relax for the journey. Steve saluted and broke into a loud rendition of *William, It Was Really Nothing* by The Smiths, something he often did when slightly under the influence of alcohol and unable to form a relevant sentence. Mattie jumped back into the car and turned to face us both, a huge grin on his face.

"Well this is it guys: the three amigos together like this for the first of many times I imagine? If Will survives this one of course; time will tell." He laughed and changed the tape in the stereo before starting the engine again. Steve sat forward in his chair, still swigging from the can of lager, and reached for the stereo before Mattie swatted his hand away.

"Steve, this stereo is now mine and this is the tape that I listen to as I journey to any festival, so do me a favour and keep your hands to yourself. If you do that we will get along just fine and I won't have to kill you." Mattie glanced in the rear-view mirror and winked at me, then pressed play on the stereo and the sound of Bob Marley's *Legend* album filled the car. Before long we were all singing along to it, all of us badly out of tune but not caring because we were enjoying ourselves. Steve was slurring most of his words and occasionally nodding off, whilst Mattie was chain-smoking and doing his most authentic Bob Marley voice, which I found entirely unconvincing and out of key. The sun was shining and the day was getting really warm; I was smiling to myself as we drove out of London, and Mattie occasionally made conversation, but most of the time stuck to smoking or singing.

"Mattie, I just wanted to say thanks to you both. This means a lot to me, you know?"

"No problem bro, we're going to have a blast. We're glad you came with us, now we have to show you how to party." Mattie was even cooler out of work; he always seemed so much more relaxed and able to be himself.

When we got to the festival site Mattie made his way round to the entrance where the cars were closest to the tents. He hated leaving his Beetle, so this way it felt safer to him as he could easily keep an eye on it. The gate wasn't open yet though, so all the cars were parked up on the side of the road in some kind of industrial estate, and everyone was lounging around waiting. The three of us found a space on the grass verge and sat down in the sunshine. I got the *NME* out of my bag, and we all looked at the lineup for the festival and who was playing. Steve decided that we should all list the five bands we most wanted to see: he was list-obsessed and always trying to get us to make them, whether it was top ten bands or favourite albums, so he went first.

"Babybird, Black Grape, Ash, Stone Roses and Billy Bragg," he said, before lying back under his cricket hat.

"Weezer, Sonic Youth, Butthole Surfers, Sebadoh and Flaming Lips," said Mattie, looking proud of his choices.

"Garbage, Sonic Youth, Sparklehorse, Ben Folds Five and The Raincoats," I said, happy that Mattie would nod in agreement and like most, if not all, of my choices. I carried on flicking through the magazine, whilst Steve started snoring loudly beside me, and looked over at Mattie who was rolling a cigarette.

"I didn't know you smoked roll-ups, Mattie."

"Haha, I don't, Will. I'm rolling a joint; please tell me you know what that is?" Mattie was looking at me like I was an alien. I suddenly felt really stupid – I knew a fair bit about drugs but I never realised anyone would do it so openly until then. I'd had a pretty sheltered life compared to a lot of other people, and sometimes it really showed.

"I know what a joint is Mattie; sorry I just didn't realise you smoked."

"Will, welcome to the world of music festivals. Whilst I'm here, there is very little I wouldn't do." With a huge grin on his face he started puffing away, and laid back staring at the blue sky above us.

Within an hour the gates had been opened and after following a slow crawl of traffic under the bridge, we had arrived. My first view of the festival was the size of the car park area, and that alone took me by surprise. In the distance I could see some form of walled-off area, but other than that it was all grass, cars and huge numbers of people with too much baggage walking around. After we'd parked up, Mattie said for me just to grab my tent first and then come back for the bags once we'd found a pitch and roped it off. So off the three of us went, Steve wobbling drunkenly, Mattie practically floating and me full of excitement and nerves. I had the same feeling from walking around here that I sometimes got in Camden; like everyone else was so much cooler than me, but I managed to stifle this and do my best to look like I was an old professional on the festival circuit. The closer we got to the main festival arena, the bigger it looked to me. Huge walls of advertising separated the tent and stall area from all the live music inside, and although there was still 24 hours before any music started, I already felt the excitement bubbling inside me.

We eventually settled on an area about halfway between where the car was parked and the arena; it had just enough room for our three tents to fit, and a space in the middle for a decent campfire. We all set up our tents and then Steve got some tape with the words *WET PAINT* printed repetitively across it, and taped a sort of triangle shape around us, allowing us our own area which would be difficult for strangers to walk through. Mattie and Steve both agreed that the worst thing about camping at any festival was the constant flow of people who, either drunk or high, cut through the middle of your patch and tripped over your tent pegs. We'd made a nice little secure area so all that was left was to get the rest of the stuff from the car.

"Have a safe voyage, my good men – I shall sit here and protect our ground. Good luck," said Steve theatrically, before collapsing onto his back and starting to snore loudly again.

"Come on Will, he's more trouble than good with unpacking anyway, and I have a present for the most helpful person here so I guess that means he's just missed out," Mattie patted me on the back and led me back to the car for the rest of the stuff.

After a couple of trips we had brought all the stuff to the tents and had everything set up like we wanted, and we'd even chatted to a couple of groups camping around us and they seemed like genuinely nice people so we felt the whole area was pretty safe. Mattie had an obsessive fear of things being stolen from his tent and when I found out what he had in there it didn't surprise me. After I'd sorted my stuff out I went to see what he was up to and found him stashing stuff in his sleeping bag, including a bottle of Jack Daniel's, a bag of weed, a small box which seemed to have all sorts of pills and powders in it, a carton of cigarettes and his portable CD player. It didn't bother me that Mattie and Steve would want to get completely drunk or take drugs; I just worried what would happen if the police raided the tents and found the stuff.

Once everything was finished and Steve had fully sobered up, we went to the ticket tent to swap them over for the wristbands they made you wear instead. As we stood in the queue I looked at all the different t-shirts people were wearing and saw everything from The Beatles to Nirvana and Pink Floyd to Oasis. The variety of people here, and their musical tastes, was amazing, but we were all equal; all here to experience some great music and maybe other things at the same time. It was the first time I'd ever been in such a huge crowd and felt like everyone was a friend; it showed the power that music had in bringing people together as it had always done, from Woodstock to the festivals of the modern age. After about half an hour, our little trio emerged with wristbands, ready to head out of the festival site and into Reading itself.

Walking to the gates showed me just how big the whole place was: we passed all manner of stalls selling everything from clothing, posters, music and even legal highs; numerous portable toilet areas and then empty space itself before reaching the gate. Luckily Mattie knew Reading quite well, from different gigs he'd been to here down the years, so was able to guide us around with ease. I'd promised them both a pub lunch as a thank-you for including me, and we figured the best time to have it was before we got all dirty from the three days' camping, and this meant that Steve could start filling up his alcohol level again. We found a place that Mattie had eaten in before and enjoyed a big meal and a couple of pints each in the luxury of comfortable seating for the last time in a few days.

Although I had worked with Mattie and Steve for three years now, I'd only socialised with them in the last year. They went out to various rock clubs and alternative nights throughout London, and I had always heard the stories at work the next day, when they were both bleary-eyed and needing headache tablets. I had always wanted to go but knew that there was no chance until I was 18 – my parents were quite strict when it came to rules and I would never have been allowed into a club before legally being old enough. Plus, I didn't look eighteen, so I had to wait to get an identity card to prove my age before I could start my social life. In the last year I had made up for it though, and had spent a fair few nights with the two of them. We'd been to gigs, parties and clubs, and over the space of the last year I had found more enjoyment in going out than I ever had in the past.

"What's the plan then, boss?" I said jokingly to Mattie.

"First, we're going to use comfortable toileting facilities for the last time in three days; then we're going to head back to the site and spend the evening listening to music and having a campfire." He had it all planned out, and Steve nodded in approval, seemingly having reached the required amount of alcohol in his bloodstream again.

We headed back via an off-licence and the stalls in the site itself, and arrived back at our campsite fully stocked with supplies of vodka, mixers, lager and firewood. Before long we all had our chairs out and were enjoying the late afternoon sun with a can in our hands and music on the stereo. Mattie had allocated us an album each so we all got a chance to listen to something, and this had started with the second playing of Bob Marley that day as he smoked himself high and daydreamed off into his own little world. Steve then had us listening to the Happy Mondays before I was allowed to put my choice on; I had chosen *Maxinquaye* by Tricky as it felt like the perfect album to listen to as the sky started to darken, surrounded by the smell of weed in the air.

The evening soon rolled in and we sat around a campfire, still listening to music and sharing one of Mattie's joints. I didn't really like smoking so I had the smallest, quickest puff I could before handing it to Steve and carrying on with my lager. Being someone who didn't smoke meant that it had a much bigger effect on me than it did on those guys, and as The Beatles' *White Album* played on the stereo, I had to bid the guys farewell and head to bed as I felt a bit sick and didn't want to ruin their fun.

"Night Will, see you in the morning. If you don't want to smoke just say so, OK? I know it's not everybody's thing and I wouldn't think any less of you for passing it over. Go get some sleep, kid; tomorrow is a huge day." Mattie was always so kind: he did that cool-but-protective older brother thing with me and it always meant a lot; I knew now that I could happily pass having the joint and there was no pressure on me. I gave him a high five and turned towards my tent.

"Yeah, it means even more for me. We're going to blow this place apart tomorrow Will, so get your head straight – you're going to need it to be." Steve saluted me, still grinning dopily as he inhaled again before passing the joint to Mattie.

"Thanks guys; sorry for turning in early, I just feel a bit green that's all. I'll see you in the morning." Then off I went, into my tent to sleep with the sound of a beautiful, crackling bonfire filling the night air.

Friday 23rd August
After a good, head-clearing sleep, I woke up early the next morning and got out of my tent for some fresh air. As I stood stretching I looked around the view from every direction and it took my breath away. As far as the eye could see there were tents and people, small clouds of smoke from campfires that were slowly dying out, and a beautiful sunny sky above. Steve and Mattie were both asleep by the sounds of things, so I decided to try and carry on resting myself for a while, as I had a feeling I would need all the energy I could get.

When I finally got fed up of lying in the hot tent unable to sleep, I gave myself a wash using the baby wipes I'd brought with me, changed my clothes and headed out into the fresh air again. The day had started to warm up nicely and I could already see swarms of people heading towards the main arena to queue for the best spots when it finally opened. I sat in my deckchair looking at the festival programme and waited for the other two to get up; it was at least another hour before they both surfaced. Mattie stuck his head out of his tent first and then Steve appeared not long after – they both looked bleary-eyed from the night before, but had at least washed and changed clothes. Eventually they stumbled out of the tent and locked everything up, Steve taping the area off again.

"I need food before I do anything else." Mattie certainly looked worse for wear, and it didn't seem a bad idea for him to soak up the alcohol with something.

"Me too, I feel like something crawled down my neck and died." Steve was holding his head and giddily putting one foot in front of the other.

I laughed as they clumsily high-fived and then carried on stumbling along with their arms around each other, singing something by The Pogues incoherently. I followed their lead, which eventually led to a lovely wooden café not far from the main arena and we all had a big breakfast and many cups of coffee before feeling human enough to rejoin the mass of bodies and start the real festival events. As I sat in the café waiting for Steve to finish flirting with the waitress I looked at the queue; it seemed to stretch for miles and I was desperate to be in there with them, awaiting the opening of the gates and whatever lay beyond. Soon enough Steve had gotten the phone number of the waitress and an agreement to meet later that evening, so we joined the queue and waited.

I'll never forget my first sight of what lay inside the main arena, after filing through the cattle grid-style line and having my wristband pulled at the security check. I stood just inside and looked out at the huge expanse in front of me, and in the distance I could see the main stage and the huge television screens either side. The perimeter held all manner of food and drink stalls, along with the merchandise stands and the toilet area, and sticking out from these rows of stalls were two huge tents, as well as another tent in the middle of the space in front of me. I looked at my little map and got my bearings, working out which was the second stage, the comedy tent and everything else before making a move anywhere. Dotted around the inside of the arena near the main gates were many more stalls, offering more beads, more clothing and more legal highs.

"Welcome to Reading, our virgin friend – what do you say we go get crazy?" Mattie and Steve both patted a hand on my back, then led me towards the main stage.

That first day seemed to go so quickly, and from the moment that the compère first stepped onto the main stage until the end of Rage Against the Machine, the day was a blur of trips to the beer tent, trips to the toilet and the most amazing amount of music I had ever enjoyed in such a short space of time, and in the course of the day we sat in the sun getting burnt as we drank lager and chatted about music or listened to it. We had soon felt the chill though as the night came in quickly, forcing us to buy a blanket each from a hippy stall, and then watched as the stars came out and various small fires lit up the arena. Still buzzing from Rage Against the Machine's set, we headed back to the campsite to carry on the rest of the night. Within half an hour of the huge mass of bodies leaving the arena, Mattie and I were sat around the campfire chatting about the sets by Sebadoh and Sparklehorse earlier in the day. Steve turned up about an hour later with the waitress from the café in tow.

"Guys, this is Helena. Helena, this is Mattie and Will." Steve seemed to be on his best behaviour in front of this girl and we went along with it. Mattie and I both looked at each other with raised eyebrows, but neither of us had the heart to make him look silly in front of her, so we carried on as normal with Steve toning down his sense of humour to a far less offensive level than usual. Helena turned out to be a really lovely girl who also had a tremendous ability to drink, and we sat around the fire chatting, listening to music and doing shots of tequila from a bottle that she had brought with her. The night rolled on with Steve and Helena getting closer and closer until they suddenly seemed to disappear into his tent without us realising it. Mattie had been smoking a joint and getting quieter by the second, until he suddenly stood up and stared at the fire.

"I am far too high," was all he said, before handing me the joint and heading off into his tent.

I sat there for a while, smiling to myself. I had been the early sleeper last night, but today I had paced myself really well and was still standing. I noticed Mattie had left his portable stereo outside, so I loaded it up with Pink Floyd's *Wish You Were Here* and finished his joint off. I found I could smoke it if I kept drinking something at the same time, and the orange juice was perfect, because it was so smooth and tamed the strong taste of the weed he'd rolled with. As *Shine On You Crazy Diamond* reached its peak, I stood up and looked around the campsite. It was like looking into outer space, with thousands upon thousands of small campfires, like stars twinkling in a dark sky. The smell of the wood burning and the sounds of all the conversations merged in my head, and I felt a complete euphoria, like I finally belonged. When the buzz of that first proper festival day had died down, I used the rest of the juice to put out the campfire and returned to my tent. As I lay there still smiling about the day, my soundtrack to sleeping was a combination of the grunts and groans coming from Steve's tent merged with the snoring from Mattie's. As I closed my eyes I started laughing out loud: I hadn't felt this alive in a long time and I couldn't wait to carry on in the morning. With this thought in my mind, the flickering shadows of other people's campfires on the wall of the tent slowly sent me to sleep.

The next two days passed even quicker than the first did. We all managed to see the bands we had come for, and before we knew it the last band of the festival had finished. Steve had suffered the most disappointment: not only had Helena never returned, but he also missed half of Ash by getting himself locked in a toilet cubicle for half an hour. Before we knew it, all the music was finished and we were back at the campsite again, making the most of the last night. The lagers had long gone, so we were all sat mixing vodka or whisky and Coke in the small coffee cups we had saved that morning. Steve and Mattie were debating the good and bad points of the Stone Roses' set, which would have been funny enough sober, but with them both being drunk and getting high it was even more ridiculous. I couldn't shake a kind of melancholy feeling that we were heading home tomorrow, and although it would be lovely to see my parents again, it felt like leaving somewhere you belong and heading to somewhere you struggle to fit in easily. Eventually the conversation turned into two children bickering so I decided to investigate the festival one last time.

"Hey guys, I need the toilet and then I just want to get a last look at everything before it's all packed up. I'll be back later; you guys just carry on." I announced it loudly, bringing an abrupt halt to the argument. Steve just nodded and carried on scowling at Mattie, who rummaged around beneath his chair.

"No worries Will — oh, here's the present I was telling you about for helping me. Don't do anything I wouldn't do." He winked as he threw me a half-sized bottle of Coke. "It's already mixed." He winked again and then turned back to Steve to pick up the argument. As I walked off, Steve shouted loudly after me.

"Hey, don't forget when you get back I need your top five bands you've seen this festival." I held my thumb up to acknowledge him and walked off smiling to myself.

"Him and his bloody lists," I muttered under my breath.

I walked around the perimeter of the campsite drinking happily from my bottle, looking at all the people sat round their fires: some laughing, some dancing, most getting very drunk or very high. Eventually I came to the stalls again — some had already packed up, but a few were trying to catch the last bit of trade from the festival-goers, and I imagined that with the amount of drink consumed, all sorts of last-minute purchases were made and then regretted in the sober light of day. The night had started to get quite cold so I bought myself an old army shirt from the closest stall and put it on over my hoodie to keep me a bit warmer, then found a spot near the main entrance which was quite quiet and sat against a tree and watched. The atmosphere was like nothing I had ever experienced before: hordes of people swarming around with each group looking cooler than the last, and all sorts of music that I loved being played from the circles of various tents nearby. It was such a wonderful feeling to just sit here relaxing and soaking everything up.

As the bottle began to empty I heard a girl singing The Doors' *Crystal Ship* somewhere nearby, and whether it was the alcohol or the atmosphere, I had to find out where it was coming from. I managed to stand up, albeit staggering rather than standing, and followed the sound of the music. As I walked along the row of tents to my left I could hear it getting louder, so I knew I was heading the right way. Eventually I saw a large open space in the middle of a circle of tents, with about a dozen people sat around watching a girl sing. The girl had dark, wavy hair and looked like someone who had just stepped out of the Woodstock Festival; covered in beads and wearing a beautiful flowery hippy dress. She was singing without any backing music at all and had a beautiful voice, completely capturing her audience and keeping them silent. As she neared the end of the song she glanced in my direction and smiled, before turning her attention back to her crowd and singing the last few words. All the people watching cheered and clapped and she thanked them before slowly standing up and walking away, a little woollen bag slung over her shoulder. I stood watching as she walked off down the path away from me, almost feline in her movements; she had a strange grace to the way she held herself, like an actress who has practised a certain walk for a movie shot over a hundred times. I walked over to the group at the campsite and got their attention.

"Sorry guys, this is going to seem like a really weird question, but who was that singing? Do you know her?"

"No idea man, sorry – she just wandered over and asked us what music we liked. I told her all the old stuff like The Doors and she said did I want her to sing, so I said yeah, sure. When she finished she threw us a joint and said thanks for listening, then she just walked off." The guy in the Rolling Stones shirt who was talking seemed even more confused by the whole event than I had been.

"OK, thanks a lot man; have a good last night."

"No problems bro; you're welcome to have a smoke with us if you want?" He seemed genuinely nice, but I had something I really needed to do now.

"I'm OK thanks man, I have to get going. Thanks anyway," I said, before heading back out onto the path.

I looked in the direction the girl had been heading and saw that she had stopped where another path crossed in front, forming a sort of T-junction, so with another swig of my confidence juice I headed down towards her. When I got within a few feet of her I suddenly had no idea how to approach the situation and tried stalling by walking slowly, which was getting more difficult as I was practically stood behind her now.

"You can sit down, you know," she said without turning round, patting the earth next to her.

"Sorry, I didn't mean to intrude; I just heard you sing and wanted to tell you what a beautiful voice you've got. That's my favourite song by The Doors and you were amazing." I tried to keep from sounding nervous or too drunk, but I think I failed miserably.

"Well, aren't you a sweetie? Here, would you give me a hand up?" She held out her hand to me and I pulled her up to her feet.

"Is this where you're camping?" I said, trying to avoid staring at her; she was very pretty and had a strange aura about her.

"No, I kind of drift really; the singing allows me to join groups for a while and not have to entertain myself all evening." She smiled and looked straight into my eyes with such confidence.

"I just wondered because you were sitting there and it looked like you were waiting for someone." I cringed internally at my supposedly subtle attempt to find out if she was with anyone.

"Whenever you reach a crossroad in life you should always sit and think sweetie; before long you will know which way to go because it will present itself to you like a sign, trust me." She took hold of my hand and rubbed her finger over my palm. "Did you want to hang out with me for a while?" she said, stroking the lines on my palm.

"Sure, the guys I'm with are busy talking about stuff anyway so I was just wandering about looking for one last experience of the festival. It's my first time here."

"Well then, experience you shall have." She smiled and turned left at the junction, pulling me along with her.

We ended up at a single tent near the edge of the camping area; it had a small area for a fire with some wood ready to be burnt and a bit of space to sit, but nothing else. I realised how all the tents faced each other and seemed to be in groups, except for this mysterious girl's.

"I'll be back in a minute, you want to light the fire for me?" she said, throwing me some matches and newspaper. So I started the fire whilst she went into the little purple tent with a peace symbol painted on the side. When she came out again the fire had just started to catch and she was carrying an acoustic guitar. She came and sat next to me on a long cushion that was next to the fire.

"I'm Alice, by the way," she said, sitting and tuning the guitar. It hadn't even registered that I didn't know her name.

"I'm really sorry; you must think I'm a freak for not introducing myself properly. I'm Will." I held out my hand to shake hers but retracted it before she noticed – I was so bad in situations where I was nervous, and an attractive girl had the ability to do that to me far too easily.

"I don't think you're a freak Will, more of a lost soul," she said, looking at me as she plucked her guitar strings. Then, satisfied she had tuned everything correctly, she started playing her guitar and singing a song. I didn't recognise it at all, but it was beautiful and I was mesmerised by her voice and the way the reflection of the fire danced in her eyes. I finished drinking the bottle Mattie had given me and laid back on the cushion just listening to her, much more relaxed and starting to enjoy this strange experience. When she finished she put the guitar down next to her and turned to me.

"That was really beautiful, what was the song?"

"*An Open Mind Can See the Future*," she replied. "I wrote it myself; I'm hoping I can get somewhere with my music one day. I mainly sing covers of songs for people, but I've written a few of my own too." She seemed almost shy when it came to talking about her music, which was strange given how talented she was.

"I like the title, and it's a gorgeous song. I love the idea too: I think living in a city surrounded by work and modern technology it's easy to lose sight of the simple things that people relied on in the past, like instinct and the power of the mind." It seemed that alcohol was finally making me waffle, and I immediately thought of how Steve was and quietened myself.

"You said you wanted one last experience, Will. Did you really mean it?"

"Yes; at the minute I'm not sure I want to leave here at all." As I spoke I started to lean in closer to her.

"Then close your eyes sweetie, kiss me and let yourself go."

I closed my eyes and felt her mouth on mine; we kissed passionately before she pulled away and spoke softly.

"Will, open your mouth; I'm going to put something on your tongue and I want you to just lay back, relax and listen." She pressed something flat onto my tongue and I did as she said. As I laid my head down, she was stroking my hair, and the last things I heard were the sound of her playing *Stairway to Heaven* on the guitar and the words that she whispered in my ear.

"See you on the other side."

I couldn't remember how I got to Parliament Hill, but I looked at my watch and it was eleven o'clock on a December morning and there was hardly any daylight. I made the familiar walk up the hill and I noticed that the sky was a sort of dark red, and that cast an eerie glow over everything. There was no sound at all: the trees seemed to be swaying gently, but I couldn't feel or hear any wind. I made it to the top and sat on the bench looking out over London, and as I looked at all the buildings they seemed to fade from my view. Slowly each building seemed to become fuzzy and disappear, until there was nothing left to see but a sort of hazy cloud illuminated with this strange, reddish glow. I tried to call out to see if anyone was around, but no sound would leave my lips — like screaming underwater, the more I tried the quieter everything felt. Above me the red was rolling over and deepening, as if someone was sealing a lid on a box I was in, and all around me the hazy cloud seemed to thicken. As I started to panic, I looked around in all directions for some help, and to the right of me a figure seemed to drift from the clouds. She was dressed in white, with long, dark hair and a beautiful face. She gently drifted towards me, holding my gaze the entire time, and stopped in front of me. Her eyes were the most magnificent blue I'd ever seen, and suddenly amidst all this chaos and confusion, I suddenly felt completely calm. As I looked at her, I tried to speak, but she just gently lifted her finger to her mouth and motioned for me to be quiet. As I stared in her eyes I felt my emotions shift from fear to calm; happiness and then an overwhelming sadness. With one finger still pressed against her lips, she moved her other hand and wiped my cheek – I was crying and hadn't even realised it. When she removed her hand, she stared at me for a few seconds and then disappeared into the clouds around me, which were getting thicker and thicker as I stood there. I tried reaching through the clouds but I couldn't get anywhere; I could see her blue eyes in my mind though and that feeling of calm washed over me again, and then everything went blank.

Monday 26th August

I woke up face-down on my sleeping bag, feeling damp and freezing cold. The noise of clattering pots and pans outside woke me, and when I poked my head out of the tent I saw Steve and Mattie creating a makeshift fry-up using the bonfire. My head was pounding and my mouth felt like a sandpit, so I grabbed a bottle of water and drained it before trying to speak.

"Well, well, well, if it isn't the dirty stop-out, finally appearing again. Where the hell did you disappear to last night, young William? We were up ages and then had a look around and couldn't find you anywhere; then suddenly this morning you're here. Care to give us the juicy details?" Mattie was studying me carefully; he had concern in his voice despite the joking around.

"I'm really sorry guys, I'm not sure – I just went for a walk and then I met this girl and we went back to her tent to chat and she played some music, then I had the weirdest dream and now I've woken up here. I think I'm more confused than you." My head was swimming with memories from last night: talking to Alice and then the crazy dream, but I didn't remember waking up again or making it back to the tent.

"Well as long as you're OK, sunshine, although it might take a while for your eyes to come down," Mattie replied, whilst giving me that 'older brother' look he often gave me when I worried him. "Sort yourself out and I'll make you some breakfast."

With my head still swimming I somehow managed to clean up and get some new clothes on, then pack my bags and tent before sitting in the chair to eat the fry-up he'd produced. I struggled to swallow the food, my head still banging and my mouth still dry, but with the help of more water I'd soon eaten it all up. Mattie and Steve were busy sorting out what stuff they were going to leave and what they needed to bring home, whilst I sat and looked out over the campsite. It was definitely the morning after the night before, with the same energetic revellers I saw last night struggling to even stand up or talk due to tiredness or hangovers. I had put my new army shirt back on over my hoodie because I felt so cold, having woken up outside my sleeping bag, and it still smelt faintly of patchouli from my time with Alice the previous night.

Eventually we were all done, and had a much smaller load to carry to the car than when we'd arrived. Within two trips it was done and whilst Steve loaded it all up, Mattie and I went back one last time to use the toilets.

"You sure you're OK, Will? You seem really spaced out today." Mattie was always looking out for me and it was something I really appreciated.

"I don't know, Matt; I feel kind of different if that makes sense? After last night everything seems clearer, but more confused at the same time." I was struggling to make sense of my own conversation, so I couldn't expect anyone else to.

Mattie laughed out loud and patted me on the back. "That, my friend, sounds like the power of LSD. I have a feeling your young lady took you on a much bigger journey than you expected last night."

I knew about drugs, but in the drunkenness of last night it had never dawned on me what had gone on. Now it all made perfect sense.

"I've got to see her before we leave, Matt; I want to give her my number or get her address or something. She was really lovely and I'd like to meet her again."

"No worries man; on the way back to the car we'll go find this crazy chick of yours." Mattie shoved me playfully and carried on striding towards the cubicles with a big grin on his face.

After using the cubicles we went in search of Alice. It took me a while to work out my bearings, but I was soon on the right track and we made it to the corner where I had sat last night. It was completely empty: there was no tent, no cushion; nothing remained of our night before, and even the campfire seemed like it hadn't been touched for days.

"I don't understand Mattie: she was here, camped on her own. I promise I'm not lying, she played *Stairway to Heaven* on her guitar, just after she'd kissed me and put something on my tongue." The more I tried to explain the story I got louder and more animated, until Mattie grabbed me with his hands on my shoulders.

"Will, I know you're telling the truth. Trust me, your eyes tell the whole story; you barely have anything other than pupils in them. Let's go – sometimes in life you meet wanderers, that's all. We want to keep everyone, but sometimes it's just not meant to be. Trust fate."

Mattie led me away and back to the car. I was still confused and a bit upset that I didn't get to see her again but what he said made sense. She had described herself like that last night, and although I wanted to know more about what had happened, sometimes you just had to accept things as they were.

An hour later after the struggle to leave the car park, we were back on the motorway and heading to London. I was struggling to stay awake as Mattie and Steve chattered away in the front about the next gig they wanted to see. As I tried to make myself more comfortable in the back seat, something inside my army shirt poked me in the chest. I stuck my hand in and pulled out a small square, realising it was a Polaroid photograph. In the photo was Alice, holding her finger to her mouth motioning for me to keep quiet, and there was a lipstick kiss on the photo itself. I turned it over and on the back was a handwritten message: *See you on the other side.* I quietly put it back in my pocket and smiled to myself, before laying back down to get some rest as the car sped back to London and normal life.

Chapter 9

September 2001 – Age 24

Can you pick a day when you think the world changed? Were you emotionally affected by something badly, even though you weren't personally involved?

I could hear her calling me over and over again; each time she called it sounded more urgent but I couldn't find her. I was running up the hill to where her voice seemed to be coming from, only for it to sound further away again and the smoke was making it impossible to see more than a few feet in front of me. When I got to the top of the hill, I could just make out the shape of the bench and slumped down on it, tired and breathless. As I sat there I heard her voice as if it was close again.

"Will, it's OK; it's not time yet. Wait for me, please."

But when I turned around, there wasn't anyone there. I was starting to get frustrated and I shouted "Sara, where are you?" as loud as I could, but there was no reply. As I slumped back onto the bench again I looked out towards London, and in an instant the smoke cleared; I could see for miles and it was all peaceful and quiet. I thought of Sara; I had to find her, she needed me. So I ran as fast as I could back down the hill, stumbling halfway down and ending up in a heap on the floor. . .

Tuesday 11th September

I sat bolt upright in bed, wide awake in an instant, the sweat running down my face as I sat there trying to work out what had just happened. It had obviously been a nightmare but it had felt so real; my chest felt tight and I didn't know whether to laugh or cry. I was so relieved that it was just a dream, but it had left me with a niggling feeling that I couldn't quite put my finger on. I looked over at the bedside clock and it said 9 am, which was a whole hour before I had planned to get up seeing as I wasn't due at work until 12 today, but I felt so hot and sweaty I decided I might as well have a shower and get up anyway. Before I did though, I booted up the computer and sent Sara an email. I wanted to check that she was all right, and though it was far too early for her to be awake, at least she could read it when she woke up. Once I'd sent it I immediately felt a bit better and went to get showered and ready, deciding I might as well go into work early seeing as I was awake anyway.

Half an hour later I was sat on the edge of my bed putting my baseball boots on and looking at the calendar, counting the days until Sara landed back on English soil again. In just ten days she would be back in my arms again and we could start planning the wedding and our future together. My eyes wandered over to the photo of her next to my bed. It was my favourite picture of her; I'd taken it when I'd visited her in New York and we had been walking through Central Park. I'd always liked taking photographs when people least expected it and I'd managed to catch a picture of her laughing and trying to hide from the camera, her face turned slightly away from me. I don't know why I loved the picture so much; I think it was because it showed such a natural innocence in Sara that people might not have thought she had.

I chucked a few things into my bag and was ready to head off, so I went downstairs and said bye to Mum before heading out into London. Although I had my car there was never any point driving it to work because of the traffic so I always walked into work. It was a lovely crisp early September day, not cold but definitely more autumnal. I stopped off in a coffee shop to have some breakfast on my way to the shop, enjoying a large latte and a couple of pastries, happy in the knowledge that I had less than two weeks to wait for Sara to return and life could get back to normal again.

When I eventually walked into the shop I was greeted by a rather grumpy Steve showing a new guy around. He only looked about 17 years old and it kind of reminded me of my first day; I knew Steve was very territorial about who worked there though, and often struggled to cope with the idea of someone new coming in. I waved at him and headed out through the back door to the stockroom. Mattie had left a note for me on the table saying he had popped out to a meeting but would be back about one o'clock, so if I could sort out some of the ordering and contacting people on the computer until he returned, that would be great. I looked at my watch: it was half eleven, so I logged into the computer to kill half an hour before I started. I brought my emails up and saw something that always made me smile: Sara's name was highlighted in the inbox with an unread message. I clicked on it and read.

Hey gorgeous,
I've started writing to you but will have to finish it later – Dad's on at me to get going. I still cannot believe I have finally let him talk me into breakfast at his work restaurant; it's called Windows Of

the World or something like that, but really, up at 7 am on my day off???? I must be mad!!!! I should be snuggled up in bed with you!!!!

Anyway honey, I promise to finish the letter later and ring you tonight.

Gotta dash,
Yours always,
Love xxxxx S xxxxx

I smiled as I read it to myself and felt better having heard from her. I logged back out again and decided to make myself a cup of tea and get working. I popped *Parachutes* by Coldplay on the stereo and set about trying to make sense of all the paperwork Mattie had left behind. It took a good hour to get it all straight and in that time Mattie had come back and gone out again, making a quick exit when he realised just how big a job he'd left me! Steve had left the new guy with Kelly training him on the till; the poor guy didn't know whether to stare at her or the keys, and I noticed Steve had managed to hang around in the shop, generally rearranging stock that didn't need moving, rather than trying to deal with him.

I was free to just carry on working out the back and that suited me fine. I liked being my own boss and being able to listen to anything I wanted was always a bonus. I decided to get stuck into the boxes of stock that had been delivered, so I put *Unplugged in New York* by Nirvana on and started singing my way through the work. Steve popped out a couple of times and threw me a glance of disapproval at my music choice – if it wasn't English then it upset him – before disappearing back into the shop again. I was more than happy just piling through the work on my own, though. Just after one o'clock I decided to check my emails again and was happily surprised to see another sent from Sara, and this time it had a file attached to it.

Hey gorgeous,

Just me again — we're waiting to get our breakfast and I wanted to send you a picture to make you smile! Dad sends his regards and hopes you are keeping well. Not long now until you have to put up with me again! Hope you've been keeping my room tidy! LOL.

Mail me back when you finish work!

Always yours,

xxxxx S xxxxx

I clicked on the attachment and smiled even more. It was a picture of Sara holding up a sign with *I love Will* written on it, and through the huge windows behind her was a startling view out over Manhattan. She looked so beautiful in the picture, wearing a gorgeous dark red and black dress, with all her bracelets on and her hair slightly wavy around her face. I sat staring at it for ages before finally deciding I should log out of my emails and carry on working.

"Ten days, beautiful," I said to myself, before returning to my work. Considering how badly the day had started I was really enjoying it now; I was glad I'd come into work early and felt like everything was starting to fall into place. Sometimes people say you are at your most vulnerable when happy, and within the hour I knew exactly what they meant.

At around two o'clock Mattie came running through the door into the stockroom. He looked as white as a sheet and was breathing heavily.

"Will, something really bad has happened; it's all over the news. There's been some sort of accident in New York at the Twin Towers; it looks awful. I don't know much, but I saw it come on the telly and rushed straight back to tell you."

"What's happened? Is everyone OK? I need to go find out what's happening, Mattie; I can't stay, I'm really sorry." I went from being frozen on the spot to blind panic in a split second; my mind was working overtime trying to work everything out. I grabbed my bag and headed for the door.

"Don't worry about this place – go home, watch the news and get in touch with Sara to make sure she's OK. Ring me later and let me know; we can manage here until things are sorted." Mattie put his arm round me, trying to be reassuring, but I could feel his doubt and worry pouring off him. I thanked him and headed out of the store, leaving through the fire exit so I didn't have to explain myself to Steve or Kelly. I just needed to get home and find out what was happening as fast as possible.

It took me about half an hour to get home, and I rushed in to find my mum sat in the living room watching the news. I stopped dead in my tracks at the pictures on the television in front of me: the Twin Towers with smoke billowing out of huge holes in both of them. My mum turned and saw me standing there; she was crying as she stood up to speak to me.

"Oh Will, it's just awful. Someone flew planes into the towers and there are people trapped in there; the towers are on fire and there's so much panic. They think people have been jumping out of the windows." She walked over to me, tears running down her cheeks. "You need to phone Sara – it's where her father works; she's going to need you," she said, struggling to hold it together.

That was the moment my heart broke. I knew that the restaurant they had gone to for breakfast was on one of the top floors in the North Tower, and the information bar on the news in front of me said that the North Tower had been hit, around the 93rd floor, at quarter to nine New York time. Sara had emailed me the photo of her in the restaurant around twenty past eight, so she would still have been there when the plane hit. Every little bit of information swirled in front of me, on the news and in my head, and then it hit me in one life-changing moment of clarity.

"Sara – oh God, no!" I fell to my knees and screamed with so much pain that I frightened my mum, who dropped to the floor beside me and held me.

"It's OK Will, you need to phone her though. She's going to need you more than ever now. You need to be strong for her." Mum kept holding onto me and talking about Sara; she didn't even know.

"Sara was in the tower, Mum," was all I could manage to say.

"What do you mean? I don't understand, Will." The shocked look on her face made me feel even worse.

"Sara went for breakfast with her dad this morning; she was in the tower when it got hit."

"But wait——" Everything was hitting her at the same time.

"Sara's dead, Mum – she's gone." Saying the words out loud made my head spin, and I rushed out to the garden and was sick in the bushes. The pain in my chest was twisting me out of shape and I was struggling to breathe. I was bent over convulsing when Mum ran out to find me.

"Oh God, Will, I didn't know, I'm so sorry." She was crying her eyes out and holding on to me as if I was the one slipping away, and in that moment I became a child again and I clung on to her for everything I could. I couldn't even speak; I was just sobbing my heart out. Everything I loved about life had been taken from me in one moment. On the news it had described the incident as a moment that would change the world and it had for me – it had destroyed mine. I knew nothing would ever be the same again. Mum and I must have stayed in that position for almost an hour, her holding me close as I shook violently with grief. She was trying to protect me but it was too late; there was nothing that anyone or anything could do to me now, I was already lost.

Eventually I knew I'd have to face the truth of what had happened, so Mum helped me up and we went back into the house. Sometime around half three, in front of my eyes on live television, the North Tower finally collapsed to the ground. Any naïve hope that I had been holding on to had now crumbled into dust. I think Mum had been struggling to deal with the situation, so she had kept going into the kitchen and making tea, tidying up and generally busying around. I sat there staring at the tragedy on the screen before me; I couldn't comprehend what had happened or why. All I knew was that the life I was looking forward to was now worthless.

After seeing enough of the same looped news report I told Mum I just wanted to be on my own and headed up to my bedroom. I closed the door behind me and the world fell still again, like everything else except for me had been carefully paused. I didn't know what to think, what to do or even where to go – thousands of thoughts were just swimming around my head. I collapsed on the bed and pulled a t-shirt out from under my pillow: it was the present Sara had given me at the airport before I flew home from New York. She had carefully sprayed her Ramones t-shirt with her scent and wrapped it up tightly for me so the smell stayed as long as possible; I had been keeping it near me in bed so I could smell her every night in the hope that we might meet up in our dreams. I carefully breathed her scent in and hugged the t-shirt tight to my chest, and once more the tears started to flow and I cried out her name in agony.

I hadn't been lying there long before I heard a knock at my door and it started to open.

"Will, I saw the news and your mum just told me everything." It was my dad; he'd come home from work and was stood in the doorway looking at me. I remember looking at him and thinking how scruffy he looked: his tie loose, his top button open and his shirt hanging loose. I looked up at his face and I could see that he too had been crying, as he looked at me with eyes that I barely recognised. Gone was the fighting spirit and cold business façade, and he stood before me as a dad, breaking his heart worrying about his only son. I stood up and he walked over to me and held me tightly against him.

"I'm so sorry Will, I really am, I'm just so sorry." He let the tears fall as he held me; I could smell his aftershave and it reminded me of being a child again and him comforting me when I was upset. It doesn't matter how old you are, in our worst moments we are all still someone's child and we long for that comfort and protection no matter what. Eventually Dad released me from his hug and put his hands on my shoulders, and he gave me that look he always gave me when he wanted to know what was going on in my head.

"I'm OK, Dad; I just want to be alone tonight." I sat back on the bed and watched him make his way to the door, wiping his eyes and trying to compose himself again before going back downstairs.

"Thank you," I said as he stopped in the doorway, giving him as much of a smile as I could. He looked at me and in that brief glance I felt everything he wanted to say or do for me all in one huge hit.

"I love you Will, and if you need me, I'm here, OK?" he said, before stepping out into the hallway and quietly closing the door behind him.

I curled up on the bed again and just lay there in the quiet, breathing in every bit of Sara's scent that I could, terrified of losing any memory, no matter how small or silly it had seemed before. As I lay there I saw the London sky change from the smoky grey it normally had at this time of year to a darker blue, and eventually turning black. The streetlights flickered into life again, dancing down the street and signalling another night in the city. I had been laying there for hours but I knew there was somewhere I should go, somewhere I had to be, and it was calling me.

It was just before midnight when I left the house. I had thrown a couple of things in a bag and left a note for Mum and Dad to say where I'd gone and that I was OK and would be back tomorrow. I carefully crept out, making sure not to wake them up, and headed to Kentish Town. When I got to Sara's house I let myself in as usual and headed up to her bedroom. The house looked spotless and the cleaner had left a note for me saying she would be back a week later if I needed anything. The note was dated 10th September. Just looking at the date made me feel sick to the stomach: one day previously everything was wonderful and I was 11 days away from getting Sara back, but within 24 hours that had all been wiped away. Now so many people, including me, were left with nothing but the pieces of their broken lives.

I walked up the stairs like an old man; each footstep was an effort. I had felt all the spirit drain out of me in the past few hours and it was a struggle just to stand up straight. I stopped outside Sara's door and the memories flooded back; all the times we had stumbled inside in the heat of passionate kissing, only to fall over something she had left on the floor. The times I had knocked on her door and when she opened it looking confused I had pulled out a bunch of flowers, or even better, a vinyl album by one of her favourite bands. Even the odd argument and door slamming swept through my head as I realised I would give anything to be arguing over something silly right then. Instead there was nothing: an absence of sound, life and love; just an empty room scattered with the memories of our romance. I opened the door and stood still inside the room, just waiting for something to happen; anything. I wanted Sara to appear out of her bathroom and say she had been here all along and it was a surprise, or to find a note that told me she had cancelled the breakfast that morning; anything that would bring her back to me.

The room looked the same but it felt so different: a sort of sadness had consumed everything in there. It was like watching a picture fade before my eyes, with everything becoming duller bit by bit. Every part of her walls had our history on them, from gig tickets to photos; little notes I'd written her to a massive framed poster of Syd Barrett I had given her for her last birthday in England. I wanted to stay locked inside this room forever – in here everything was as it should be; we still existed. There was nothing that the real world could offer me anymore, nothing that could excite me or make me feel the way Sara had. She was my heart and now it had been torn out for good; she was all I knew and all I wanted.

I sat on the bed and opened up my bag, taking out her t-shirt and a half-bottle of whisky. I got some Coke out of the mini fridge in the room and poured myself a large drink; more whisky than I liked but not half as much as I needed. I found her CD of *Various Positions* by Leonard Cohen, put *If It Be Your Will* on repeat and turned the television on so I could watch the video of her. As I sat there I carried on drinking and slowly my mind started to calm as the alcohol took hold and made everything hazier and less painfully harsh. As the music filled my ears I watched Sara on the television; I had put it on slow motion so her every move was captured almost frame by frame. I watched, mesmerised, as she blew a kiss at the camera one more time; you could see the spark in her eyes. As the screen went black I felt the warmth of the alcohol cover over me like a blanket, and I lay down hugging her t-shirt again, letting sleep overtake my tired body.

Wednesday 12th September
I stood in front of the site and my heart ached. The scene of the destruction was deathly quiet, with no signs of life, just rubble everywhere and smoke damage to the surrounding buildings. I couldn't understand why there was no one else here; I thought there would have been hundreds of people sifting through the remains of the buildings, looking for any clue as to what happened to their loved ones. Instead there was nothing, just me stood alone in this eerie silence, knee-deep in the chaos of a worldwide disaster. Thick clouds of dust still hung in the air and made it difficult to see clearly, whilst the amount of debris underfoot made it almost impossible to navigate around safely.

"Sara," I called out as I walked around, longing to hear a noise to signal that she was trapped under something but still alive. The louder I called her name, the quieter the whole area sounded. I hadn't seen a single human being in the time I'd been there, and there was no traffic noise either, just this ghostly silence amongst the dust.

"Sara, where are you?" I called out louder, struggling to stay on my feet whilst climbing over all the bricks and mortar.

"Will, I'm here." A voice came back at me through the clouds; I knew straight away it was Sara. I tried to move to where her voice was coming from, but the quicker I moved, the further away it seemed to sound.

"I can't find you, Sara. Where are you?" I was getting more and more desperate to find her; I needed to save her.

"I'm here, Will," she said, placing her hand on my shoulder and turning me around.

I turned to see Sara wearing the red and black dress from the photo she'd sent me; she looked immaculate, as if nothing had happened at all. I went to hold her but felt like I couldn't move, as if I was rooted to the spot.

"Will, I'm not here anymore, but I'm okay. I want you to stay strong for me, get on with your life and do the things you want to do. Never give up and always fight for what you believe in; I'll always be here for you and I will wait until that day I can hold you again. I love you; I always did and always will."

As tears welled up in my eyes, I threw myself forward with all my strength and went to embrace her, but instead I passed straight through her and headed towards the rocks that covered the floor in that huge empty space.

I shocked myself awake, face-down in the pillows, startling myself into reality. Again that dream had been so vivid it really shook me, and I struggled to pull myself together and snap out of that sleepy mindset. As my mind started to clear, the reality of the situation hit me again and I laid there staring at the ceiling. I didn't know what to do without her; it was different when she was in New York because although I was alone here, I felt like she was always with me. As I laid there I looked around at her room and all our memories stored in it; I knew I had to get up but I didn't want to move. I wanted to stay here, trapped in our bubble until things got better; the only trouble was I couldn't imagine they ever would.

It was early afternoon before I got ready and left Sara's house. I had to go home and see my parents to let them know I was OK, and I needed to ring people so they knew what was happening. I couldn't face work or anything really, so I just wanted to put everything on hold until I could cope with it. As I took one last look around her room it struck me how this room would stay locked forever in this moment: there wouldn't be any more conversations or kisses in here; it was like a museum of our time together. I closed the door behind me and headed home.

When I got home, Mum gave me a big hug and started fussing around me to see if I was OK and if I needed anything. She was supposed to be going out shopping with her friend, but said she could cancel if I needed her with me. I didn't want anyone with me, though; I just wanted to be alone to work out the best way to deal with everything that had happened. Everything was still so raw and hard to comprehend, and I wasn't in the mood for any company. After Mum had repeatedly offered to stay, I told her to go shopping and I would just get on with things I had to do. Then she told me Mattie had rung, and I realised immediately that this meant that he knew about Sara. I wasn't even in the mood for speaking to anyone, but I knew I needed to speak to Mattie to sort work out and see if I could have some time off to get myself back together again. I rang him on his mobile whilst I sat in the garden, starting my second packet of cigarettes that day.

"Hey Will, how are you? You didn't have to ring." He sounded far more sombre than usual; I got the feeling he was as uncomfortable receiving this call as I was making it.

"I'm not sure how I feel really, kind of numb I guess. I just wanted to sort work out and find out where everything stood, that's all." I didn't want to mention Sara; I just wanted to get off the phone as quickly as I could.

"As far as I'm concerned we'll cover your shifts and keep on covering them until we know any different. Ollie has really taken to the place and wants lots of shifts before he goes travelling next year, so he can fill in for you. I don't want you to worry about any of this until you're ready."

"Thanks Mattie, I'm going to take a couple of weeks and see how I feel then. I can't really make any decisions yet, I don't know where my head is." I didn't know why but I couldn't help feeling jealous at hearing that Ollie, who I guessed was the new guy, had settled in so well. It seemed a stupid thing to be thinking, but I couldn't help how I felt.

"That's no problem, just concentrate on yourself OK, and if you need me for anything, just ring me any time of day or night and I'm there for you." Mattie did a good job of being like a big brother to me and I knew that he was always as good as his word.

"Thanks Mattie, I'll be in touch soon."

"Will, I promise you that you will be OK. You're not alone. Speak soon."

"I will, Mattie." But when I finished the call I realised that's exactly what I was: alone.

Friday 14th September
The days were passing so slowly. Every day brought fresh reports on the news about the attack and the fallout from it. Part of me wanted to read the papers and learn as much as I could, but the other part wanted to ignore all of it and pretend it wasn't there. I had spent the last two days at Sara's just because it was easier to be alone there, and it was the place I still felt closest to her. Through all the tears and hugging her t-shirt, the scent of her had started to fade, and the thought of her slipping further away from me every day often surfaced. I was sat on her bed flicking through one of our old photo albums when the phone rang downstairs,

slicing through the silence like a knife. I wanted to ignore it but the ringing just kept on and on until I had to go and stop it.

"Hello?" I'd never answered the phone at Sara's house before and it seemed alien and awkward.

"Hello, I need to get a message to Will, please. Is he there?" The voice on the other end sounded Hispanic.

"I'm Will. Who is this, please?"

"Oh God, I'm so glad I've managed to get hold of you. I'm Antonia; I live in New York. I was the housekeeper for Sara and her father; I wanted to call you to say how sorry I am for your loss. I know Sara loved you very much and she spoke about you often." She sounded very tearful, and I wasn't sure how I was going to be able to cope with this out of the blue.

"Thank you. I hope you're OK? I don't really know what to say about all of this, I'm struggling at the minute. Did you need something from me at all?" I didn't want to sound rude but the last thing I wanted at that moment was to talk to a complete stranger about Sara.

"I'm sorry, I know this must be a very hard time for you; it's just there's something I wanted to tell you. I've been here for the last two days sorting the house out, but while I was sorting out Sara's room I found a letter that she'd started writing but not finished and I thought you should know. I wanted to speak to you rather than just send it as I thought it would be less of a shock this way."

It hadn't dawned on me that there could be anything from Sara other than the last email, so this came as a complete shock anyway. I tried to think of how to react, but without thinking, the words just came out.

"Do you have it there? Could you read it to me please?" The minute I spoke, part of me wished I hadn't.

"Yes, I wasn't sure if you'd want me to. Hold on, here it is:

"*To my gorgeous man,*

I am starting this letter now and will finish it when I get back home tonight. I hope you're doing well and haven't got any of those London girls hanging on your every word whilst I'm stuck here eating pancakes and getting chubby! I need to tell you the truth. When I come back on the 21ˢᵗ, it isn't to visit: I'm coming home! I spoke to Dad and he agreed it would be best for me to move back to London so we can be together, make all our plans, and be as happy as we can be. Me helping him settle in here has meant the world to him, but I think he realised how sad I am without you and that's not what he wants. So there, you aren't getting me back for a couple of weeks — you're getting me back for good! I've been desperately trying to keep this to surprise you when I got back, but I just can't do it. New York is amazing, but it's nothing without you and I need to be in your arms again for good. You and I belong together and I love you more than anything or anyone in the whole world. I hope that this. . .

"I'm afraid there isn't any more. I just thought you should know." Antonia was in tears as she read the letter out to me.

"Thank you," I said, before dropping to the floor and crying out with all the pain that had been building up inside me. I could still hear Antonia trying to talk to me on the other end of the phone, but eventually she said how sorry she was and the phone went dead. I curled up tightly in a ball and cried my heart out. When my mum came home later she found me still curled up on the floor, sobbing. She ran over and hugged me as I lay there in the foetal position, rubbing my back gently with her hand like she used to do when I was sick as a child.

"I just don't know what to do without her. I'm so lost and it feels like nothing will ever be the same again. I miss her so much."

"I know Will, I know, but it'll be all right, I promise. We're all here for you and we'll get you through this. You can't give up; you need to keep fighting. Things won't ever be the same, but maybe in time you can accept the difference and start feeling better. It all takes time; you need to stop putting so much pressure on yourself." I could hear the sadness in Mum's voice and realised how difficult it must have been for her to see her only child so broken.

"I just miss her so much, Mum."

"It's OK honey, I know – just let it all out."

I sat up a bit and hugged Mum back, clutching on to her in a way that I hadn't for years, letting all the hurt flow out as she comforted me. Even though I was 24, I was still her little boy, and she held on to me until I started to calm down.

"I'm so tired Mum; I just feel sick."

"You need to rest, Will. I know what you're like with analysing everything and you're going to make yourself ill if you don't give yourself time to heal. Let's get you up to bed and I'll make you a cuppa. You don't need to do anything other than take some time out for yourself." Mum helped me to my feet, wiping the tears from my cheek with her hankie, and walked with me upstairs and into my bedroom. I took my boots off and climbed onto the bed; I felt exhausted, and curled up with my head on the pillow. Mum got a blanket from the drawer and laid it over me, before sitting next to me stroking my hair.

"Just try and get some sleep Will, you need your rest." She carried on talking softly to me, but I was already falling asleep. Before I drifted off I heard her say "Your dad and I

love you Will, and we'll do anything to make it all better."
And then I drifted off.

Friday 21st September
I'd spent the last week trying to keep myself busy. I'd been
to the doctor and told him everything that had happened, and
he'd offered me grief counselling but I had politely refused,
saying I just needed some help to sleep, so he'd prescribed
some sleeping tablets for me and I'd been taking them when I
needed. Some nights I was so exhausted that I managed to
drift off naturally, but other times my mind was working
overtime and I really needed the help. Mum and Dad both
thought counselling was a good idea, but I didn't want to talk
about Sara to everyone: part of me felt like if I had
counselling then it would heal me and I'd start to forget her
and that scared the hell out of me: I felt like if I held onto the
grief then I kept her with me in some strange way, and that
was all I wanted.

I'd been in her room looking over old letters she had sent
me, and different things from our time together. Looking at
the things she'd written and how she was feeling; finding that
I had missed so many little bits she had put in the letters and
envelopes about music and books. So in the last week I had
been making notes of different books and music that Sara had
recommended, and started looking into them. She'd always
said that I should be studying things, and because I was such a
thinker she had found lots of books in all sorts of genres,
from philosophy to the esoteric and everything in between,
like conspiracy theories. I tried to immerse myself in the
words to keep my mind occupied, but somehow my thoughts
always went back to Sara and the huge loss I was feeling. I
was finally able to listen to some of our music again, and

although certain songs still reduced me to tears, I was able to remember some of the good times and celebrate what we had together.

Today had been the day I was dreading the most, though: the day that Sara was supposed to have returned from New York and surprise me with the news that she was staying for good and we could start planning our life together at last. Instead there was just me, surrounded by memories and trying to pick up the pieces of a beautiful dream that had been completely smashed.

At some point in the early afternoon my mobile rang. I was going to ignore it, but I saw it was Mattie and figured I'd better speak to him so he didn't worry.

"Will, it's Mattie. I hope you're OK? I've got something that the guys and I want to ask you, but feel free to say no." he sounded almost nervous.

"Hi Mattie. I'm doing all right really – bit up and down but I'm getting there, I think. What did you want to ask me?" I wondered whether he was going to try and talk me into coming back to work.

"Well, all of us have missed you so much man, and we were thinking about the date today and how we all loved Sara too and were glad to be a part of you guys. We were thinking of having a small gathering for Sara, kind of a remembrance thing, tonight and wondered if you would join us? Wherever you want to do it is fine and if you don't want to then just say no and we'll understand."

I didn't know what to say. His question had hit me from nowhere, and it was the last thing I had expected. I'd spent so much time thinking about my loss that it hadn't even dawned on me that anyone else would be feeling it too; especially the guys at work, although thinking about it now it dawned on me how much time we'd all hung out together in the past. Maybe it was time for me to let people in rather than hide myself away.

"Will, are you still there? I'm really sorry if I upset you buddy, I wasn't sure whether I should ask you or not but the guys wanted me to check."

"You know what Mattie – I'd love to. I want Sara to know how we feel about her, and I can't think of any better time to do it than today. Can you guys get some bits and pieces for me and I'll meet you at the top of the hill at eight o'clock?" As I said it, I tried to stop thinking and let my real feelings answer for me. I was grieving her loss, but this was a chance to celebrate her life, our life, no matter how short it had been.

"That's great, text me what you want later and we'll meet you there. It'll be great to see you again bro, it's been far too long."

"You too Mattie; see you later." Part of me felt good at arranging something, but the other part of me almost felt scared to be around people again. I'd spent so long locked away on my own that I'd almost forgotten how to act around other people, and tonight would be the first time in ten days that I'd spoken to anyone other than family. A while later I sent Mattie a text asking for a few things, before starting my own preparations.

I reached the top of the hill 15 minutes early and found the gang already spread out on the grass near the bench Sara and I had often called our own. Somewhere in the weather-worn surface you could see an S and a W in a love heart, scratched into the wood. I'd felt so nervous at being around people again that I'd had a few drinks at Sara's before heading up to meet the guys, so by the time I got to them I was already feeling a bit more confident. As I swigged the last of my bottle of cider I waved at them and made my way to their little gathering.

Mattie got up first and gave me a huge hug, closely followed by Steve, and even Kelly took a break from her cool persona to give me a kiss on the cheek and check I was OK. When they walked me over to where they were sitting, I could see all sorts of things ready for our evening together. They had loads of little tealight candles, drinks, some Chinese takeaway, cigarettes, a few joints and a large envelope with the word *Secret* written on it.

"Thank you guys; this is all really wonderful. I know it would've meant the world to her." I struggled not to say her name: I was so overcome with the occasion that I needed to gather my strength first.

"What can I say man, you both mean the world to us." Everyone looked at Steve; they weren't used to him not being sarcastic. He was being genuine though, and you could see that he had tears in his eyes. I smiled a thank-you at him and he nodded back in reply.

The whole evening was an emotional rollercoaster, with us laughing together one minute and then fighting back the tears at the next. The drink and cigarettes were consumed at an alarming rate, as was the food. When it started to get dark, Kelly lit all the candles and we sat surrounded by this beautiful dance of the flames; such a strange contrast to all the electric lights you could see in the distance lighting up London. Something about the setting reminded me of the different festivals we'd been to as a group in the past, and it made me sad to think that I'd never be able to go to a festival with Sara: it was one of the things we'd always wanted to do. At some point late in the evening, Mattie handed me the envelope.

"This is for you Will, from all of us. Open it in your own time and it'll make sense once you see it. You don't have to do it now." The sympathetic smile he gave me when handing over the envelope made me think twice about opening it, so instead I thanked him and slipped it into my bag.

Eventually the drinks had almost run out, the food was gone and Steve was out of joints, so the evening drew to a close. I still had a couple of bottles of cider left and was enjoying the last flickering of the candles, so I decided to stay for a bit longer.

Steve stumbled to his feet and gave me a big bear hug. "I miss you man, I hope you come back soon. There's no one for me to take the piss out of anymore. They're all too sensible."

"Thanks Steve, and thanks for tonight. I'll be back soon I promise. You better start finding some new material though." I smiled at him and patted him on the back; ours was a strange relationship but I knew he cared deep down, and I cared about him.

"You take care, OK Will? Don't forget she was lucky to have you too." Kelly gave me another kiss on the cheek before helping Steve stagger down the hill safely.

"I guess I better go too then, mate. It's been really good seeing you again. I'm always here for you, just remember that." Mattie hugged me and started to walk off after the others.

"You can stay if you want, Mattie. I mean, if you want to get home then that's fine, but if not then you're welcome to sit with me for a while?" Although I wanted to be alone, I knew Mattie was the one person who I could happily let see me cry, and I was frightened of what might happen if I was left alone with so much emotion running through me.

"Only if you're sure, Will."

I motioned for him to join me, so he walked back and we sat on the bench, partly to get away from the ever-dampening grass beneath us and partly so I could look out over the view and reminisce. I opened the last two bottles of cider, gave him one and we clinked an unspoken toast to Sara. As I rummaged around in my bag, I put my hand on the envelope and took it out. I looked at Mattie and he shrugged as if to say *it's up to you*, so I opened it. Inside was an A4 photo of Sara and me, which had been taken on our last trip out in London with all the guys from work. It was a beautiful photo of us stood at the bar in the Camden pub, sharing a quick kiss whilst I waited to be served. The picture managed to capture us in such a natural moment, and was so clear that it had to be the best one I had of us by far. I slipped it back into the envelope and into my bag for safekeeping, just as the tears started to roll down my cheeks.

"She's never coming back Mattie, and I don't know whether there's a me without her."

"Will, you made each other. She knew that and we knew that. You meant everything to her and she never went anywhere; she's stored safely in here." Mattie took his hand and gently touched me on the left side of my chest.

I smiled through the tears and he put his arm round me, and as we sat on the bench overlooking the beautiful view of London at night I thought of Sara and I knew what Mattie said was true. It had never mattered where she was – London, New York or anywhere else – she had always been in my heart and always would be. As if he'd read my mind, Mattie stood up and started to walk down the hill slowly, giving me time on my own to talk to her.

"I don't know whether you're up there or right here with me, but I just want you to know that I love you. There's never been anyone in my life like you and I know there won't ever be again. Promise me you'll wait for me beautiful; one day I'll hold you again, and we can both feel complete. I miss you so much Sara, sleep well princess." When I finished talking, I wiped the tears from my cheeks and followed Mattie down the hill. Eventually I caught up with him and he put his arm round me again, pulling me in briefly just to let me know he was there. I turned one last time to see the last of the candle flames dancing into nothing, and something about the way the smoke hung in the air at the top of the hill gave me a strange feeling of déjà vu. I turned back and carried on walking. I only hoped that Sara had seen the evening somehow and had known just how much she was loved.

Chapter 10

October 2003 – Age 26

What do you believe in? Have you ever lost yourself so badly that you struggled to find yourself again without help?

The big drinking binge I had gone on at the beginning of April 2003 had been the start of a slippery slope for me. Waking up that next morning, face-down on the couch with all the previous night's memories slowly flooding back, should have put me off drinking completely, but instead I was heading further down a dark path.

It had been seven months since I'd lost both Mum and Dad, and I was no closer to getting on with my life than I had been back then; if anything I was moving further away from any positives and losing myself in the bottle. After losing Sara I had struggled to find reasons to carry on and had relied heavily on my parents, and their love, to keep myself going. Once they died there really was nothing left for me – I had the guys from work but it was a different kind of relationship; there was no one to give me a hug when I needed it or to deal with my mood when it hit a heavy low. Maybe if I had still been working with Mattie and Steve it would've been different, but once I had made the decision to take some time out it had become increasingly more difficult to face nights out with them, and the shop banter that I was no longer a part of. I had spent time getting my flat together and trying to make a home for myself, but it always felt so empty and night after night I would end up drinking to pass some of the time and give myself some comfort. The warm taste of whisky had replaced the warmth of a human hug, and I had withdrawn even further from the rest of the world.

Friday 10th October

As with most of my days over the last few months, this one had started with a hangover and I found myself having a couple of drinks in the morning to cure it. This would have been my mum's birthday, and it was my first major test since losing her. I'd spent a lot of time the previous night looking through old photo albums, struggling to come to terms with how I felt and had heeded the all-too-familiar call of alcohol to numb the pain. Now the day was here and I felt even worse, suffering from the grief of the occasion and the blues brought on by the previous night's drinking. I decided to take a trip up to the hill later and sit for a while to pay my respects, but I hadn't decided what to do with the rest of my day. Even though I had spent a lot of time at home drinking, I had been keeping myself occupied by reading a lot and studying things that I had taken an interest in. I was still working through the books that Sara had recommended, and had found all sorts of interesting things to research on the internet to keep myself busy. I had even started looking into the various world religions and was attempting to reacquaint myself with the Bible, which I had read as a child but not taken much notice of ever since.

My parents had both been religious to an extent, but were never the sort of people to force their beliefs on you, so over time my knowledge and understanding of faith had gotten so slim that it barely existed at all. I'd had lots of theological conversations with Steve at times, mostly when he was high, but couldn't ever really say where my true feelings lay. I had a lot of interest in spiritual things, but also a mathematical brain so I was sort of caught in the agnostic area; I wanted to believe but felt I needed some sort of proof. Reading about God's children had caused a lot of inner conflict at times; I couldn't understand the reasoning, given all the losses of good people that I had witnessed, and that's what I had spent the morning mulling over in my mind. After a cooked breakfast and some coffee, my head had cleared enough for me to return to my study. I had been looking on the internet at different arguments regarding the existence of God, and what reasons could be given for all the bad things that happened in the world, if he existed. I had gotten deeply into the heart of the argument from all different perspectives and had found it heavy enough to warrant me pouring myself a late morning drink.

After a few hours of going backwards and forwards over the same old arguments I'd drunk my way through half a bottle of whisky, and found my head starting to swim with everything I'd read and everything I felt, so I decided to give up the search for answers and listen to some music instead. In the last few months I had turned to anything to try and keep my mind away from all the loss I had suffered, and a little dabbling with different drugs had now turned into a daily smoking of joints and even the occasional line of cocaine when I could get my hands on it. As it was only quite early in the day I felt I needed to sober up a bit, so I searched the cupboard for the last bit of coke I had and, after splitting it into two lines, snorted one of them off the kitchen worktop. The rush was instant and immediately my head felt clearer, so I used my new-found energy to shower and get dressed for what was left of the day. I'd started to feel twitchy and knew it was time to get out of the flat, so I gathered my stuff together and headed out towards Camden. I hadn't ventured out much at all for the last few weeks, partly because I just wanted to be alone, and partly because every time I went out in public I found myself feeling anxious and hiding from other people's glances. Ever since the funerals, I had found people looking at me in a different way; no one seemed to treat me the same anymore and I felt that behind my back they were whispering about how tragic everything was and pitying me. So I'd felt safest locking myself away in my flat and only going out when I had to, but today I felt like I needed some air and the coke had given me enough of a confidence boost to manage it.

When I got to Camden I suddenly felt like avoiding the shop: I didn't want to bump into Mattie or Steve as they were always trying to get me to go out with them and I just didn't feel like it, so I jumped on the Tube and got on the Northern line heading towards Highgate. When I got off I headed for the closest pub I could find and decided to get something to eat and have a couple of drinks. The anonymity offered to me by places that were close enough to home but still in quiet areas was a great comfort to me at times. As usual it didn't take long before a pint over lunch became the start of a session, and before long I was starting to feel that familiar fuzzy feeling again. I was sat at a table in the corner on my own listening to the conversation of the two guys on the table next to me.

"It's all bullshit man, there isn't any major terrorist group planning to attack the world and there never was. It was an inside job, I'm telling you. You read all the stories about illegal wars and stuff; this gave him the perfect reason to invade, and Hollywood couldn't write a better script." The guy in the skate clothing was getting animated as he explained his theories, most of which he'd probably just read on the internet.

"No way man, that's crazy. Next you're going to tell me that it was all a setup and nothing really happened." His friend was hanging on his every word, and found the argument even more exciting with every pint he had.

"You never know man, stranger things have happened. Maybe it was all one big story. If you can't fight over religion then you need to find something else to start a war."

I drained the rest of my pint quickly and stood up, leaning one hand on their table. I looked the skater guy in the eye but couldn't find the words I wanted to say to him. Visions of Sara flooded my mind and as hard as it was to walk away, I did just that, leaving him and his friend giggling between themselves behind my back. The alcohol had really kicked in now, and the effects of the drink from the morning had started to seep back. That was the thing with coke; it didn't sober you up, it just made you feel sober for a while. The problem was when it all caught up with you and suddenly you were hit with a huge alcohol surge all at once. I needed the toilet anyway, so I staggered to the gents' and shut myself away in the cubicle. As I stood peeing, I felt around in my pocket and found the small bit of foil which I had scooped the last line of coke into before I left. I spread it out on the back of the toilet stall, snorting it all up, and when I left the pub I was feeling sober again and my mind was slowly sharpening.

Then I decided to visit Highgate Cemetery. I had always loved the statues and it was somewhere I remembered taking

Mum when I was younger and Dad hadn't been able to get out of work. The day was chilly but dry, and the autumn leaves always made the cemetery look that bit more magical. There was hardly anyone in the cemetery and it left me free to walk around in peace; I was fascinated by the imagery of graveyards and they didn't get much more impressive than this one. I was planning on visiting Paris to see Jim Morrison's grave at Père Lachaise, but for the time being I would be able to lose myself in the peace without having to leave London.

After a while of wandering around, I sat on a bench to have a smoke. Opposite where I was sat was a lovely white statue that was almost shimmering in the autumn sun. As I stared at the statue I noticed it was a mother holding a child, and my mind filled with vivid images of my mum. For the first time in a long while, I started to question why I'd lost her and then Dad as a result of her death. As the images started to come to life in my head I thought I saw the statue move; it looked like the mother held her child tighter for a brief moment, and I walked over to it and touched the mother's face. The cold stone felt strange beneath my fingertips, and it shifted my thoughts of Mum when I was younger to her time near the end, when all the life was seemingly draining out of her before our very eyes.

"Mummy, wait for me – my lace is undone." The voice broke my daydreaming instantly. I turned to see a small boy, only about six or seven, part-running and part-hopping along the path through the cemetery, trying to catch up with his mum who had stopped at the exit and was waiting for him. I stood frozen, watching as he caught up with her and she helped him do his lace up, ruffling his hair and holding his hand as they walked out of the cemetery together. I don't know why but I followed them out; I'd been walking about for a long time anyway and was ready to head to Parliament Hill to sit and speak to Mum, and there was something about this mother and son that reminded me of my own childhood. I remembered going on so many outings with Mum, and even though she was the grown up and I was a child she let me feel like I was protecting her, and this mother and child seemed to have the same relationship. The more I followed behind them the more of their conversation I overheard, and the more I tried not to listen, the harder it got.

"Where is Daddy now, though? Can he still hear me?" The little boy was staring up at his mum through a mop of blonde hair.

"Daddy's in heaven watching over you, and he can hear everything you say to him. He's always with you." I could see tears in her eyes as she explained to the little boy, and it seemed like it wasn't the first time that she'd had this conversation.

"Will we see him again?"

"One day we will, but for now we know he's always there for us. You don't have to worry about him; he's happy and loves you like he always did." I could see how upset the lady was, but she was fighting hard to be strong for the child. A chill blew through me as I thought once more of my parents, and how much harder it must be with a child being so young when there's a loss.

"You won't leave too, will you Mummy?"

The lady knelt down next to the boy and brushed the hair out of his eyes. I'm not going anywhere. It's you and me OK, and we're a team." She hugged him closely and gave him a kiss on the cheek, before starting to walk off down the road with him again.

I stood still, watching them walk down the road and suddenly my chest felt tight: the whole road seemed to be spinning and I couldn't breathe. As the panic rose in me, I knew what I thought I needed to do and ran for the closest off-licence I could find. An hour later I was sat at Parliament Hill, drinking a half bottle of vodka and thinking about everything I tried to block out on a daily basis. The hill was silent as I sat there in the dark, but the noise in my head was loud enough that I felt like anyone nearby could hear it. My mind was constantly flicking through my life, from Sara to Mum and Dad; all the sadness and all the anger slowly rising to the surface. The thoughts of religion and everything I'd read in the last few months came crashing against everything I felt and wanted to know reasons for, as my mind and mood started to slide further into the abyss.

"I miss you all so much, why am I still here? I just want to be with you," I screamed into the night air, angrily emptying the bottle and throwing it in rage towards the London skyline. I don't know whether it was the alcohol, the coke wearing off, or a combination of both, but I had a fixed idea in my mind of what I needed to do. So I got up from the bench and headed away from the hill, looking for a church and determined to find some answers at last.

I made it to Hampstead in next to no time, the anger making me walk at a determined pace. The streets around were quieter than usual, and it allowed me to walk without any disturbance at all. I wasn't in any mood to bump into people or have to converse with anyone. When I got to the church I marched up to the huge wooden doors and knocked heavily. I waited for someone to answer, but there was nothing. I knocked again, my knuckles grazing on the wood as I heard the loud thuds echo inside the church. I took a step back and searched any windows I could see, looking for any signs of life; I didn't even think to look at my watch and see what the time was. All I wanted were answers.

"Where are you? If you want to offer me some help then now is the time. Come out and see me, or are you too busy hiding behind all the lies you spit out at us? Where is God if this is his house?" The words were spilling out of me as I screamed at the top of my lungs, but still nothing happened. I made my way around the side of the building, which was full of beautiful stained glass windows that were twinkling like stars under the light of the moon. There didn't seem to be any signs of life at all; no one to speak to me and no help from above. I slumped to the floor crying with my head in my hands, the alcohol starting to make me feel dizzy and nauseous as I sobbed my heart out.

As I sat there, I looked up and everything started spinning. The church appeared to be looming over me, and all the scenes in the stained glass windows seemed to be moving like a slowly-animated film. I could hear a noise that sounded like laughter, and the rage in me grew. I stumbled to my feet and threw myself at the church wall, my right fist going straight through the window. I didn't even know what I was doing or what had happened until I heard the loud smash and saw the blood spilling down my hand and arm.

"I just wanted some comfort," I shouted, sobbing, as I pulled my arm back and cradled it against me. The last thing I remember is seeing my blood seep into parts of the glass that remained in the window frame, casting an eerie red glow over everything.

Saturday 11th October
I woke up in bed with no recollection of getting home. My head was throbbing, and when I went to roll over I felt a

surge of pain through my right hand which brought everything flooding back. I opened my eyes and was greeted by the sight of blood covering my bed: somehow in my drunken state I had managed to use an old t-shirt to bandage my cut hand, but the blood had seemingly seeped through that and onto the sheets. I laid there for a while, piecing together all the events from the night before, and every little thing I remembered made me feel sicker by the minute. Eventually made it to the bathroom to get cleaned up, and I managed to wash my hand and make it as clean as I could without actually looking at it; scared of what I might see. A combination of the pain surging through it and the blood made me realise how much damage I'd done, and I knew looking would only make it worse. If anyone had known they would have made me go to the hospital, but I didn't want to trouble anyone else – it was my own stupid fault and I felt like I deserved to be in pain for what I did.

It took me a while to get ready and bandage my hand up properly before I could eat something and have a strong coffee to help me get myself together. I sat having a cigarette, drinking my coffee and thinking about last night. I felt so bad about the church window and knew I had to make amends somehow. I decided I'd go to the church and find a way to slip a letter in to apologise, and some money to go towards the repair or church fund; anything that might in some small way make up for my actions. I typed a letter of apology using my computer and printed it out, slipping it into an envelope before taking some money out of the shoebox I had in the cupboard. Most of my money was in the bank, but since I'd stopped going out so much I'd decided to draw a chunk out and keep it at home; I figured it was safe there as I was always in anyway. I counted out £500 and put it into the envelope with the note, sealing it shut before addressing it to the reverend. I knew the church had things going on Saturday mornings but nothing after that until the early evening, so I pulled my jacket on and headed back to where I had fallen apart the night before.

When I got to the church, it was as quiet as it had been the night before. I slipped the envelope through the door of the warden entrance and walked round the side of the building to see what damage had been done. The window was boarded up, and there was a trail of blood-drops heading further round the back. I followed the trail, trying to remember what had happened after I broke the window, around the back and through a gate to the small graveyard. There was a small stand just inside the gate which I could see housed a paper calendar of events at the church, and I noticed that the blood-drips seemed to stop there, so I walked over and was shocked at what was waiting for me. Written in large letters on the calendar's plastic cover were two words – *HELP ME* – and they were written in blood; my blood. I stood there with tears welling up in my eyes, partly coming down from the night before and partly with shock at what I'd seen. I stumbled to a bench nearby and sat there amongst the graves with my head in my hands, sobbing to myself.

"I hope you don't think I'm being nosy, but are you OK?"

I hadn't even been aware that anyone was in the churchyard, let alone sitting next to me, and I looked up through teary eyes to see a dishevelled older man sitting there.

"I don't know really, I don't know what to think or what to feel. All the loss, it's all just too much." I hadn't planned on telling him anything but in my vulnerable state it just came out and the tears started flowing again.

"I know how you feel lad, trust me I do. I've come to this churchyard for the last ten years and sat here during the day; sometimes I've even slept on this bench at night. I get cups of soup given to me sometimes by the people who work here, but generally they just let me keep myself to myself. I try not to cause them any problems or embarrassment and they keep an eye on me, generally making sure I'm OK." The man's eyes showed years of sadness and hurt; his face weathered and worn and half-hidden under a wiry, greying beard.

"Why, are you homeless?" I didn't mean to be rude, but I felt like I needed to know more about this stranger.

"I get called many things lad, but I guess homeless sums it up. I try to take as much care of myself as possible, but I just don't care really and haven't for years. Ten years ago I lost my wife and my two kids when our house caught fire; I was working nights so I was safe, and that was the end of everything for me. People paid their respects and told me I was lucky to be alive, but I didn't feel lucky. I'd lost my family, my home and I didn't see the point in carrying on so I gave up. I didn't drink or smoke and still don't; I just walked away and didn't want anything to do with the world after the funerals." He sighed to himself before carrying on. "All three were buried here and ever since then I've visited them every day. On the days when I feel really low, I even sleep here sometimes; I just want to be with them as much as I can. I lost everything I cared about and I never wanted to go back to that kind of life with a house and a car and stuff – what was the point? So I gave up and became as I am now, and at least this way I can still be as close to them as possible." His voice sounded worn down by the years and all his pain, and I could see that he'd given up all hope completely.

"I'm sorry for your loss, that must have been terrible for you. I've suffered a lot of loss myself over the past couple of years and I don't know what to think anymore, about faith or anything. I just want them back; I'm not sure how to carry on without them." I didn't want to tell him too much about my life, but felt I needed to explain why I seemed such a mess.

"The thing about faith is it's your own; you don't need a church to believe. For every bad thing that's happened to you there must have been some good, and that's what you need to hold onto. I've given up on the world and humans in general, but I still have my beliefs. Something looks after me even though I sleep rough and something lets me be as close as I can be to my family. Sometimes it's not the answer you need but to know the right question to ask."

"I think it's amazing how you can stay so strong though, when even you admit you have nothing left to live for. How do you do it?" I needed to know the secret if there was one.

"I read a lot in what I call my previous life. I had my own personal library at home with books about everything, and it's taught me one thing: this is all going to end one day; we'll end up killing the planet and ourselves in the process, and then I get to be with my family again. I know they're waiting for me on the other side, wherever that is, and I will get to join them. In the modern age we use science to prove or disprove everything, but the ancient civilisations seemed to have known more answers than we ever have, and lots of their texts hold the key to what they think is the end of days. Take the Mayans for example; see what they had to say about the end and you might feel less troubled than you do now. We all go home eventually, trust me, lad. Sometimes you have to think: if all you have is now, are you truly happy or would you do things to change your life?" He spoke so calmly and eloquently, I could imagine him doing great things with his life had he not suffered all the sadness ten years ago.

"Are you happy though?" I had to ask.

"I'm happy that I'm free to come here; stay here even, spend time talking to my family and tending their graves, but most of all I'm happy that I can count down the days until I see them again. Make the most of what time you have lad; I promise you it all works out in the end. Once you know the right question, you'll get the right answer." With that he patted me on the back, stood up and walked slowly away from the graveyard.

I watched him turn the corner out of the main gate and head down the road. Part of me wanted to know more, but the other part had probably been told enough. I wondered if he had been here last night and seen me, but either way he didn't seem the sort to cause any trouble. I stood wearily and headed out of the churchyard myself, deciding it was time to go home and maybe get some more sleep. When I turned out of the gate I looked down the long road, but the old guy was nowhere to be seen.

Later that evening, I got up from having a nap and sat thinking about the guy I'd met. I was listening to Neil Young's *Harvest*, and as *Old Man* came on I was suddenly reminded of something he'd said, so I booted up the computer and typed five words into the search engine – WHEN WILL THE WORLD END – and hit enter. As the results came up on my screen I poured myself another drink and grabbed my cigarettes.

"Once you know the right question, you'll get the right answer," I said to myself as I sat back and lit a cigarette. I stared at the picture of Sara, taken on that fateful day two years ago, and spoke directly to her.

"I'm coming home, beautiful."

Chapter 11

November 2012 – Age 35

If all we have is now, are you happy? Or would you change things to make your life better for yourself or others?

It was a cold, grey day in London, and at the top of Parliament Hill there was no sound except for the wind. On my walk here I hadn't seen a soul; no traffic on the road and no one out walking – it was deathly quiet. I wasn't even sure what day it was; all I knew was that hundreds of people were gathered here for something. As I looked around there were people sitting everywhere, all in silence, listening to music through headphones and looking out over the hill at the view of London. Some were sitting on blankets, others directly on the grass, dampened by the winter weather. Everyone seemed fairly calm, almost as if they had just accepted the obvious, and they were all sitting, waiting for the end. I walked quietly through the crowds of people and looked out over the view. Rolling in silently from the distance was a dark red cloud, blackening the sky and the city at the same time. It was rolling in like a huge, silent wave and leaving everything behind it lifeless. The closer it got to the hill, the more I could sense its awesome power, and even though it was completely silent, there was something about it that was raging with anger and pain. I looked at all the people sat around and was suddenly struck by the sadness of all this death and destruction that was soon to happen; I was ready but somehow I felt they all deserved more time. I held my right hand up in front of me as if silencing a crowd and concentrated on the scene before me, thinking and wishing for this to work. As I watched intensely, the thick red cloud swirled into a shape like a tornado and appeared to be sucked into the palm of my hand, leaving everything illuminated by light and life. When the last of the cloud had been sucked into my palm, I looked at my hand and saw that it was glowing, a fiery red colour. Then there was one massive flash of light, and I automatically closed my eyes, but when I opened them again the scene atop the hill was subtly different. The same people were still sat around everywhere, but instead of being shrouded in darkness, it was a lovely sunny da,y and instead of sitting solitary and listening to their headphones, they were talking to each other and seemingly having a lot of fun. I started to walk back, away from the view of London, and as I did I passed straight through a couple sat on the floor. Thinking that I had kicked them, I instantly apologised, but they didn't hear me, and then I realised I couldn't see my feet. I went to raise my hands to look at them, but they weren't there either. It appeared that I didn't exist; that I had sacrificed myself to save all these people. They all carried on as if nothing had happened, and I headed away from the hill, smiling to myself.

Sunday 4th November
The vision I'd had last night had been playing on my mind all morning. I'd spent the last eight years thinking and researching the end of the world, and now it was so close and starting to penetrate my dreams. It was nearly lunchtime and I was sat in my lounge, drinking coffee and going over some plans for the shop. Something about the dream made me

reminisce over the last few years, and how far I'd come. I'd been sober now for over seven and a half years, and the only drugs I took were from the cupboard full of sleeping tablets which I had acquired over that time. Sleeping was the only thing that still caused me trouble, and it had taken regular trips to the doctor and multiple attempts before finding anything that worked well for me. I should've thrown all the others out but I hadn't bothered; instead I had just let them pile up in the cupboard until my kitchen resembled a pharmacy lockup. Part of me couldn't believe it had really been so long since those awful years, but then part of me felt that was a different life altogether.

The biggest thing to happen to me in the last few years had been in late 2009, when Mattie had phoned me to say that Love Music had gone bust and they were shutting all the stores before the end of the year. I hadn't worked there properly for years, but had managed to save my friendships with all of the guys after losing myself for a while, and was in touch regularly during my sober years. I knew how much the shop meant to those guys, and to me before everything went wrong, so I tracked down Dad's old financial colleague Kevin and together we formulated a plan using some of the money I still had stored away. By the start of 2010 I had bought the London shop, and using the same staff, turned it into an independent music store. The original plan was just to have records, but we knew that would struggle in the modern age so we bent the rules and catered for CDs, but with a special area for vinyl and always making sure that any special edition records were either stocked or could be ordered easily enough. By the end of January, Camden Rocks was open for business, and I handed the running of the store over to Mattie and just acted as a silent owner. The plan had worked on many levels: it had preserved our standing as a passionate music store in London, kept all of the guys in work and also repaired any bridges I thought I'd burnt during my lost years. I'd even become a fairly regular visitor there, just to see the guys and chat about different ideas with Mattie and Steve, and on more than a few occasions they had tried to get me back in there on a daily basis, but I never agreed. I was used to my fairly solitary life now, and didn't have any plans to change that.

It always made me smile when I thought of the crazy journey we had been on as a group, and how our passion for music and doing what we believed in had always gotten us through in the end. This was exactly the thinking that snapped me back to the present day, and made me decide on my next move. I'd done more than enough sitting around and reminiscing that morning, and now it was time for action. Looking at the calendar showed me I had less than seven weeks to complete all my plans and wait for the end; seven weeks could go so quickly and I knew that I needed to start now. After getting myself together I headed out to Hampstead in the direction of the church that had created the path I had been following ever since.

As I turned into the main gate of the church, the memories of all those years ago appeared as fresh in my mind as if they had happened just last week. The door to the church was open, and I saw the reverend talking to a group of people just inside, so I headed around the side and towards the graveyard. As I walked past the side of the building I stopped and looked at the stained glass windows, remembering that awful night and the damage I had caused, and noticing that they had all been all beautifully replaced. The original story they told was still there, but in newer, crisper glass. As I started walking again I felt that familiar ache in my hand that I always got when the weather was cold. I'd always assumed that was my karma for what I'd done in the past, but felt better knowing that at least I had tried to make amends with my donation, and hopefully that helped with the replacement work. I hadn't been back to this graveyard since that day in October 2003, when I'd spoken to the homeless man who had taught me so much and to whom I felt I owed a lot. Now, nine years later, I was sitting on the same bench and hoping that he would show up again. Although it was freezing cold, the sun made the day bright and bearable, and with my earphones in I was able to sit huddled up and wait for him to appear. I sat listening to Nerina Pallot's *Year of the Wolf* on my iPod, watching a couple of robins flying after each other through the hanging tree branches, and suddenly I a chill permeated my layers of warm clothing. During the song *Grace*, my eyes wandered to the graves of the stranger's wife and daughters and I noticed there was a fresh stone next to them. I got up and walked over to the graves, almost too scared to look, and saw that the third stone couldn't have been more than a couple of years old. It had a man's name on it, and as I bent down to take a better look, a lump formed in my throat.

Albert Byrne, beloved husband and father, back in the comforting arms of his family. 1952–2010.

I cleared some leaves off his grave, and those of his wife and daughters, when I felt a hand on my shoulder. Startled, I turned around to see the reverend standing behind me. I took my earphones out and smiled politely at him.

"I'm very sorry sir, I didn't mean to surprise you like that. It's just I noticed you come round here and I hadn't seen you before, so I wanted to make sure everything was OK?"

"No, I'm fine really; I haven't been here for a few years and I was looking for someone I met here. It seems I'm too late though." I glanced down at the gravestone and felt the tears stinging my eyes as I tried to blink them away.

"You mean poor Albert? Yes, it was very sad. He was a regular round here and almost part of the church itself in many ways. It was a terrible thing, but at least he is with his family now – we all knew how much he missed them. Did you know him well? I've never met a friend of his in all my years here." The reverend seemed surprised rather than suspicious; this was such a small church that it probably always had the same congregation and visitors, so a stranger would be quite a rarity.

"I met him here once and he helped me a lot; I was very lost and he put me on the right path. I came here today to thank him. Do you mind telling me what happened to him?" As I spoke it dawned on me that he hadn't been any more than a stranger to me, yet possibly also the most important person I had met in the last few years.

"That's very kind of you, and you're right – Albert was a lot like that. He often helped people out by giving them all sorts of advice, but sadly he never took any himself: he was destined for something in his own mind and that was all he cared about, really. It was one morning in December when I found him: he was curled up on the bench there asleep, and I tried to wake him so I could offer him something warm to drink, but he wouldn't wake at all. I phoned for an ambulance, but he was already gone. He died in his sleep and the hospital said it was almost certainly hypothermia; the sad thing is that I had spoken to him the previous evening, concerned about the predicted frost, and he said he would be going back to the shelter that night. Part of me thinks that he never planned to go back; maybe he knew exactly what he was doing. All I know is that he's with his family now, so he's found peace at last." The reverend seemed to struggle with a bit of guilt and a lot of relief as he spoke.

"Thanks for your time; I just want to have a quiet moment with him and then I'll be on my way. Thanks again and for everything you did for Albert; I know he appreciated it."

"It was my pleasure. I shall leave you to your thoughts, but may I say you are welcome here any time you want." Then he smiled and headed back to the church.

As he walked off I called after him, finally seeing the chance to ask the question that Albert had started me thinking about all those years ago.

"You say Albert is with his family now? Are you sure that's what happens?"

The vicar turned and nodded. "We all know when it's time to be with our loved ones again, and they are always waiting for us with open arms." Then he waved, before heading off again.

I sat on the bench, got my notepad and pen out of my bag and started writing. I wasn't sure whether Albert would ever get the message, but it was something I had to do for myself if nothing else.

Dear Albert,

It's been nine years since we met and you comforted me in my darkest hour. I came here today to thank you and to find out how you were, but sadly I have come too late. Ever since I spoke to you that day, I have known what I had to do, and now the reverend here has confirmed it for me. I need to thank you for being there when I needed someone and to tell you how lucky your family are to have you back again. Your presence in this world was something that can never be replaced. I'm glad you've found your peace and I hope I can do the same very soon. Maybe we'll get to meet again? I sincerely hope so!

Your Friend, Will

I folded the note carefully and poked it gently into the earth of his grave. I had read about different cultures sending messages to the other side by burying them or setting them alight, and all I could hope was that he would get this message and know just how much his words had meant to me. I stood and looked at the three graves, all together like a proper family.

"Goodbye Albert," I said, and then headed out of that memorable churchyard for the last time, the words of the reverend still repeating in my head.

We all know when it's time to be with our loved ones again, and they are always waiting for us with open arms.

Monday 5th November

It was early morning when I sat in the lounge looking at my finances. I had a lot of money in savings bonds, and other bank arrangements that I didn't really understand without the help of a financial advisor. With the clock counting down I had decided to get rid of as much of my money as I could in the hope that it might do people some good in their last weeks on earth. I had phoned up and arranged various transfers that morning so I could stockpile all the money I had in my current account. The money I had coming in from the shop I didn't touch – I had plans for that at a later date – but all my other money was in one easy-to-reach place at last.

I sat thinking about Albert, and decided I was going to donate to the homeless shelter that looked after him when he wasn't at the graveyard, so I did a search on the internet for the closest homeless shelters to the church in Hampstead. The search gave two possibilities, but one of them was more likely given that it was just a couple of roads away, and I couldn't imagine Albert wanting to be too far away from his family, so I made a note of the address and started getting ready to go out.

Within the hour I was stood opposite the homeless shelter, finishing my cigarette and watching the different people coming and going. It struck me as sad; the range of ages of the people who were using the facility. I'd always assumed that they would be older people, but some of them were barely out of school and yet living rough on the streets of a great city like London. There was something about the scene that reminded me of Victorian times like you'd see in films, and it made me wonder whether progress had really been made at all, or if the rich still got richer while the poor died on the streets, nameless and faceless.

I stubbed my cigarette out and walked across the road, heading for the reception desk just inside the building. I spoke to a lady behind the desk and explained that I'd like to speak to someone in charge, and she told me to take a seat and she'd get Thomas for me. I sat there, still watching the people coming and going; it was great that this kind of service would be provided but it still struck me as sad that it was even needed in the first place. Although my money and ability to live comfortably had come from awful events, in so many ways I was still so lucky to not have ended up in the same situation as the poor people I saw here.

About ten minutes later a man walked through a side door and headed my way. He was dressed casually, but had his official identity badge clipped onto his shirt pocket.

"Hi, are you Will? I'm Thomas, pleased to meet you. Do you want to follow me up to my office? It's quieter there, so we can have a chat." He seemed very approachable, and after a quick handshake we were heading to his office.

Although it was small, the office was well laid out, so it made the most of the space available. It had been a long time since I had sat in any sort of office, and I was pleasantly surprised how at ease this one managed to make me feel. Thomas sat opposite me and leant back in his chair, looking relaxed but interested in what I was doing there.

"So Will, what can I do for you? We don't often get visitors here in the business sense; well, not unless they're selling something anyway." He had a sort of cynicism about him that I found strangely comforting.

"Well, it's two things really. Firstly, I wondered if this was the place where an old friend of mine used to stay? His name was Albert and he spent most of his time at the church a couple of roads away from here." I didn't want to lie about knowing him better than I did, but I figured they wouldn't give any information to a complete stranger.

Thomas leant forward on the desk, pinching the bridge of his nose after removing and cleaning his glasses. "Ah yes, Albert stayed here for a few years before his sad death. I didn't even know he had any friends; how did you know him?"

"I met him once and he gave me so much help that it changed my life. I only found out that he was dead when I went to the church yesterday, but I wanted to find the place that looked after him so well." I didn't have any reason to lie once I found out that this was the place that Albert had stayed; that was all I needed.

"Albert was good at advice. He counselled a lot of the younger street kids we had here during his stay with us – a very clever chap, and if fate had dealt him a better hand he could have done so much more with his life. It's so sad to think of someone as special as Albert being reduced to such a wasted life, and in the end all we have of him is this one photo." Thomas reached into his desk drawer and pulled out a photo of Albert with his family, posing on a beach somewhere. I held the aged photo in my hand and noticed how much of a spark he had in his eyes at the time the picture was taken. It was obvious how much of his life was devoted to his family, and it made me feel sad to think of him when I met him, dishevelled and with that spark long gone. I slid the photo back to Thomas and reached into my pocket, pulling my chequebook out and laying it between us on the table.

"I think it's time I told you about the second reason I'm here. On behalf of Albert and his family, I've come to make a donation to your shelter. You might think this is a joke but it's not, I promise you. All you have to do is pay it into your account and then use it for whatever would help your organisation. There might not be much time to use it though, so you might want to get started pretty soon." I took a pen out of my pocket and wrote a cheque for twenty thousand pounds before handing it to him.

He had such a confused look on his face, which turned into amazement when he read the amount. It hadn't seemed strange to me, but I guess it wasn't every day a complete stranger turned up and donated twenty grand to his shelter.

"Will, I don't know what to say, I'm in shock. Are you sure about this?" He tried to slide the cheque back across the table to me, but I stopped it with my hand and slid it back his way, nodding at him as if to say it was OK.

"This is for Albert. Please make sure everyone gets to enjoy it, and thank you for everything you all did for him. I know he would thank you in person if he could." I shook his hand one last time and promptly headed towards the exit.

"Thank you," I heard him say – he sounded choked and I was glad I had made a swift move; none of the good deeds I wanted to do were for people to thank me and make a fuss. All I wanted was to do something positive while I still could. People probably thought I was crazy but it didn't bother me; money couldn't buy me what I wanted so instead I'd hoped it could benefit others.

It was early afternoon by the time I left the shelter, but I didn't want to go home – something about doing such a good deed had really given me a buzz, and instead of locking myself away in the flat again, I decided to pop into Camden and see the guys. On that walk after I left the shelter, I felt lighter than I had done in such a long time, and I thought about that picture of Albert and smiled to myself as I pictured him with his family again and that old spark back in his eyes. Something told me that these next few weeks would be some of the most constructive I had ever had, and part of that was thanks to Albert. I pulled my jacket collar up to keep out the cold November breeze and headed towards Camden and the next step of my plans.

Saturday 10th November
"I can see what you're thinking buddy, I really can, but I just think it's a bit nuts, that's all I'm saying. I mean, who's gonna buy CDs if the world's really about to end?" Steve was attempting to carry far too many bottles of beer back to the table, and trying to have a conversation with me at the same time.

"Steve, I know what you're thinking – I'm not drunk or high; it's just something that came to me when I was thinking about a new promotion for the shop. I've researched the end of the world for God knows how many years now, and even though you guys don't believe it, I do. This got me thinking about how I would spend the end, and for me it would be listening to music. So why don't we have some kind of promotion for it and get people involved?" I was arguing my case very soberly against a rather drunk Steve, who had spent the last 19 years thinking I was nuts anyway.

On the way back from the shelter at the beginning of the week I had come up with the idea of a soundtrack to the end of the world. I'd been planning what I was going to do on that day in December and I figured that I would listen to music, and then I got to thinking about Steve and his lists, so I came up with the idea of choosing 20 songs that you'd most want to listen to before the end. This idea I had pitched to Steve and told him to think about and discuss with Mattie, and it was now five days later and we were spending Saturday night in a pub in Camden discussing the pros and cons of the idea.

"What do you think, Mattie? I mean don't get me wrong; I love the list idea, but the whole end-of-the-world thing? Aren't we just gonna end up looking like a bunch of cult freaks or something?" I had to laugh that Steve was worried about other people's opinions of him whilst also debating the possibility of the world ending. Mattie looked at me and shook his head, laughing.

"You know what Will, I think you're a nutcase but I think you might be onto something here. Ultimately you own the shop so it's your call anyway, but I say let's go for it." With that he clunked his beer bottle against my glass of juice and sat back in his chair again, continuing to watch the girl behind the bar.

Steve eventually gave in too, and any arguments about the idea completely disappeared when we all started talking about what would be on our lists. There were just the original four of us around the table – Mattie, Steve, Kelly and myself – but Mattie had employed a couple of weekend staff whom he could get involved, too. As everyone sat arguing about what they'd have to put on the list and what wouldn't make the grade, I zoned out a bit and thought back to when the gang of us had been sitting in a Camden pub all those years ago. It was the last time any of them had seen Sara, and I wondered if any of the guys were thinking about it; in fact I couldn't even remember us all being together since. I got up from the table and headed towards the bar calmly.

"Where are you going?" Steve shouted at me from the table.

"I need a drink." I'd said it, *a drink*; I'd been sober for so long now and with just a few weeks of the world remaining I wanted to see if I had conquered my biggest adversary: alcohol. When I returned to the table both Mattie and Steve were staring at me as if I was holding a grenade that was likely to explode any minute.

"It's OK guys, I just want to prove that I beat it, that's all. Carry on with your lists; I'm not going to flip out." I smiled to Mattie and he smiled back, nodding to Steve and then returning to the manic scribbling of band names and song titles. As I sat there, tasting the first drop of alcohol in so many years, I felt a real buzz about the idea, and enjoyed watching all the gang back together again, creating something. They all argued about what they should and shouldn't choose and whether 20 songs were enough or too many, but eventually seemed happy with their choices even though they wouldn't reveal their final lists to each other. We agreed that the best time to start would be the first of December, and that it could act as a twenty-day shop promotion until the end, although all the gang were agreed that I was nuts and we'd be sat around on the 22nd of December laughing about all this madness. I sat and listened without arguing, and inside I smiled as I thought about everything I had heard, read and learnt over the past few years. I knew that everyone had a time to go and I didn't need to argue about that: this was a time to just enjoy being with the guys again, talking about music, like we always did.

Thursday 29th November

It had been over seven years since I had been to an AA meeting, or even to the building itself, but all those years later I was sat at a coffee shop nearby, waiting for the lunchtime meeting to finish so I could find Joey and do my next good deed. The last time I had any contact with him was when I'd received the package from him in the post, and it was over seven years since then. I'd been thinking about him more and more recently though, and when I looked at the people who had done me good during my life, he was one that definitely deserved recognition. I sat finishing my coffee and preparing for my next move. I felt nervous at the prospect of seeing Joey after so much time, and hoped he'd be glad to have me wander back into his life.

As I walked down to the hall I could see people leaving and knew that the meeting must have just finished. I was surprised to see that the majority of the people attending were younger rather than older and figured it must have been a sign of the times: whenever money caused stress for people it seemed as if the amount of drink and drug problems often increased. As I waited for the hall to empty I recognised a lady from years ago when I went to the meetings; she'd always been an assistant to Joey so I decided to speak to her and see if he was about or expected anytime soon. The minute I caught her eye, her face lit up and she headed over to me, giving me a huge hug.

"Hello stranger, what an unexpected surprise! How are you? It's been a long time." She was beaming as she spoke to me and it showed how much she must have cared.

"I'm doing well thanks; I stayed sober and haven't touched any drugs since I left here over seven years ago. I've had a couple of beers recently, but just to prove to myself that I can control it." I had to admit to the beers otherwise I'd have felt like a fraud.

Not everyone remains completely sober; as long as you don't feel yourself slipping back into the old routines again you should be OK. It's really good to see you again. You've just missed the meeting, though."

"I didn't come for the meeting; I was trying to find Joey. We lost contact not long after I stopped coming here, and I wanted to speak to him." Something about being back in this hall again made me feel uncomfortable, and I just wanted to see Joey and get out again.

"I thought you knew? Joey passed away not long after you completed your year and left us. It was very sudden and incredibly sad. I would have gotten in touch with you, but I knew you two were close and just assumed that you would have known straight away. I'm very sorry Will, this must be such a shock for you." The lady reached out and held my hand to comfort me whilst I stood there trying to think of something to say.

"He can't be. I was in touch with him after I left here, and we even met up a few times." As I spoke my mind returned to the last time I'd spoken to him, and then how often I'd rang and he'd been busy, before eventually getting no answer at all. The note he'd sent me in the parcel with the Velvet Underground album suddenly sprung to mind:

I have some things I need to do, so it's time for you to open your wings and fly solo. Onwards and upwards my friend! Forever in music, Joey.

Suddenly that message seemed far more sinister than when I'd received it originally, and a cold shiver ran down my spine. I needed to know more; this was all such a shock and made very little sense to me.

"What happened to him?" There was no point hiding from the question; I needed a straight answer.

"To be honest, we've never known exactly. His body was found in the Lock but there were no signs of any violence – all we know is that he had been drinking. Apart from that we never got any other information; it was ruled as an accidental death in the end but I always had the feeling that he took his own life. He'd struggled with the drink for so long, and sometimes it's such a constant battle that it can haunt you and no matter how strong you are, you cannot completely beat it. I think he just ran out of fight in the end, it was so very sad and we still miss him now."

My mind returned to that night when I listened to the CD Joey had sent me, and the news report about the man found in the lock. I got that cold chill down my spine again as I realised it was probably him, and at the time I hadn't even known it. I felt so sad, but having had so much grief in my life I was almost too exhausted to cry. The lady was still holding my hand and looking at me with a worried expression on her face.

"We set up a lovely tribute for him at the back of the hall on one of our noticeboards, and it's been there ever since. We update it with notes and flowers when we can. I'd like to show you if you have time?"

I nodded and followed her to the back of the hall, where I was greeted by a large photocopied picture of Joey in the centre of the noticeboard. Pinned all around it were notes from other people in recovery who had been helped by him or felt moved by his death. I glanced briefly at the notes but didn't want to read them, it felt ghoulish after all these years and I knew what I felt for Joey; I didn't need to use other people's words instead. I noticed a small photo on the bottom corner of the board and it was Joey and I hugging at our last meeting together here. Looking at the picture brought back so many memories of our time here and I could feel my anxiety increasing the longer I stood there.

"It's only a little tribute but we can't do more here unfortunately as the hall gets used for other things too these days. We might even have to relocate completely if we don't get ourselves sorted soon."

I remembered from my time here that so much was done voluntarily, and it always put a strain on finances when people needed the help but just couldn't afford to pay for them. With the financial situation in the country being as bad as it was it meant that lots of places wouldn't survive at all, and people would end up stuck in bad situations needing help, but unable to get any.

"I can help with that." I reached into my wallet and pulled out my chequebook, certain that donating money here would be one of the best things I'd ever done, and wrote out a cheque for twenty-five thousand pounds. I handed it to the confused-looking lady with as little fuss as possible, and she stared at the cheque and her expression changed from confusion to pure shock.

"I can't possibly take this; it's far too much money." She held the cheque between us, waiting for me to take it back. I put my hand over hers and looked straight at her as I spoke.

"I want you to take it. Joey and everyone connected to this place did so much for me, and this is my thank-you. If it can stop people getting as close to rock-bottom as I was then, it will be well worth it. Please take it; I want you to have it, for Joey if nothing else."

The lady looked down at the cheque again with tears welling in her eyes, before throwing herself at me and giving me the sort of hug that only a mother can ever give. I could hear her crying with shock and happiness into my chest.

"Thank you, thank you, thank you. Just wait until the others hear about this. Wait here and I'll go get them so they can thank you in person. You really are a special human being." The lady wiped her eyes and scuttled off out the back towards the office. I remembered sitting in there once with Joey after a meeting whilst he finished up some paperwork and we chatted about music and life. I never had any intention of staying and seeing the other people there. I wasn't doing the good deeds to get thanks; I was doing what was important and what was right. I watched the lady close the door behind her and made my move. I pulled the photo of Joey and I off the noticeboard, putting it in my jacket pocket before hurrying back out of the hall into the cold November air, and towards home. The lady must have been bemused when she returned and I was gone, but I hoped she would forgive me for not staying: all I cared about was the donation and hopefully that would make up for my disappearing on her.

"I don't get it though buddy; seriously, I actually think the idea is kind of cool but tomorrow? It's the first of December, people don't wanna be thinking about the end of the world, they wanna be thinking about Christmas!" Steve was on his umpteenth beer and still arguing about the direction of the December shop promotion, whilst a bemused Mattie just kept quiet.

"Steve, trust me. I know what you're saying but I really think we can stand apart from everyone else with this. We don't have to ignore Christmas at all; you can do what you want with that if it makes you happy. All I'm saying is that this is what I want us to focus on: a twenty-day interactive promotion and a huge display of all the different lists from us and the customers we encourage to do them. It's lists, Steve; you know how much you love lists!" I wasn't prepared to let my idea be rolled over; it was what I wanted for the shop as my last statement.

"OK man, whatever you say; I do love the lists, I must admit. So tomorrow morning it starts and it ends on the 21st? You're not still on your world-ending kick are you? Don't you think there'd be something in the news if it was true?" He wouldn't give up, but that was one of the things I loved about Steve: he was constantly debating everything.

"I'm not saying anything – we all have our own beliefs and we all make our own decisions, and they don't have to make any sense to others. I've got loads of stuff printed up for it and will bring it in tomorrow before opening so we can get it all set up. I need to get home now though, so I'll see you both in the morning. Don't stay out too late!" I winked at Mattie before high fiving them both and heading out of the pub. I looked back to see Steve still moaning to Mattie, and Mattie rolling his eyes at me. Tomorrow the promotion would start and that would be my role in the shop finalised: another thing to tick off on my list.

Later that evening, after gathering all the posters and flyers for the shop together, I sat relaxing in my lounge. I'd been listening to *Grace* by Jeff Buckley and looking through a box of memories: it was full of things like old notebooks of things I'd written; all sorts of notes, poems and story ideas. I don't know whether it was because December was so close but I was feeling quite nostalgic and thinking about all the different people in my life at different points, especially those I'd lost. I took an envelope out of the box and tipped the contents onto the coffee table; it was a few photos I'd put away to keep safe. There was a picture of Mum and Dad, one of Sara, and the picture of Joey and I that had come from the noticeboard at the hall. It dawned on me that I didn't have a picture of Albert, but the one that Thomas had shown me was so clear in my mind that it didn't matter too much anyway. I put *Unplugged in New York* by Nirvana onto the CD player and lit a cigarette, and as I sat there looking at the pictures I could still feel every bit of loss resonating through me. All such special people, and all gone too soon in my eyes. I walked over to the window and glanced out at the night sky, wondering where they were and if they were somehow all together, waiting to see me again. Whilst I stood and watched the clouds blocking out the bright November moon, the words of Albert and the reverend echoed through my head. So many questions, soon to be answered.

After a while I saw a group of people down the road: they were all obviously drunk, shouting and singing at the tops of their voices. I drew my curtains and headed back to the peaceful solace of my lounge and my memories. I dug through my music and found the perfect song to suit my mood: *It's Just a Little Bit of Everything (That's Brought Me Down to This)* by Steven Jesse Bernstein, pressed play and walked back to the sofa. Before I sat down I looked at my watch and noticed it was just past midnight, so I walked over to the calendar and turned it to December. I took a marker pen from the drawer and put crosses through every day after the 21st, then returned to the couch to sit and listen to the song. I let the words penetrate my mind whilst I looked at the pictures and thought about the date. Only 21 days to go, and still so much to do.

Chapter 12

December 2012 – Age 35

If you had time to listen to 20 songs before the world ended, which songs would you choose?

Saturday 1st December

"I can't believe you've managed to get us here at seven in the morning! Man, we must really love you." Steve was still moaning as he alternated between yawning and sipping his take-out coffee.

"I told you, this has to start today so we've only got a couple of hours to get it all set up. Enough of the moaning already, let's just get this done." I had everything we needed and wasn't in the mood for all my plans to be messed up by Steve's desperate urge to sleep after a night out.

I hadn't gone to bed much earlier than one in the morning myself, but had been the first to arrive at the shop that morning with a box full of promotional material that a local print store had made from my design for me. All the posters and flyers had the same message: *20 songs to hear before the end of the world; which 20 would you choose?* The display was going to include highlighted albums from the lists that myself and the guys had chosen, and if we could encourage customers to give us their lists, then they would go up on the promotional wall too. I had some postcards that Kelly was going to hand out in Camden, and we had cleared space on the main wall to display the whole promotion. The signs included an apocalyptic-looking view from Parliament Hill that had been digitally altered and looked striking, and simple wording so the message was sharp and to the point. Once the display was on the wall I was even more convinced that we were onto something, and all of the guys seemed excited too.

"Why are there four empty frames on the display?" Steve stood looking puzzled at the display wall.

"Our lists," Mattie said with a grin, and patted me on the back. "I think you've hit on something really cool here buddy. We always prided ourselves on how alternative we were as a shop and this sort of thing really gives us the chance to prove it. I love it man, well done." Even after knowing him for so long, it still gave me a huge buzz to get a compliment from Mattie.

"Who's gonna go first then?" I asked all of them, holding out the first of the empty frames. I already knew who couldn't wait to show off and so did everyone else – that's why we all turned to look at Steve.

"Well, if I have to." Steve was grinning from ear to ear and already had his list printed out and in his hand. I took the list from him and secured it in the frame, before putting it up on the wall beneath the display. Mattie and Kelly gathered next to me, desperate to get a look at his list, and as usual with Steve, it didn't disappoint. Steve's musical taste very rarely spread outside of the UK, so as predicted he had a wealth of British talent, from older bands like The Kinks and Pink Floyd to more recent nineties bands like Blur and Dodgy. As soon as his list went up, I could see that the vertical rack in front would have an awful lot of very cool home-grown talent promoted there, and would be really popular, especially in London. We all agreed that it was a very cool list, and Steve just shrugged.

"Like I say, you've either got it or you haven't," was his only comment.

Mattie stepped forward next and handed me his list, and again I put it in an empty frame before securing it on the wall. He stood back this time and Steve joined Kelly and I, huddled in front of it. Mattie had always been very much into the alternative American music scene, and his list did it proud: most of the tracks were taken from the big early nineties explosion and included Nirvana, Pearl Jam and Sebadoh amongst others, but there was also the odd nod to the older generation, via Iggy Pop and the Stooges and Mother Love Bone. We had such a diverse customer base that I knew this would be a popular list too; there was a common misconception that musical trends died out, but we knew there would always be people who still held that genre close to their hearts and this would act as a great trip down memory lane for some of them. Mattie didn't say anything about his list; instead he stood there whistling the American national anthem and nudging Steve playfully in the ribs.

"The floor is all yours, Kelly," I said in a mock announcer's voice. Kelly was by far the most confident of all the workers at the store, but now she seemed shy about handing her list over.

"You can all make your jokes about being a lesbian now or whatever; I've heard them all before, OK." She thrust the list at me and then leaned back against the wall of the shop nonchalantly. Kelly had always been known as the angry girl of the shop and her music leant towards punk, so her list wasn't that much of a surprise really, but on paper it showed us just how cool she was. The list contained a large amount of music from what had been dubbed the 'riot grrl' movement, including bands like Bratmobile and 7 Year Bitch, but also had older acts like Joan Jett on it, alongside Patti Smith. Steve, Mattie and I all studied the list before turning to Kelly, who was staring at her shoes.

"You are one cool cat," I said to Kelly who looked up at me to check I wasn't making fun of her. "With music like this, it's no wonder you are our favourite little rock chick," I added, and that was met with her poking her tongue out at me and scrunching her nose up.

"Well buddy, there is one more space: time for you to unveil yours, then?" Steve was desperate to see my list, so I clipped it into the final frame and popped it up on the wall with the other three. My list had been chosen from different parts of my life, from being a child growing up, to the periods of loss I suffered and ending with a few select songs from modern times. I knew one or two of the choices would raise an eyebrow, but it was my list and I didn't care whether it was deemed cool or not. The guys stood eyeing the list and I could see how parts of it were uncomfortable for them to comment on, knowing me as long as they had and being aware of the songs that were related to my parents' funerals or to Sara and I. They all turned to look at me at the same time, before speaking to me individually.

"That's the bravest and most honest list of all; you never fail to amaze me with your strength," Mattie said, patting me on the back.

"They'd all be so proud of you, Will," Kelly said, giving me a quick kiss on the cheek.

"Lana Del Ray? Really, Will?" Steve was always going to be the ass – it was a role he played so well and he used it most when he was too nervous to know what to say. He came over and high-fived me anyway though.

"It's all down to personal choice guys, that's the only rule of this; completely non-judgemental. Now if you don't mind, you guys need to open and I need to get going, so I shall leave the last bit in your capable hands."

I said bye to all of them before heading out of the shop's front door and into Camden High Street. I watched through the glass as they started filling up all the display gaps in front of the four lists; the display looked just as I'd planned it, and as I headed away from the store and down the road, I ticked another job off in my mind.

Friday 7th December
I'd spent all week creating a time capsule and had finished it just in time for the next task I needed to complete. I'd managed to track down an old metal tin about the size of a medium coffee jar, and it had a lockable lid so was perfect for what I needed. I had chosen to fill it with the most important people from my life up to now, so inside it were pictures of my family and Sara, and the picture of Joey as well as all the guys at the shop. I'd also put in the order of service leaflets from both Mum and Dad's funerals, the note that Joey had written me, and a printout of the last email I got from Sara, with a copy of the picture taken in the restaurant. The missing piece was something from me, and it had taken me ages to decide what to do. In the end I wrote a poem and popped that into the tin, alongside a pack of my favourite cigarettes and a lighter. Anyone finding the capsule would have laughed at some of the contents and possibly cried at others; it was a fitting snapshot of my life and how I'd spent it with these loved ones, so in the end it was perfect. I sealed

the lid and locked it shut; put it into my bag and headed somewhere I hadn't been in a very long time.

Standing outside my parents' house for the first time in over nine years was such a strange experience, especially since the house itself had hardly changed in all that time. It had been painted, and the front garden was arranged slightly differently, but looking at it brought everything flooding back as if it was only yesterday. I'd found out that it was still owned by the couple that had bought it from me originally so I had phoned them earlier in the day and asked if I could take one last look at the place and they'd agreed. I told them I was emigrating and that I just wanted to look at the garden one last time before I left, and they'd offered me a chance to look at what they'd done with the rest of the house, but there were too many ghosts in there for me to deal with and I didn't feel up to it.

I remembered the inside of the house as I wanted to, but the garden had always been special to all of us as a family, and they were the memories I wanted one last reminder of. The lady who owned the house now was really friendly and kept offering me cups of tea or something to eat, but in the end she showed me through to the back and said she'd leave me to it, realising I just wanted to be on my own for a short time.

I sat on the bench, which was still against the kitchen wall, and looked at the garden. As a child it had seemed huge to me and now it seemed tiny, and I was amazed that it had hardly changed at all. Sitting there lost in my thoughts I could almost see my mum hanging the washing out as I dug through the grass looking for strange insects, or my dad building a snowman with me or kicking a football about. The amount of times my mum had called out that dinner was ready, or as I got older, shouting for me to come and grab the phone call that she'd answered for me. Had it really been over nine years since I'd smelled Mum's perfume or Dad's aftershave? So many years since I had felt their arms around me, giving me a comforting hug? It's so strange to think of all the things you take for granted at times as a child; you think it will always be there waiting for you when you have time for it, but it's not. Life has a nasty habit of taking things from you before you've even had time to enjoy them, or tell people how much you love them. We'd all like just ten more minutes with someone, and I realised now that the trick was not to waste the ten minutes with them in the first place.

I sat there for about an hour, lost in my thoughts, before the lady came to check if I was OK. It was time for me to be heading off anyway, so I said goodbye to my childhood memories and headed for the front door.

"Have a safe journey when you go, Will. Have you far to travel?" The lady was asking out of politeness more than anything as we said goodbye at her door.

"Not really, it's not so much the travelling; it's more about going home." I waved goodbye to her and couldn't help but notice the quizzical expression on her face as she contemplated my cryptic remark. I took one last look at the house that had started me on this journey, swallowed away any sadness, and headed to fulfil my tribute with the time capsule.

It didn't take long to get to Parliament Hill, and by late afternoon I was sat on the bench holding the time capsule in my hands. Although it was dry, the sky was dark and stormy-looking. There wasn't anybody about on the hill so I decided to bury the capsule before anyone could notice; I didn't want somebody to come along and dig it up for a laugh. I wanted it to stay there untouched, as a tribute to everything I'd been through and the beautiful people I'd lost along the way. I walked over to a tree near the bench and moved away the leaves which had fallen at the base and were carpeting the ground at the base of the trunk. I'd brought a small trowel from home and dug as far down as I could without causing too much trouble, before gently laying the capsule in the hole I'd made and covering it back over again. I said a few quiet words to myself and swept the leaves back over the disturbed earth, covering the fact that anything had been done there, and went back to the bench and sat quietly. This place had meant so much to me throughout my lifetime, and apart from Albert, every other person represented in the capsule had a link to here too. I remembered fondly the times spent here with Mum and Dad when I was a kid, the times Sara and I had spent here that were both happy and sad. This was the place where Joey first appeared to me and got me the help I had so badly needed, and then there was the evening that I had spent here with the gang from work, all saying goodbye to Sara's memory in our own special ways. I had always known that this was the place where I would see the end of my world, and coming here now just confirmed it. I looked at the ever-darkening sky and thought about all the people I'd lost.

"I'm coming home soon; you won't have to wait much longer. I think about you all every day and I can't wait to be back with you again. I love you, all of you." I spoke the words aloud as that old, familiar ache in my chest reappeared; the truth was that nothing had ever really felt right since I'd lost Sara, and I'd struggled to carry on. Once I lost my parents I had no reason to really care anymore, and as hard as I'd tried to find a reason, everything had remained so pointless. I took heart from the fact that in two weeks' time all the pain would be gone and I could feel weightless – something I had longed for since 2003. Wearily, I got up from the bench and headed home, happy that I had left my mark here on behalf of all those special people.

Monday 10th December
I'd been thinking long and hard about what to do with my flat and any money left over after I'd finished my last few good deeds, and had come up with the idea of setting up some kind of foundation in memory of my mum. As the days grew ever closer to the 21st, I realised how many people were carrying on as normal and like nothing was going to happen, but I figured there wasn't any time left for messing around. I'd called Kevin over to the flat that morning and he was looking through all my finances with me, seeing what was possible and how much I could help, whilst I was showing him the plans I had for the foundation.

"What you've got here is really wonderful Will, but I don't see how you're going to survive if you give everything away? You're not still on the end-of-the-world kick are you? I mean, if it is the end of the world then surely no one is going to need this anyway?" Kevin had been hesitant to say anything negative, but had my best interests at heart and didn't want to see me destitute. I'd realised for a couple of weeks now that it wasn't a good idea to keep talking about the end of the world though, because people didn't understand where I was coming from. I'd started to make excuses for all sorts of things, like saying I was going abroad to the lady when I visited my parents' house, and it had worked well in stopping people worrying about me or trying to get me to change any plans I had. I knew what was going to happen though, so I kept my head down and carried on with my plans.

"You don't have to worry Kevin; I'm renting the flat above the shop and get a good income from there anyway so I won't struggle. This is just something I have to do; I want people to get the help they need and for people to be at peace in their time of need, like Mum was." I'd made sure to have an answer for everything, so there was no comeback at all.

"Well I'm more than happy to set things in motion for you, but only if you can assure me that you are still set up OK. As long as everything is detailed and done legally then you've got no problems. I've left some notes for you here, so just get the stuff all drawn up and then we can start arranging it. Give me a ring when you're ready and I can get it started for you." He stood up and shook my hand; I still felt like he was looking at me strangely but carried on as if everything was normal.

"I'll make a start on it tonight. I'm not moving for a couple of weeks but will make sure it's all sorted so you can start everything off." I showed him to the door, wanting him to leave before he asked anything too awkward.

"I'll wait to hear from you then, Will. I think it's a really lovely thing you're doing, and your folks would be so proud of you. I'll see you soon."

"Thanks Kevin, for everything. You've been such a support and I really appreciate it. Give my love to your family for me and I hope everything goes well for you." I didn't mean to sound so final; it just slipped out and I could see the frown on his face as he stopped and thought about what I'd said, so I quickly added "I'll see you soon though, OK," to throw him off-track.

"No problem Will – you take care though and remember if you need anything I'm always here for you, any time." He slowly turned and headed down the stairs towards the entrance to the flats, and I closed my door. I slumped down to the floor and breathed a sigh of relief, both at getting things sorted and not creating any problems for myself.

I spent the rest of the day looking over my plans. I'd worked out that with the money I could pay for a special set of trained carers and nurses to help more terminally ill people get the help they needed at home, whilst also providing some form of counselling for the relatives that were affected by the issues surrounding losing a loved one. I had everything I could possibly arrange all written up, and would leave it to be done after the 21st; I was safe in the knowledge that I could trust Kevin to see that my plans were completed as I wished. It wasn't until late that night when I went to bed, having written up everything I needed and making sure it was all legal. I'd been forced to fake a couple of signatures on documents, hoping Mattie would understand, but other than that I had been able to do it all myself. I could sleep that night happily, knowing that once my world had ended there would be something special remaining: a legacy left by me, but in memory of my mum and dad; something that could help people long after I'd gone.

Friday 14th December
It had taken some hard work to arrange and convince the club owner to agree, but it was finally happening. The final part of my work promotion was to hold an end-of-the-world party, with music being picked from all the different playlists that we'd collected in the last two weeks. I'd got some flyers

printed up and Kelly had been passing them out around London on her travels, as well as putting some up in the store next to the promotion section. The club owner had agreed to us hosting the night as long as we could promise to fill at least half the club, and that had turned out to be no problem at all – in fact the club was busier than he'd seen it in quite some time. The guys had come straight from the shop to help me set up, and Steve had provided a DJ who was helped by a stack of song lists that we had acquired from the shop. It was amazing to see how well the promotion had taken off, and after all the doubting, even Steve had to congratulate me on how good the idea was. The guys had been saying how so many people coming in to the store had brought up loads of music they wouldn't necessarily have heard of it if haven't been for this promo, and they'd been getting all sorts of lists from people, and some posted through the door anonymously too.

By ten o'clock everyone at the club was really buzzing, and some amazing music had been played, ranging from The Doors right up to Ed Sheeran, and everyone seemed to be having a great time. Steve kept dragging me over to speak to people I didn't know, and tried to get me to start telling them all about how I came up with the idea, but I kept sneaking back into the darkened corner of the club where I could be more of an anonymous spectator. For the first time in over seven years I had a constant flow of drinks and was slowly falling back into that feeling of happy numbness. I had to hide half of them when Mattie or Steve came over, but the rest of the time I was free to do as I pleased.

I'd made sure that my song list wasn't included in the songs to play because it was so personal to me and I didn't want to hear them played in a party atmosphere, so instead I was enjoying listening to all the crazy diversity that the other lists offered. Mattie had spent all night checking up on everyone as usual, making sure people were having fun and that there were no issues that needed sorting, and Steve had spent most of the night playing air guitar on the dance floor to anything remotely English, but I hadn't seen Kelly anywhere all night. Somewhere around midnight the drink was really starting to hit me, and I was lying back on the sofa lost in my thoughts and the music when I heard someone come and sit next to me.

"Hey handsome, you leapt off the wagon then?" I looked up to see Kelly sat at the table with me, swigging from a bottle of red wine.

"Hey, yeah, kind of – don't go telling the guys though otherwise I'll get all sorts of lectures. I just needed it tonight, that's all." I sat up and tried to make myself look fairly presentable and I noticed how great Kelly looked. I was so used to seeing her in all her punk 'statement' clothing, as we called it, that I was surprised to see her wearing a dress. It was black with a low top and shredded-looking hem; it came down to just below her knees and underneath she had on fishnet tights and shiny knee-high boots. "You look great. Who are you out to impress tonight?" I nudged her with my elbow, but she didn't look up at me.

"It doesn't matter, he won't notice me anyway. You think I look OK though?" She seemed a lot more sheepish than usual, and I was worried about her.

"Don't be mad honey; you'll knock his socks off! How could you not? Who is he anyway, do I know him?" Kelly was a lovely girl and I figured I could put in a word for her if she needed help; anything to make her happier.

Kelly took a big swig from her bottle and looked up at me. "You really don't know, do you Will?"

Suddenly it dawned on me; something that had never even crossed my mind. Kelly liked me. I felt really awkward and didn't know where to look or what to say. I took a swig from my drink and tried to speak, but nothing came out.

"It's OK Will, I kind of knew what you'd say anyway, so don't worry. I didn't mean to say anything tonight; I just couldn't help myself. I've been hiding away near the bar and watching you; I just can't stand to see you so sad and lonely, and I just want to make you happy." She was pouring her heart out to me and I really didn't know what to say.

"I never knew Kelly, I'm sorry. I don't know what to say. I've never looked at anyone since Sara; it's not you, and I don't want you thinking that." I was babbling and Kelly reached across the table and held my hand, which had started to shake.

"I know Will, that's why I never wanted to say anything, but I got drunk tonight and now it's all spilled out. Don't hate me."

"I couldn't ever hate you, Kelly. You've always been so wonderful to me and I know Sara thought the world of you. I'm really flattered to be honest, but there's some damn lucky guy out there waiting for you." I smiled at her and she smiled back, shuffling over next to me on the couch.

"I do love you Will, I just want you to know that. I want you to do whatever makes you happy – you deserve that and more."

"Thank you – same to you though; you need to show the world how amazing you are. Stop hiding yourself away because you're a star that needs to start shining." I gave her a huge hug and she kissed me on the cheek. "Now go and enjoy your night; show those guys what they're missing." I grinned at her and she curtsied to me before heading into the crowd on the dance floor.

I spent the rest of the night drinking alone, watching everyone rushing around dancing and chatting to each other; many still talking about the promo and how they decided what songs to pick and why. I felt proud that I'd created something which had taken off so well and involved others who were able to enjoy it, and this would be the last party I'd ever go to so I'd made the most of it. By the time Mattie sat down next to me most of the people had cleared out and I was drinking water to try and rehydrate myself.

"Hey chief, what a night! I didn't imagine so many people would show up. You did really well, and being here made it perfect so thanks for that. You should see how much business we're doing and it's all down to you and this crazy idea." He patted me on the back and laughed to himself.

"It's a team effort Mattie, always has been. Thank you for putting on such an awesome night, it's been really great and I've had a brilliant time." I actually had enjoyed myself despite being so out of practice with social events, but now I needed to get home. "I'm gonna head off now bro, I hope you don't mind? I've got some things to do; if you need help clearing up I can stay though?"

"You've done more than enough chief; you get home and we'll clear up, it won't take long anyway. See you soon though, don't be a stranger." He high-fived me and I slipped away quietly. Steve was busy talking to the DJ and Kelly was sitting on the step next to the dance floor, so I waved at her and headed off. I wanted to say a proper goodbye to her but after the conversation tonight I didn't want to make anything worse. All I knew was that with all the drink it was time to get home. The cold early morning air hit me as I stepped out onto the pavement and stumbled slightly all the way home.

Over the last few weeks I'd managed to complete all my plans without any trouble at all, but as I sat outside a coffee shop near the store, I knew this would be the hardest part of all, and my hands were shaking as I chain-smoked and thought about everything. It had taken some work to set up the last plan, but it was ready and all I had to do was cross the road and head into the shop. It was such a strange sensation walking into the store, knowing it would be my last time, but seeing the window display of the 20 songs promo made me smile to myself and without further thought, I pushed the door open and walked in. I was greeted by the sound of the Yeah Yeah Yeahs and knew it must be Kelly working behind the till. Before I got a chance to get any further her head popped up from behind the counter, and when she saw me she smiled but looked a bit nervous.

"Hey lovely, how are you?" I tried to sound as relaxed as possible so I didn't make her feel awkward.

"Hi, I'm good thanks, just enjoying a bit of freedom for a change." She laughed, nodding her head to the back door, seeming happy to be left on her own for a change. "About the other night, I didn't mean to—"

"Did you have a good time the other night? I can hardly remember it; that's the danger of getting drunk! Now I remember why I don't drink anymore." I'd cut her off to save her any embarrassment of having to apologise when she didn't need to.

"It was great; I really enjoyed myself. It was good to see you." She seemed like she knew I was lying, but was grateful that I'd taken the effort to make her life easier.

"I've got a favour to ask: can you and the guys come meet me after work tonight? I've got some stuff to show you and I thought we could have a quick drink before you all head home. If you let Mattie and Steve know for me and give me a ring if there's a problem?"

"Sure, no problem — we'll meet you about seven?" I noticed she'd been fiddling with her nails the whole time she spoke to me.

"Sounds great. I gotta dash, but have a good day and I'll see you later." I headed out of the store, but she caught me just before the door closed.

"Will?"

I turned back to look at her, and she had her mouth open as if she'd meant to speak but thought better of it. "Doesn't matter. I'll see you later."

I hurried away from the store just in case she came out and caught up with me. Kelly was beautiful and I was really flattered by her interest but I hadn't thought about anyone since Sara, and it wasn't something I could do. No one could replace Sara; she had meant everything to me and still did. I was relieved to have sorted the first part of my plan though, and headed home to gather the things I needed for later.

Around half seven, I was sat at our usual window seat in the pub, watching the guys ordering their drinks. They were the funniest bunch to watch because they always looked like they were squabbling about something, and no one would have ever guessed we were all so close. I was sat slowly sipping a cider, promising myself I would behave, with my bag next to me full of the evening's surprises for everyone. After the usual banter and shop talk which we couldn't help but get involved in, the floor was mine.

"I've got some stuff for all of you and it might all seem a bit crazy, but just bear with me OK? I've been doing a lot of thinking and you know how I feel about the end-of-the-world stuff, but it's made me look at everything I want and need and the things I don't, so I've made some decisions." My palms were sweating and I kept taking sips of my drink to stop my mouth from getting dry. All the guys were sat staring at me, silent for once and all confused and apprehensive. I got three envelopes out of my bag and slipped the first one across the table to Steve, then one to Mattie, and finally the third one to Kelly. They all looked down at the envelopes, then at each other, and then at me.

"What's all this about bro?" Steve asked first, always the most inquisitive.

"Open it and take a look," I said, leaning back in my chair.

Steve tore the envelope open and looked through the papers that were inside, his eyes wide, before putting them down and looking at me.

"What the hell bro? Is this for real? You're crazy; this lot must have cost a bomb." Steve was half-standing in amazement, causing everyone else at the table, and practically the pub, to look at him.

"It's for your band; you guys need decent instruments so I'm getting you some because I can. They're already bought and of no use to me so you have to take them." I calmly carried on sipping my pint before relaxing back in my seat again.

"I don't know what to say bro, this is mind-blowing! A Gibson SG, are you serious?"

"Calm down matey, you're gonna have a heart attack and then the instruments will be wasted," Mattie was laughing as I carried on.

"I've heard you guys are serious, and being in London, you're in the best place to get interest if you do it right, so with decent instruments I figured you could do it."

Steve came over to me and hugged me, a very rare event, then sat down again to look at the other instruments on the list of things I'd got for him and his bandmates.

"It's all getting delivered to the shop tomorrow so make sure you can find some space for it, and go make a name for yourself." Now that Steve had calmed down, I looked at Kelly. "Your turn, Kelly."

Kelly opened the envelope and started beaming from ear to ear, and I threw my car key onto the table for her. "Again, I won't take no for an answer. I know you need a car and I haven't used it in ages anyway, so it's all yours – it's a present of freedom if nothing else!"

"I'm speechless Will, thank you so much." Kelly jumped off her chair and wrapped herself around me, nearly squeezing the life out of me, and planted a huge kiss on my cheek. "You're amazing," she said, and then sat down quickly as if she hoped no one had heard.

All eyes turned to Mattie and he shifted uncomfortably in his seat. I didn't need to say anything – I just looked at him, and he slowly opened the envelope. It was almost as if he feared what was inside, alternating between looking at the envelope and at me the whole time. He pulled out half a dozen sheets of paper and read through them.

"No way Will, that's ridiculous! What the hell is this all about anyway?" He sounded angry, but I think it was more concern in his voice. He passed the papers back to me and walked over to the bar to order a drink.

"What was that, man? What are those papers for?" Steve was desperate to get the gossip.

"It's the shop; I've signed it all over to Mattie. I've got other plans and I know he'll make it work and he deserves it; it's something he's worked so hard for over the years."

Mattie walked back to the table with a tray containing pints for all of us and sat back in his chair, just staring at me.

"You know I always said you had the worst signature in the world, Matt? Take a look at the papers; it's already done."

Mattie picked up the papers and checked the back page: his signature clearly accepted the transfer of ownership, except it wasn't his signature at all; I'd forged it and signed my own name before getting it completed legally.

"I don't care Will, I won't take it; it's too much. What the hell are you gonna do if you don't have the shop?" Now his concern was showing even more and I was pleased to realise it wasn't just anger.

"I've hardly been there since I bought it, man; you guys run it and I just come in occasionally to see you all. I don't even do the financial stuff, it's already your shop and this just makes it legal. I won't back down, so take it and stop hurting my feelings." I wasn't prepared to budge an inch, and sat there waiting for the inevitable.

"I'll only say yes on one condition: if you change your mind then I sign it straight back over to you, no messing around." He was staring straight at me as he spoke.

"No problem; I won't change my mind, so you wanna say thank you now?" I joked, to try and lighten the atmosphere around the table.

Mattie came over to me and hugged me, whispering in my ear. "I love you bro; this means the world to me, so thank you." Then he returned to his seat and started handing the pints out.

I looked at all three of them and held my pint out towards them. "That's it guys – my presents from me to you as a thank-you for everything all of you have done. Cheers." We clinked glasses and I sat back down again, more relaxed now that everything was out in the open. All three of them alternated between looking at their papers, looking at me and starting to speak but not saying anything. Eventually I managed to steer the conversation round to the party and how the promotion in the shop was doing, and we managed to find some sort of normality, although there was still a sense of strangeness in the air. When I finished my pint it felt like the right time to go; I'd managed to hold it together this long and I didn't want to ruin everything now. I had started putting my jacket on and standing up when Mattie spoke.

"Are you sure you're OK though Will? I'm worried about you, and this all seems so final. Is there something you're not telling us?" He never was the sort to give up.

"Look at it this way guys: there's two days left so I don't need this stuff, and if you think I'm wrong then so be it. All that means is that in three days' time I've got less stuff that I don't need anyway and you guys get to enjoy it."

"You really think the world's gonna end in two days bro?" Mattie still couldn't get his head round it, and the other guys were shaking their heads in agreement.

"We've all got to go sometime," was all I said.

"So what's the deal with giving this all away, then? If the world ends it's pointless anyway; or is this some sort of redemption for something, like in the Bible?" Steve never did mince his words. I looked at him and smiled before calmly replying with one sentence.

"We're all looking for redemption." And then I gave him one last hug and wished him well with his band. I hugged Mattie and told him to turn the shop into the best damn record shop in England, let alone London; and then I hugged Kelly and told her to remember what I'd said about stars. I wished them all the best and headed out of the pub, and as I went I heard Steve shout after me.

"Yeah man, we'll see you on the 22nd when you come looking for a job!"

I turned and saluted him before heading down the road. Holding back the tears was starting to sting my eyes, and my throat felt like it was burning. Just before I lost control, I heard a voice behind me.

"Will, wait." It was Kelly; she ran up and hugged me tightly. "I want to tell you that I love you but I understand. Whatever you do I hope it's what you want and you've thought about it properly. I only ever wanted you to be happy." Her eye makeup was smudged on her cheeks, and I wiped it off carefully with my thumb.

"Thanks Kelly, you never needed to apologise for anything. Any man would be crazy not to want you; you just had to pick the crazy one." I smiled at her and tucked her hair behind her ear.

"Will, if the world is about to end, I've got nothing to lose." And she kissed me full on the lips, before stepping back and putting something in my hand. "I'm really going to miss you." And then she turned and started walking back to the pub. I stood there beneath the streetlight, watching her walk all the way back to the door, and just before she entered the pub she turned my way and waved, with tears running down her face. I quickly waved and turned into the blackness of an alleyway, sliding down the wall and crying my eyes out. Sometimes when you had no reason to want to stay somewhere, you found a reason for never wanting to leave either. I picked myself up and began that familiar walk home, back to my flat, the clock ticking ever more loudly in my head.

Thursday 20th December

I'd woken up that morning with such a headache from all the emotion last night; I'd been so upset by the time I got home that I hadn't even carried on drinking, just sat down and listened to some music. The last thing I'd remembered hearing was *Hurt* by Johnny Cash, and looking at what Kelly had put in my hand. It was a curious necklace with a tiny bottle tied to the cord, and in the bottle was an even tinier bit of paper with one word written on it: *Hope*. I wasn't sure whether she'd bought it somewhere or made it herself; either way it was beautiful and I felt quite sorry for her and her longing to save me. I wished she hadn't seen the sadness, like most people, but after our conversation last night I felt like she almost knew what was coming.

I spent the morning boxing up the last of my possessions in the flat and labelling certain things that I was leaving out, like my CDs for the guys at the shop. By mid-afternoon I was done, so I left the flat and decided to have one last look at London, one of the greatest cities in the world; my London. There was a snowy feeling in the air as I walked around and it made Christmas time come alive with all the hustle and bustle of the shoppers. Camden was heaving with people; everyone who passed me had more bags than the last, and the smells of cinnamon from the various Christmas sweet treats on sale in the market hung in the air. I pulled my collar up to protect me from the cold and crossed the road; I wanted to walk past the store but didn't want anyone to see me – I'd said my goodbyes and didn't want to have any more upset. I stood at a stall buying myself a sweet waffle and looked over the seller's shoulder at the shop window, and I nearly laughed out loud when I saw what they'd done, with the full window display now cut down to half. Instead of just the end-of-the-world promo, someone had added the words *but if it's not* at the top of the other window, and put a Christmas tree up and a glowing *Happy Christmas* sign. The words had been added using fake snow which I thought was a very festive touch, and I knew it must have been Steve. He got his Christmas display wish in the end, and I headed on down the road, still grinning.

I hopped on a few Tubes and spent the afternoon taking in as much of the great city as possible. I started off by walking along the Thames and did everything I could, from seeing Big Ben to sitting in Hyde Park for a while and watching the world go by. By the time early evening had come I was starting to get tired and decided to take one last walk around Piccadilly Circus, always one of the busiest places in London but one of the most impressive at this time of year. I found a coffee shop and sat outside drinking and having a cigarette, just looking at the beauty of all the Christmas lights. I watched all the families walking around together, mostly chatting and laughing; all the couples lovingly wrapped up tightly together and fending off the cold as they headed wherever they were going, and finally the awe on the children's faces as they looked at all the illuminated pictures of Santa and snowmen. So much happiness amongst so many people and it all felt so alien to me – these were all reminders of the things I'd lost over the years and of things I'd never have, and although the lights were beautiful, I decided to call it a day and head home. In my head I said goodbye to London, such a crazy but beautiful city, and the only place I had ever been able to call home. I jumped on the Tube and headed back to my flat for one last night in my most familiar surroundings.

It was the strangest evening I'd ever spent in the flat. Most of my stuff was all boxed up and labelled either for charity or if I had someone in mind who might make use of it. It was like moving in, except I knew the place like the back of my hand, with all the boxes everywhere and only the essentials left out. I spent the evening looking through my box of memories and listening to as much of my music as I could, drinking tea like it was going out of fashion, and smoking cigarettes. Even in my flat I had started to feel anxious now, and for a while I had been watching television and looking on the internet for news regarding the end of the world, but there was hardly anything and I'd gone through a stage of thinking it was a conspiracy to stop us knowing anything in advance. I had spent time reading the information I had found before, over and over again, looking for any mistakes or any clues that would give me more details, but there were none. Everyone I spoke to thought I was mad, but I remembered that conversation with Albert like it was yesterday and I knew what it meant. It would be the end of the world tomorrow, I was certain of it. At least it would be the end of my world and at last I could relax.

That night I got everything ready for the morning so I wasn't rushing when I got up. I had my favourite Converse, my flares, Sara's favourite shirt of mine, a hooded top and my fur-lined winter jacket all laid out neatly on top the bed. I had an envelope to post in the morning and a couple of things I needed, but other than that I was ready. I looked at the clock and realised it was nearly midnight, so I sat and listened to a copy of the compilation I'd made for Sara all those years ago, and wrote a letter. When I finished, I put the letter in an envelope and left it on the kitchen worktop before wearily heading to bed. My mind and body were so tired now and I knew it wasn't the late nights; it was all the constant fighting I'd had to do over the years just to survive. As I laid my head on my pillow that night, I relaxed like never before, happy that it wasn't long before I could stop fighting. The last thing I remember going through my mind before I fell asleep was the strange dream I'd had a month ago. I remembered appearing to save everyone from the end of the world by sacrificing myself, and as all the vivid images from the dream rushed through my mind, it made me feel even more confident that I was doing the right thing.

Friday 21st December
"We're all waiting for you, Will. Don't be scared, we're here and we're ready for you."

The alarm woke me from my dream at seven in the morning. All I could remember of it was all the smoke and the voices calling me, and with tears rolling down my cheeks I headed to the bathroom to have a shower and start preparing. I didn't want to hang about in the flat long so once I'd got dressed I made sure everything was ready for me to leave. I grabbed the stamped envelope addressed to Kevin, my shoulder bag which was light with hardly anything in it and the pot of tablets by my bedside, before saying goodbye to the flat in my head and locking the door behind me. Once the flat was secure, I popped the front door key into the envelope and sealed it, heading down the stairs and out into the street.

I posted the envelope in the first letterbox I found, before heading to the local coffee shop for a quick breakfast. Apart from the man behind the counter I didn't see anyone else at all and sat on my own outside, sipping my coffee and smoking as usual. Whilst I sat there I reached into my bag and pulled out the photo of Sara that I had taken years ago when I visited her in New York; the one where her face was shyly turned away from the camera. It was still my favourite photo after all these years, and I traced the outline of her with my finger as I thought about how much I'd missed her and how long I had spent wishing I could hold her again. It was so close now I could almost feel it. I looked at my watch and it was just before half past eight, so I took my coffee with me and started walking to Parliament Hill.

By just after nine I had made it to the top of the hill and was sat on the bench. The wind was blowing steadily from the west, and it brought even more of a chill to the already wintery conditions there. Looking out over London I could see no signs of movement: no trains running anywhere and no traffic noise. The blowing of the trees was such a contrast to the stillness of the city; it was like nature's last stand against a man-made world. There was a sense of calm inevitability about what came next and for the first time in years, all the sadness and loneliness was replaced with a sense of hope. I looked through my bag and got my iPod out ready; all that was left in the bag was my wallet and the empty tablet pots. I put the bag on the floor and took the last two remaining tablets in my hand with another swig of my take-out coffee. I was ready for the end of my world, but I was only going to leave while at one with the music. I looked at my watch and it said 9.35 am. It was the beginning of the end.

2012 – Epilogue

So today is the day: it's Friday 21st December 2012, and I've had a long time to prepare for the end. For the first time in years I guess I feel lucky. I have nothing to lose and everything to gain. My world stopped when I lost Sara and now hopefully I can finally get to see her again. It's time for me to go home, feel her warm body against mine and kiss those lips that I have spent the last 11 years longing for. A chance to see my parents at peace, not ravaged by disease or depression; to have all our hearts fixed again and to be able to smile one more time. I have had more than my fair share of loss and now there is nothing more to fear. I will be safe in the arms of love.

As I looked out over the city, I was expecting my final view of London to resemble a beautiful monster destroying the last remnants of business and religion, like nature turning against its creator and making God bankrupt. Instead there is quiet, such quiet, and a strange sense of calm. I look around the hill and can see the blurry outline of others sat here near me; I hope they have the same sense of hope and homecoming that I do. I feel for others who face losing people now, but at least they are leaving together; safety in numbers. I have been a lonely soul, wandering aimlessly, for too long now. I have had my music to comfort me and guide me home safely. As the last few seconds of my music runs out, I can feel the end is near. The dark red cloud in the distance resembles an old cinema curtain as it rolls heavily towards me, ready to finish the show. As I sit here on the bench, it feels like someone has taken my left hand in theirs. I smile to myself as I raise my right hand and hold it out towards the skyline, just to see what would happen. This is me, Will – I existed, I was here, I lived, I loved, I lost, but ultimately I survived. Now I am ready. As Sara's face appears, smiling, in my mind, a solitary tear rolls down my cheek. I'm coming home, baby. I look at my watch. It's 11.11 . . .

Will's 20 songs list for the end of the world, and reasons why

1. *Separate Lives* by Phil Collins
(Reminds Will of his childhood and his mum's music)

2. *Hello Again* by Neil Diamond
(Reminds Will of his childhood and his dad's music)

3. *Bohemian Rhapsody* by Queen
(Favourite song from the first cassette he ever bought himself)

4. *Imagine* by John Lennon
(Will's favourite song ever)

5. *Jeremy* by Pearl Jam
(Comfort during school troubles)

6. *The Crystal Ship* by The Doors
(Reminder of his first festival experience)

7. *Where Is My Mind?* by The Pixies
(Reminder of his first nights at rock clubs)

8. *Gorecki* by Lamb
(First time he met Sara)

9. *Yellow* by Coldplay
(First day spent with Sara)

10. *Sloop John B* by The Beach Boys
(First night with Sara)

11. *With Or Without You* by U2
(Sara leaving for New York)

12. *Something* by The Beatles
(Asking Sara to marry him)

13. *Hear You Me* by Jimmy Eat World
(Losing Sara in 2001)

14. *This Woman's Work* by Kate Bush
(Played at his mother's funeral)

15. *Freebird* by Lynrd Skynrd
(Played at his father's funeral)

16. *The Ghost Of Tom Joad* by Bruce Springsteen
(Comfort after the loss of his parents)

17. *Sophia* by Nerina Pallot
(Reminder of how much he loved Sara)

18. *Zebulon* by Rufus Wainwright
(Modern day reflection of how it felt losing his mother)

19. *Video Games* by Lana Del Ray
(Modern day reflection of how he loved and lost Sara)

20. *No Sound But The Wind* by The Editors
(His perfect song for the end of the world)

Michael's 20 songs list for the end of the world

1. *While My Guitar Gently Weeps* by The Beatles
2. *Only Living Boy In New York* by Simon & Garfunkel
3. *Where Did You Sleep Last Night?* by Nirvana
4. *Naked As We Came* by Iron & Wine
5. *If It Be Your Will* by Leonard Cohen
6. *A Change Is Gonna Come* by Sam Cooke
7. *Country Feedback* by R.E.M.
8. *After The Gold Rush* by Neil Young
9. *Passenger Seat* by Death Cab For Cutie
10. *Raining In Baltimore* by The Counting Crows
11. *Ruth Marie* by Mark Kozelek
12. *Wichita Lineman* by Glen Campbell
13. *Hallelujah* by Jeff Buckley
14. *Samson* by Regina Spektor
15. *Stairway To Heaven* by Led Zeppelin
16. *Love Will Tear Us Apart* by Nerina Pallot
17. *Brothers In Arms* by Dire Straits
18. *Cold Water* by Damien Rice
19. *Daydream Believer* by The Monkees
20. *Rainbow Connection* by Sarah McLachlan

Many people asked me how or why I chose my 20 songs. They're not my favourite 20 songs in the world, or particularly linked to memories, the answer is quite simple though. I picked 20 songs that I felt fitted the end of my world.

Thank you to the following artists who have supplied me with their own personal 20 end of the world song lists.

Nerina Pallot
The Wombats
Kristin Hersh
Kate Miller-Heidke
David Bason
Brian Viglione
Jesse Malin
Shaun Keaveny
Matthew Priest
Calm Of Zero
Martin Rossiter
Dubstar
EnglanE
Amy Studt
Rumer
Let's Go Safari
Mouth Of Ghosts
Sound Menagerie
Eric Hehr
The Folk
Simon Taffe
Miles Hunt
Elijah Jones
Bruce Driscoll
Coyle Girelli
Ami Barwell
John Twelve Hawks

Sophie Pointer
Sean Taylor
Alaska Cole
Jennifer Left
Natalie Curtis
Hilary Jay

A huge thank you to anyone who has sent in lists since this
went to print; sorry I didn't get to mention you.
All these lists and more can be found at
www.michaellinford.co.uk

What 20 songs would you choose?
(Send your list in and get featured online)

For more information on this novel or the author, follow:

www.michaellinford.co.uk
www.facebook.com/TwentyTwelveBook
www.facebook.com/MichaelJamesWriter
www.twitter.com/cupidmagicpoet

Or email direct at **info@michaellinford.co.uk**